"WILL YOU NOT CALL ME ADAM?" HE ASKED SOFTLY.

His fingers left her ear, only to brush down her cheek for a fraction of a second.

Startled, Helena met his eyes, very close still, although he was no longer touching her. Adam's gaze, under long, dark lashes, was the dark navy of the jacket he was wearing. The intensity of the look took her breath away, and she could only stammer, "But, m-my lord, we..."

"If you are going to tell me that we have not been properly introduced, I shall have no patience with you, Helena! Come, I thought you had more spirit than to be cowed by the conventions. Who is there to hear us?"

Francesca Shaw is not one but two authors, working together under the same name. Both are librarians by profession, working in Hertfordshire but living virtually side by side in a village in Bedfordshire. They first began writing under a tree in a Burgundian vineyard, and although they have published other romances, they thoroughly enjoy writing historicals. Their shared interests include travel, good food, reading and, of course, writing.

THE ADMIRAL'S DAUGHTER
FRANCESCA SHAW

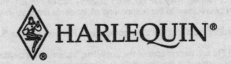

TORONTO • NEW YORK • LONDON
AMSTERDAM • PARIS • SYDNEY • HAMBURG
STOCKHOLM • ATHENS • TOKYO • MILAN • MADRID
PRAGUE • WARSAW • BUDAPEST • AUCKLAND

ISBN 0-373-51169-8

THE ADMIRAL'S DAUGHTER

First North American Publication 2001.

Copyright © 1999 by Francesca Shaw.

Chapter One

The man's bare feet, brown and braced on the bleached planking of the yacht's deck, were what first caught the eye of Miss Helena Wyatt from her vantage point perched on the quayside bollard. She gave the vessel a closer, curious look: Siddlesham Mill quay was not of such a size that gentlemen's yachts were commonly to be seen, even one as plain and workaday as this large converted cutter appeared. The name *Moonspinner* was visible on the bows.

If only she had brought her sketch pad and pencils, for the sailor would make an admirable study as he stood there, head thrown back to watch the rest of the crew in the rigging. He was the sailing master, she guessed, her artist's eye travelling up the strong musculature of his calves revealed by the canvas duck trousers. His hands were on the broad leather belt which encircled his waist and his white linen shirt flapped in the idle breeze rippling across the harbour.

Helena studied his face, committing to memory the tanned skin, the chiselled planes marred only by a nose which had obviously been broken at least once in the past. If only he would move a little closer towards the

bow so she could see his mouth more clearly, for already
the picture was taking shape in her mind. The April sunshine was suddenly dimmed by a black cloud passing
overhead and a flurry of wind lifted the man's sun-
bleached hair and caught the edge of her plain straw bonnet. With an exclamation of annoyance, Helena put up
her hands to straighten her hat and found herself looking
directly into dark blue eyes regarding her with quite bla-
tant admiration.

Miss Wyatt might be only nineteen years of age and
raised with the utmost propriety, but even so she clearly
understood the message that insolent stare was sending
her. Furious for having put herself in a position to encourage such familiarities, she swiftly averted her gaze
from that other penetrating one.

Through her confusion she suddenly realised that she
had not seen her young brother for quite ten minutes.
Trusting that the brim of her old sunbonnet was hiding
the blush which was rising hectically to her cheeks, Helena scanned the dockside. Long experience of John's
uncanny ability to vanish into thin air tempered any alarm
she might be expected to feel on finding a lively ten-
year-old no longer within view. He would be in one of
the warehouse sheds, no doubt, hunting for rats amongst
the sacks of corn landed for the mill, or plaguing the
fishermen with questions or wheedling one of the old
sailors into showing him yet another knot. For John,
young as he was, was obsessed with anything to do with
ships or the sea, and counted the days until, thanks to the
influence of his uncle, Commodore Sir Robert Breakey,
he could join the fleet as a midshipman.

His widowed mama might have been expected to show
more anxiety about her only son's marked lack of dili-
gence in his studies relating to anything other than math-

tleman. Helena was aware that she was looking unflatteringly stupefied and hastily shut her mouth. The angry retort on the tip of her tongue was cut off by the embarrassing realisation that she was appearing as a veritable hoyden before a member of Society. To be escorting her young brother while dressed in an old gown and bonnet was one thing—to be found wandering around the dockside attracting the attention of sailors was quite another. She had no intention of having her name bandied about over cards in some exclusive gentlemen's club. For whoever this man was, and however eccentric he might be in working with his own sailors, he was quite clearly of the Quality.

Her mother's blue-stocking approach to girls' education and preoccupation with her own academic studies might have delayed Helena's come-out, but that was not to say that Miss Wyatt was careless of propriety or unaware of the damage to her own reputation this man could do her if he discovered her name and chose to gossip.

She dropped her violet eyes and murmured, 'Yes, sir, I am sorry, sir. John, come here this minute!' The boy scuttled to her side; Helena longed to put her arm around him but, conscious of his dignity, only rested one hand on his shoulder and pushed him down the gangplank in front of her.

Furious with everyone concerned—herself, her imp of a brother and most of all that domineering man—Helena propelled John with more force than necessary along the quayside towards the ferryman's hut. She could feel those hard blue eyes burning into the nape of her neck: either he was laughing at her or he was ogling her and Miss Wyatt found both equally unpalatable. Well, she had no intention of giving him the satisfaction of looking back.

'What, going back over already, Miss Helena?' The ferryman got to his feet from the bench where he had been mending crab pots and steadied the rowing boat for her to climb in. 'Fine day like today, I'd have thought you'd be walking back right round the harbour, same as usual.'

Helena took his hand as she climbed over the gunwales and settled her skirts tightly around her knees as she sat in the stern. 'Thank you, Ned, but the wind is getting up. John, sit down directly and do not fidget under Ned's feet! I do declare, I have had more than enough of your conduct today.'

The old sailor looked up in surprise from his oars as he pushed off. Not like Miss Helena to come all snappish with the lad! Something had put her out of countenance for sure. He backwatered to allow a fishing smack to go out on the falling tide and glanced sideways at her heightened colour. Always healthy looking for Quality, unlike those mimsy females who came down from London for the air and spent all their time under a parasol. But, none the less, he'd never seen her cheeks so flushed, nor that sparking anger in her eyes—a right pretty colour that violet…

The few moments it took for the boat to reach Selsea Ferry House was enough to make Helena rue her irritation with her brother. He was only a child—high-spirited and adventurous, just as a boy ought to be—and she was too fond of him to stay cross with him for long. She felt in her reticule for a coin and pressed it into John's grubby fist. 'Here, please pay Ned for me.' John shot her a worried look, then seeing her face relax into a smile, squeezed her hand.

'Do you think I should have offered to pay for the damage to the deck?' he asked anxiously. 'Only I think it would take my allowance for months, and I do not know if Mama would advance me all that, especially not,' he added thoughtfully, 'as I still owe for the parsonage window and Mr Willoughby's chickens.'

Helena laughed at the recollection of the farmyard race which had led to the escape of the neighbouring farmer's poultry. 'No, I should not worry. That man can more than afford to put right a few scrapes on his deck.' They climbed ashore and John scampered off down the shingle beach, all cares forgotten. Helena sighed and followed him, wishing her own equilibrium could be restored as easily.

'Please, can we go down to the shore?' John pleaded as they trotted through the winding lanes towards home. Helena nodded absently and continued past the gate of Norton Manor and down the track to the beach. The morning's expedition was entirely to entertain John and give her mother a little peace and quiet: it made no difference where they went until it was time for luncheon.

She should have put the sailor in his place, of course, for being so open in his admiration of her face and figure. She was quite capable of depressing pretension even though she was not yet out, for local society held many admiring young men. None, however, had managed to advance beyond the coolest social contact, or the granting of Miss Wyatt's hand for a country dance at one of the informal local parties.

And yet this man...this man had shaken her composure to the core. Was it the boldness of his manner, the blatancy of his admiration of her looks or the unconventionality of his attire? She thought again of those strong, long legs, the bare feet, his toes flexing on the planking as he balanced easily against the swell...

Angrily Helena shook herself, realising that the old

pony had stopped in his usual place where the track ran into the shingle and that John had jumped down and vanished once again. The panicky eruption of a flock of ducks from the marsh bordering the beach told her where he must be and she resigned herself to taking him home not just grubby, but thoroughly muddy to boot. Not that Mama would give it a thought, for she was deep in a new translation of the poems of Sappho which would no doubt be well received by literary circles in London.

'Helena, come and see what I have found!' John's excited voice came from where the marsh drained to the sea. Helena saw he had discovered an old rowing boat tied up at the mouth of the stream. With a sigh she picked her way over the stepping stones and joined him. 'A French frigate!' he announced, his eyes shining. 'You shall be the captain, asleep on watch, and I shall board and capture you and your vessel! I will sail it with a prize crew to join Uncle Robert's squadron and will be made a lieutenant!'

'Very well,' Helena replied placidly, climbing into the boat and resigning herself to the complete ruination of her skirts. She was too used to John's imaginary adventures to protest. 'Where am I to fall asleep? Here in the bows?'

'Anywhere, for you have drunk too much brandy.' John crept away up the beach and disappeared stealthily into the undergrowth.

Helena settled herself as comfortably as possible in the boat, which had seen better days and was sadly in want of a coat of paint. However, it seemed to bob safely enough at the end of its rope, despite the sucking of the falling tide and the slapping of little wavelets raised by the wind.

Closing her eyes was as far as she was prepared to go

in imitating a drunken Frenchman, she decided firmly, finding it rather soothing to sit in darkness with the sunlight warm on her eyelids and the boat rocking. Helena fell to dreaming, her mind turning once more to the yacht and its owner. Now that would be the way to go to sea, cresting the sunlit waves with the wind in her face and a strong arm round her waist keeping her secure and safe…

These highly improper thoughts were broken into by the sound of surreptitious footsteps over the shingle, followed almost immediately by a bloodcurdling yell, a crack and a yelp of pain. The rowing boat rocked wildly and Helena found herself tumbling backwards off the plank seat into the bottom of the boat.

Indignantly she scrambled back into a sitting position to find the boat adrift, the shore already several yards away and John sprawled on the beach where his attacking leap had obviously broken the mooring stake. 'Helena! Come back!' His face was white and pinched with fright at the consequences of his playacting; the need to reassure the frightened boy kept her calm.

'It is all right, John,' she called more cheerfully than she felt. 'See, there are oars, and you know how well I row!' As she spoke she fitted the oars into the rowlocks, not without difficulty for the wood was splintered and old. The insidious sucking of the tide was taking her away from the beach with alarming speed, but she made herself sit squarely in the centre of the boat and raise the oars steadily. Helena dug them into the water as her father had taught her and pulled hard. To her relief the little boat responded, but she needed to turn it to row back to shore. She lifted the starboard oar clear of the waves and dug hard with the other. The boat began to turn, then, with a loud crack, the rotten wood gave way and the oar broke. As she had been straining with all her strength against the oar, the sudden release of pressure precipitated her backward with some force. The last thing she was aware of was an intense pain in her head and John's cry of alarm, then the world went black.

Helena woke to find, confusingly, that she was lying on her back in a pool of water which was soaking into her gown. She blinked up at the sky through a lancing pain in the back of her head and, for a moment, could only gaze in bewilderment at the clouds scudding across the now fitful spring sunshine. Shakily Helena eased herself upright until she was sitting. But nothing prepared her for the wave of dizziness which made her retch over the side of the boat.

The sea slapping hard against the sides of the rowing boat brought her to reality with a shock as unpleasant as the pain in her head. Frantically she cast around for a sight of land, anything to tell her where she had drifted to and how far out she was. The low headland of Selsey Bill loomed to her right all of a mile away. Helena gave a gasp of horror and for several minutes was quite beyond any rational thought as panic swept through her. Gradually she regained some control, but no one from a seagoing family, living as close to the ocean as she had always done, could be in the slightest doubt that she was in peril of her life.

The other oar had fallen back into the boat but Helena, although taught at an early age to row, had never mastered the skill of sculling over the stern. Nor had she any confidence that this oar would not be as rotten as the other. She scanned the horizon for other craft, but could see no sails. She forced herself to think calmly and recall her father's words when he had spoken of sailing in small craft around these waters. The Owers, treacherous reefs, extended for three miles around the south and south-east of the Bill and, although her little craft was in no danger from the rocks, any seagoing vessel would give the area a wide berth. Helena realised she would need to be carried around the tip of the Bill before she had any hope of encountering the fishing fleet.

The wetness around her feet recalled her to a more immediate danger: the old planking was far from watertight and water was seeping through the perished caulking. She looked around wildly for something to bail with, but the litter floating in the bottom of the boat contained nothing which would hold water. Desperately she pulled off her stout leather half-boot, thankful that her habit of walking over even the roughest ground meant she had not come out in the dainty footwear usual to a woman of her class. The well-polished boot proved to be an efficient, although small, bailer and, after ten minutes which left her breathless, the water had diminished below the bottom boards.

Helena looked round again, relieved to see she had been carried no further out and was still being swept by the prevailing tide to the south and west. But her relief at being taken towards open water where the chance of rescue was greater was rapidly countered by her dismay at how rough the sea was becoming. From the deck of even a small fishing smack it would have seemed no more than a good swell, but for the small rowing boat, designed only for creeks and harbours, it was dangerously high. Soon Helena was bailing again, water splashing over the sides adding to the seepage from below.

By the time the little boat was swept around the southern tip of Selsey Bill and she could see, distantly, the outline of the Isle of Wight, she was sobbing with exertion from the effort of keeping the water at bay. She slumped over, the breath rasping painfully in her lungs, and almost gave way to despair. But as her vision cleared she saw the red sails of a fishing smack half a mile away to the west. The sunlight caught the little ship and she got to her feet, waving and shouting at the top of her voice. For a moment she had hope as the profile of the sails changed, then she saw it had moved on to another tack and was heading away from her, not closer.

Helena let out a cry of anguish. No wonder they had not seen her: without sails, all she was was a brown dot on the dark sea. The next ship she saw, she must attract their attention, must signal by some means. She had the single oar—if only she had a scrap of sail to tie to it! In that instant she thought of her petticoat and, without hesitation, wrenched it off. With trembling fingers she ripped off the narrow lace edging and used that to bind the cloth fast to the end of the oar.

She had to break off several times to bail as the water rose to her ankles again, but finally she had a signal ready. As if in answer to her prayers another sail appeared to the south of her, scudding along in the brisk wind, topgallant sails and royal set. Helena raised the unwieldy oar and waved it, ignoring the strain to her arms from the weight of the wood and the wet cloth. She shouted, too, although the wind snatched away the words as soon as she uttered them. For long desperate minutes it seemed they had not seen her, then the ship came round into the wind and began to take in sails.

'Oh, thank God!' she whispered, sinking down and dropping the oar into the bottom of the boat. The sailing ship was tacking under reduced canvas, making its way towards her. Now it was less than a quarter of a mile away and she could see they were making ready to swing out a boat.

Her eyes glued to her rescuers, Helena quite forgot to bail. The boat's crew scrambled down into the craft and now they were close enough for her to hear the sharp words of command carrying across the water. The sailors pulled hard on the oars and the gig leapt forward, eating up the distance between rescuers and the sinking craft.

For sinking it was: Helena looked down in horror as a plank finally gave way and water gushed over her feet. The boat stopped tossing and began to founder. Helena jumped to her feet and screamed, 'Hurry, oh please, hurry! It is sinking!'

Her cry of anguish must have reached the ears of the boatmen, for a tall figure stood up, pulling off his jacket. For the briefest of seconds he stood poised on the gunwales, then he was cleaving the water in a shallow dive. Helena had no opportunity to watch her would-be rescuer, for with a lurch the sinking boat slipped sideways under the waves, precipitating her into the freezing water.

Helena could swim, but the warm shallows of Brighton beach with a bathing machine close at hand was a far cry from the cold, choppy Channel. To add to her terror, the soaked cloth of her skirts wound itself around her legs, the weight imprisoning her so she could not tread water. She struck out towards the dark head forging towards her through the waves, only to be slapped full in the face by a wave.

Stinging salt water blinded her, filled her nostrils and cascaded down the back of her throat. Choking, she knew she was sinking…

A hand seized her hair, ruthlessly dragging her into the air. Helena was pulled up and back on to a broad chest and found herself held hard, her breasts crushed under the muscular forearm of her rescuer. He lost no time in striking out for the boat; Helena forced herself to relax into the grasp, knowing that if she struggled she would take them both under the murky waves.

It seemed forever before they reached the side of the boat, an eternity before willing hands were lifting her out of the sea. Dumped unceremoniously into the bottom of the craft while the men made room for her rescuer to haul himself back on board, Helena choked and scrubbed painfully at her salt-encrusted eyes. The swimmer was on board before she could focus and she found herself abruptly lifted and turned over his knee while the water was ruthlessly thumped from her lungs.

Eventually she found enough breath to protest, 'Stop! Enough!' and was turned back to sit on the man's knees. Words of thanks died on her lips as astonished recognition took over. 'You!' she gasped.

It was unlikely that he could recognise the young 'governess' he had seen just a few hours before as the half-drowned female he had just plucked from certain death. But Miss Wyatt recognised the master of the cutter only too clearly. His blond hair was dark with water, plastered to his head; his chest rose and fell with the exertion of his rescue and the linen shirt clung transparent to the strong planes of shoulder and upper arm.

He looked somewhat taken aback at the vehemence of her expostulation. He raised one eyebrow but said with considerable formality, 'I am sorry, Miss...er...have we been introduced?'

'No, we have not, sir! But it did not prevent you from shouting at my little brother this morning!'

'So...not the governess after all.' His eyes moved appreciatively down from her face. 'How could I not have recognised you?'

Recalled to the clinging cloth moulding itself to her body, without even a petticoat between her shift and her gown, Helena blushed furiously, tugging up the neckline in a futile effort at decency.

Her confusion was cut short by the gig bumping against the side of the cutter. Before she could say or do anything else her rescuer commanded 'Eyes front!' The rowers, shipping their oars, obeyed instantly. He stood, grasped her around the knees and tossed her lightly over one shoulder before seizing the rope ladder and scaling it.

Winded, flustered and scandalised, Helena found herself deposited unceremoniously on her feet on the deck of the cutter under the interested eyes of the rest of the crew, who had obviously decided that the order to the boat crew to keep their eyes to themselves did not apply to them.

'Sir!' Helena stormed at him, eyes sparking. 'How dare you handle my…my *person* in such a manner?'

The man turned from giving orders to the boat crew and enquired amiably, 'Do you object to being saved from drowning and prevented from choking or to being assisted safe on board, madam?'

Helena discovered that stamping one's foot, when one was wearing only one sodden boot, was both undignified and uncomfortable and glared at him. 'I am, sir, most deeply obliged to you for rescuing me, for I would have undoubtedly drowned…'

'Undoubtedly,' he echoed drily. 'Can I assume from your lack of concern that your small brother was not with you in the boat?'

'John! Oh, he will be frantic with worry… No, no, he was not in the boat, I was quite alone. He was pretending I was a drunken French captain, you see…' A snort of amusement escaped from the tall man and she added irritably, 'I do wish you would tell me your name, sir!'

He smiled and bowed slightly. 'I agree, madam. Nothing is more frustrating than to try and quarrel with someone when you do not know their name. Adam Darvell, ma'am, at your service.'

'*Lord* Adam Darvell?'

'The same, ma'am. You appear to know my name.'

'Er…yes. Why, you are almost a neighbour of ours.'

'And you have been told by your mama that I am a notorious rake and you should have nothing to do with me should we meet?'

'Oh, no, it was not my mama, I mean…' Helena stopped in confusion. She could hardly tell him the scandalous tales the Vicar's daughter had regaled her bosom friends with, having been within earshot of one of her mama's afternoon tea parties. 'I am sorry I sounded so ungracious—it was a very frightening experience and I am truly sensible of the service you have done me.' She was rather pleased with the dignified manner she achieved.

'Might I hope, unconventional though the circumstances are, that you will tell me whom I have the pleasure of welcoming on board the *Moonspinner*?'

Helena pulled herself up to her full five feet five inches, raised her chin and said properly, as if she were at Almack's and not shivering on the deck of a cutter in mid-Channel, 'Helena Wyatt, sir.'

'Miss Wyatt, it is indeed an honour to have been of some small service to the daughter of such a distinguished naval hero.' He was obviously sincere in his reference to her father and Helena warmed to him. Perhaps all the things she had heard about Adam Darvell had been wild rumours.

The sun disappeared behind a cloud and the wind got up sharply, sending Helena's wet skirts flapping about her legs. She shivered and at once he was at her side, ushering her towards the companionway leading below decks.

'What am I thinking of, you will catch your death of cold.' He glanced over his shoulder and called, 'Jenks, get us back on the same heading as before and have someone brew some coffee.'

Adam ushered Helena into a small, yet luxuriously furnished, cabin. She could stand upright but he had to bow his head below the deck beams and she realised he must be well over six feet tall. His presence in the gloom made Helena a little uncomfortable and she looked around her with an assumption of interest while he lit the two oil lamps hanging in gimbals. The bed was built in with cupboards below and the panelled walls were lined with lockers. There was a table with two chairs and a massive sea chest at the foot of the bed.

Helena shivered again, no longer certain it was with cold and shock. His lordship threw open a small door in the panelling and, peering in, she saw, with some relief, a private closet and a washstand with an ewer and basin. He handed her a towel and threw open one of the lockers. 'Here, some of this must fit you.'

The women's garments he tossed so carelessly on the foot of the bed were all of the finest quality and some of them of such an intimate nature that Helena blushed to look at them. Adam caught her eye and saw the colour mantle her cheek. 'And you were thinking all the stories you had heard about me were just malicious rumour,' he said mockingly, his voice low. 'I like to make my guests comfortable.'

It seemed to Helena that he was looking at the bed behind her, but she forced herself to stare straight ahead and say with a fair assumption of calm, 'Thank you, sir,

I am sure there will be something suitable. If you will leave me I would like to change.'

With a mocking bow and a smile which showed white teeth in the gloom, Lord Darvell opened a locker, removed a shirt and trousers and let himself out of his cabin.

Helena sat down on the edge of the bed with a thump and let out a long shuddering breath. Her heart, she realised now, was fluttering. Who would have thought that shock could make one feel so very flustered? But she was honest enough to admit that the way she felt could not be entirely attributed to being cast adrift and half drowned.

After a moment she began to remove her gown. She looked at the door and almost stretched out her hand to throw the latch but then checked the movement. Lord Darvell was a gentleman, knew her to be a lady; to lock the door would be to display an insulting lack of trust.

Washed, dry and clad in the most sober of the available gowns with a fichu around her shoulders Helena felt rather more herself. However, when it came to her hair, she had to admit defeat. She could not wash the straight mass of dark brown hair in the small basin and pinning it up with an inadequate mirror and no maid proved impossible. In the end she tugged Lord Darvell's comb through the tangles, plaited it into one long braid down her back and tied the end with a ribbon unthreaded from a petticoat.

She had just completed her toilette when there was a knock at the door. Helena caught herself tugging self-consciously at the damp tendrils around her forehead and sat on one of the chairs before calling, 'Come in!'

'Ah, Miss Wyatt, quite restored, I see. Did you find everything you needed?'

It sounded a curiously intimate question in that confined space and she bit her lip before saying quietly, 'Yes, thank you, my lord.'

'I have brought you some coffee. We will eat soon.' He had changed into shirt and trousers with a dark blue reefer jacket against the wind but his feet were still—disconcertingly—bare.

He waited in silence, sipping his own coffee, apparently content to let her speak first. The brew was bitter, but reviving and warming as it slipped down her sore throat. Helena had been pushing all thoughts of her mother and brother's anguish over her disappearance to the back of her mind, but now she could suppress them no longer. 'How long will it be before we return to Siddlesham sir?'

Lord Darvell considered. 'Several days—ten or so perhaps.'

'Then you will be landing at the next port?' she asked anxiously.

'I have no plans to make land until I reach St Mary's,' he replied.

'The Scilly Islands!' Helena put down her mug with a thump. 'But how will I get home?'

'I will take you back in the fullness of time.' His smile was scarcely reassuring.

'Until then, I will do my utmost to make you tolerably comfortable.'

Chapter Two

'The Scilly Isles!' Helena was aghast. 'My lord, if this is some form of jest on your part, I can assure you it is in very poor taste!' She stood up in her agitation and held out a hand to him. 'Please, sir, do not jest with me—assure me you will return to Siddlesham at once. My mother and my brother will be believing me drowned—think of their torment. You cannot be so unkind!'

For a moment, looking into those imploring violet eyes, Adam Darvell almost relented, then hardened himself against their innocent appeal. It was evident that, in her concern for her family's feelings, it had not occurred to Miss Wyatt that her position was indeed precarious. Even the most liberal member of Society would regard her as being hopelessly compromised already—a few more hours or even days alone with him at sea could scarcely make things worse than they already were. And he had very good reasons for wishing to reach the port of Hugh Town on St Mary's by tomorrow evening.

'I cannot turn back now, but I will make sure a message reaches your mother by tonight. You have my word on that, Miss Wyatt,' he added with a smile, taking her outstretched hand and squeezing it reassuringly.

Helena snatched it away, far from reassured. 'Sir, I cannot believe you realise how serious this is! How can you undertake to deliver a message to my mother, yet refuse to take me to dry land?'

Adam Darvell's mouth twisted wryly. 'Believe me, Miss Wyatt, I fully realise what a predicament we are in.' He turned to the door, adding under his breath, 'Even if you do not.' He lifted a heavy boat cloak from a peg by the door. 'Here, wrap this around your shoulders and come up on deck. We will make rendezvous with a small vessel off the Needles presently: they return to Siddlesham this afternoon and the master will deliver a message, you have my word.'

'Then give me pen and paper and I will write to Mama myself,' Helena demanded on a rising note of impatience. Then the absurdity of this talk of messages struck her. 'But if a boat is returning, why cannot I go back to Siddlesham with it?'

'I have no intention of entrusting you to a small fishing smack with a crew of...rough seamen.'

Helena's eyes narrowed in suspicion. 'Rough seamen? More likely your acquaintances are smugglers, are they not, my lord?' she demanded.

'Smugglers?' His grin was almost wolfish. 'What *do* you take me for, Miss Wyatt?'

Any retort Helena could have chosen to make was cut off as he closed the door behind him.

She threw the boat cloak onto the bed and sat down with a thud. Grateful though she was to have been plucked from the jaws of death, why, oh, why did it have to be by this man! Adam Darvell, by all accounts, was a rake and a roué; now it seemed he was in league with smugglers to boot!

Having lived all her life on the south coast, Helena

was all too familiar with the hair-raising tales of such as the Hawkhurst gang, who had terrorised the county for miles around in her grandfather's day. Smuggling was a less violent occupation these days—and many a respectable household would find a cask of brandy on their kitchen doorstep in return for 'watching the wall as the gentlemen went by' with their loaded pack-ponies—but becoming involved in the 'trade' itself was quite another matter!

Her agitated reflections were interrupted by a tap at the door and the entrance of a respectful sailor who handed her an inkhorn, quill and sheet of paper. He tugged his forelock and left as silently as he had arrived. Well, at least she could write and set Mama's mind at rest, she must be distracted with worry. And poor John must be believing he was responsible for his sister's drowning.

Helena scribbled a few reassuring words, avoiding all mention of the sinking boat, stating that she was well and safe, but unfortunately could not be returned to shore yet.

...please do not worry, dear Mama. Lord Darvell has offered me every comfort and consideration possible. He has pressing business on St Mary's, it appears, and cannot alter his plans to land me, but assures me he will return me to you as soon as may be. Please give all my love to John.

Your dutiful and affectionate daughter, Helena.

There was no way of sealing the letter, but she folded it and wrote her mother's direction clearly. As she did so there was the sound of raised voices and a bump, signalling the arrival of the expected fishing boat. Helena snatched up the cloak and made her way up the steep companionway to the deck.

The wind whipped cold around the flimsy muslin of her borrowed skirts and she huddled gratefully into the heavy oiled and felted wool of the cloak. Adam Darvell was leaning on the rail, quite at his ease, exchanging shouted banter with the crew of the smack tossing alongside. Suddenly he threw back his head and laughed, his throat in a strong line that drew Helena's gaze and held it. His dark blond mane blew in the wind and she thought he needed only a gold earring to look the perfect pirate. The realisation that she was staring shamelessly at this man filled her with sudden confusion and sent the blood rushing hectically to her cheeks.

She dropped her eyes, but found her confusion deepened as she took in the lithe body, strong thighs and those bare brown feet braced on the deck. Never before had Helena found herself aware of a man's body. True, nobody who had been brought up surrounded by fine classical sculptures could remain ignorant of the male anatomy, but cold marble was quite another thing from live, warm flesh and blood.

Her cloak flapped and snagged on a nail protruding from a crate by the mainmast. Her exclamation of annoyance attracted Adam's attention and he left the rail to saunter over, his foothold sure on the pitching deck. 'Miss Wyatt! Are you warm enough?' He freed the cloak and pulled it around her, his arm around her shoulders for one brief moment. Helena shivered, but not with cold. 'Walk up and down in the lee of the wheelhouse, you will be sheltered from the cut of the wind there.'

Adam took her arm and walked her round to the far side, finding her a patch of sunlight and, she realised, shielding her from any view of what was going on with the boat alongside.

'Is that the letter for Lady Wyatt? I will put it with

mine to her.' He made no offer to let her read what he
had written, folding one within the other as he returned
to the rail. The bosun handed him a battered leather
pouch, already well stuffed. Adam tucked the letter in
and tied the flap shut before dropping it down to the
waiting boat.

Helena was suddenly overtaken by a wave of tiredness.
More crates were stacked alongside the wheelhouse and
she found a sheltered corner and settled down, pulling
the cloak tight around herself in a comforting hug. Now
that she had the chance to reflect in tranquillity, relieved
of the worst of her anxiety about her family, she could
comprehend how very near she had come to death. Looking out over the cold, grey, slick surface of the sea, she
knew she would have survived only minutes more without help. She was uncomfortably aware that she had appeared less than grateful to her rescuer, and to cavil at a
few casks of smuggled brandy or some rolls of Lyons
silk or whatever he had in the hold, was ungracious in
the extreme.

Lulled by the rocking, she fell asleep thinking of Adam
Darvell and was awakened with the smell of savoury
stew in her nostrils. Helena opened her eyes and found
him standing before her, a plate in each hand.

'Oh, I am so very hungry!' she exclaimed, sitting up
and pushing back tendrils of salt-sticky hair from her
brow.

'Would you like to eat up here? The weather is much
better now.' And, indeed, the cutting wind had dropped
and with it the swell which now sparkled in the late afternoon sun. At her nod of assent, Adam sat down beside
her and handed her the pewter plate which, beside the
stew, had a thick slice of bread and cheese and a battered
spoon.

Helena ate with more urgency than good manners, digging into the meat and vegetables with an appetite heightened by exertion and a total absence of food since eight that morning. By the time the stew was gone, she recalled her social graces and nibbled at the bread and cheese with more decorum, conscious of the man by her side.

'Our cook will be gratified to see a clean plate,' he remarked. 'Do you feel a little more yourself now?' Adam was still working his way through his own plateful, as Helena was suddenly all too aware.

'Forgive my haste,' she apologised. 'I had no idea how hungry I was until I smelled that stew. Do you bring your own chef aboard, my lord?'

Adam laughed. 'Jean-Pierre is a most superior French chef and would sooner be disemboweled than set foot on a boat again. Fleeing the Revolution and having to cross the Channel in a storm left a lasting impression upon him. It is as much as I can do to persuade him out of London and down to my country estate. No, our cook is one of the seamen, but he does a fair job for the men, and when I am in port I send ashore for my meals.'

He took the plate from her and put both dishes on the deck. 'What would you like to drink? I have no tea on board, I would not recommend the ale—but I do have a very respectable burgundy, if you would care for a glass.'

Helena was not accustomed to drink wine, but there was little choice and her throat was still parched from the sea water she had swallowed. The warm heaviness of the red liquid soothed her throat as it slipped down and the fruity flavour deceived her palate into thinking it more innocuous than it was.

Lord Darvell made no move to refill her goblet, however. He watched her with quiet amusement as the wine brought a sparkle into her eyes and the colour back into her cheeks. The breeze had tangled a curl round the filigree of her modest earring and he leaned over suddenly, unexpectedly, and began teasing the dark hairs free with surprisingly sensitive fingers.

'My lord!' Helena gasped.

'Be still, it will hurt if you pull away,' he commanded, his face intent as he concentrated on the task. 'Will you not call me Adam?' he asked softly as his fingers left her ear, only to brush lightly down her cheek for a fraction of a second.

Startled, she met his eyes, very close still, although he was no longer touching her. His gaze, under long, dark lashes, was the dark navy of the jacket he was wearing. The intensity of the look took her breath away and she could only stammer, 'But, my lord, we…'

'If you are going to tell me that we have not been properly introduced, I shall have no patience with you, Helena! Come, I thought you had more spirit than to be cowed by the conventions. Who is there to hear us?'

He got to his feet, pulling her gently to hers and tucking her hand under his arm.

'But your crew—!' she began to say, allowing herself to be walked forward to the bows.

'They are about their business. And,' he added drily, 'very well paid to be both deaf and blind when it suits me.'

Helena was nettled by the implication that the crew would bracket her with the sort of woman his lordship habitually entertained on board. 'From the sight of the female garments in your cabin, my lord, I imagine they have much practice in discretion,' she remarked tartly.

'I think you must own, Helena, that both the clothes and the discretion of my crew are beneficial to you, placed as you are.' He paused at the bow where the bowsprit met the rail. 'Now, if you are not too cold, let us admire the sunset.'

Infuriating and improper though he was, Lord Darvell was quite correct and Helena allowed herself to admire the flaming red of the sky as the sun began to sink in the west.

She did not notice as the air became cooler, nor protest when his arm went around her shoulders, pulling her closer to his side. The red wine was heavy in her veins and she felt light-headed, warm and very safe. The light faded fast and he moved beside her. All at once Helena became very aware of just how close and how big he was. She felt safe and lulled, warmed by his body heat even through the cloak.

That morning—a hundred years ago, it seemed—she had chided herself for dreaming of standing like this in the shelter of his arms, watching the sea slip by under a wide sky. Now it was happening and she had no desire to break the spell, no matter how improper.

Without speaking he began slowly, insidiously, to stroke down the column of her throat with one long finger. Helena gasped as a wave of sensation tingled to the very tips of her toes. 'My lord!'

He pulled her round to face him, laughing down into her flushed face. 'Adam—call me Adam. It is very hurtful that you should be so formal, considering the circumstances of your arrival on this vessel.'

Miss Wyatt was too inexperienced in flirtation to recognise when she was being teased. Stricken that he might think her both ungracious and ungrateful, she raised an anxious face to his. 'Oh, Adam, I did not mean...'

Her unconscious invitation was too much for his lordship's carefully maintained willpower. Reflecting that it was really more than flesh and blood could stand to resist the innocent provocation of those wide violet eyes and the promise of those full, soft lips, he bent his head and kissed her full on the mouth.

To be kissed for the first time under such circumstances robbed Helena of both her breath and any desire to resist him. She found herself overcome by a wave of entirely new physical sensations: his skin smelt clean with a tang of salt and where his lips moved on hers she could taste the salt through the sweetness of the wine. Her hand lifted to his cheek, tracing the tautness of the skin over the high cheekbone, moving down, exploring the sensation of stubble under her questing fingers.

Adam's kiss, had she any experience to judge it by, was restrained in the extreme, but it was enough, innocent as she was, to shock Helena to her senses. She pulled back, turning her face from his questing lips, her cheeks burning with shame and embarrassment. Adam let her go immediately, watching her as she took a trembling hold on the rail a few yards away. A rueful smile played about his lips as he reflected that flirting with virgins was a different game entirely to the dalliance he normally enjoyed with the sophisticated married ladies of his acquaintance.

He had had no intention of frightening Helena, and he knew enough about women to guess that what had alarmed her was not his kiss but her own response to it. But at least she had shown him that she was not averse to him which, in view of the fact that the only possible outcome to this little escapade was marriage, was indeed fortunate!

The rail was smooth and cold under Helena's grasping hands as she gazed unseeing over the darkening sea. No wonder, she reflected shakily, that Society placed so many barriers between young ladies and young men! She was honest enough not to blame Adam for what had just passed between them—it was not so much that she needed protecting from him, more she needed saving from her own responses!

Helena turned to face him with a social smile firmly on her lips. 'Why, how late it has got, and how chilly now the sun has gone down. I must bid you goodnight, my lord, for I am very fatigued.' It was true, suddenly everything felt flat.

'Of course. Let me find you a lantern. Have you everything you require for the night?' His neutral tone as he escorted her below belied his annoyance with himself. Adam Darvell was not used to nursemaiding anyone, least of all very young ladies, but he should, he told himself severely, have realised that she was exhausted, confused and frightened, however well she concealed it. And Miss Helena Wyatt was a far cry from the experienced and demanding ladies who flitted lightly through his life with commitment on neither side to anything but passing pleasure and entertainment.

He went before her into the cabin and fixed the lamp into its gimbals so that it hung safely, however the boat tossed or rolled in its passage down the Channel. He cast a swift glance around the cramped space to check that all was well, then saw the set of Helena's rigid shoulders as she looked everywhere but at the bunk which took up most of the space. Sensing her unease, he wished her goodnight and closed the door quietly behind him. He stood for a moment, listening. Then he heard the click of the latch as she secured the door and was surprised by the swift stab of chagrin that she did not trust him.

Helena, expecting her anxieties to disturb her rest had no sooner climbed between the sheets than she fell into a deep and dreamless sleep. Unknowingly she slept the clock round while the *Moonspinner* drove through the crested seas, scudding before a brisk following wind and making better time than even the most optimistic sailor could have predicted towards Adam Darvell's rendezvous on St Mary's.

Lyme Bay, Portland Bill and Start Point all fell away on their starboard side while Helena slumbered. Thrice during the night Adam went up on deck, to the surprise of the crew who were used to being trusted to stand their watches alone.

'Not like him to be so restless,' the helmsman muttered to his companion on the watch. 'I 'spose he's missing his nice soft sheets, him having turfed the bosun out of his bunk!'

His companion laughed coarsely. 'It's not his nice soft bed he's missing—more like what's in it!' The laughter reached Adam who was staring ahead into the darkness, and he turned to stroll back towards the wheelhouse. Both men fell silent under his decidedly frosty eye.

The next morning Helena woke with a start and sat up in the stuffy shadowed room. Her heart thudded against her rib cage and for a moment of pure panic she had no recollection of where she was. Then the slap of water against the wooden planking and the dim light filtering through the salt-crusted porthole brought realisation.

Hastily she slipped out of bed and into the tiny closet, thankful that his lordship's concern for his own comfort gave her privacy. She splashed her face with cold water from the ewer, gave up the hopeless task of getting a comb through her sticky hair and pulled on her borrowed gown and slippers.

The muslin gown dipped scandalously low in front no

matter how much she tugged it up and, despite two petticoats, clung to her form. Helena reflected as she pinned
a shawl around her shoulders and across her bosom that
she must take care not to allow the spray to dampen the
skirts or it would become quite indecent.

The sunlight was flooding down the companionway as
she emerged from the cabin and climbed up on deck.
Moonspinner was running under a full set of white canvas, fairly dancing over the blue sea and Helena could
see no sight of land in any direction.

Adam was in the bows, a long spyglass to his eye,
scanning the waters ahead of them. Helena hesitated,
seized with uncertainty about how to approach him after
that kiss the night before. Her fingertips brushed her lips
where his had pressed and she shivered with remembrance. It seemed impossible that they could carry on a
normal, everyday conversation after that degree of intimacy...

'Please ma'am, I'm to ask you, ma'am, if you want
any breakfast.' The cabin boy, a ginger-haired urchin,
gazed at her anxiously. He wasn't usually permitted anywhere near his lordship's ladies, but this one looked nice
and kind. Helena smiled at him and he grinned back,
reminding her painfully of her brother. Had they received
the letter telling of her safe rescue or had John and her
mother endured a sleepless night, believing her lost?

'Yes, that is very kind of you. I am indeed hungry and
would enjoy some breakfast. Will you show me where to
go?'

The lad blushed to the roots of his hair. In all his thir-
teen years, no pretty lady had addressed him, never mind
so kindly. Utterly smitten, he stammered, 'I'll bring it to
you, ma'am, if you care to make yourself comfortable by
the wheelhouse out of the wind.'

Helena settled herself and watched with amusement as he ran off to the galley, returning a few minutes later with a loaded plate. Helena reflected that cold herring, a slab of odorous cheese, hard bread and strong coffee was not what she would choose to break her fast, but she accepted it from him with a smile and a word of thanks which quite enslaved the lad. He sat down cross-legged on the deck at her feet, 'Just in case you want anything else, ma'am.'

Helena was so hungry that she managed to clear her plate, although the cheese had to be shared with the cabin boy, who confided that his name was Billy. Helena was being regaled with the entire, if short, life history of her young admirer when his narrative was cut abruptly short by the arrival of the mate.

'Billy! Where've you got to, you little b— Morning, ma'am! Didn't see you there. What are you doing annoying the lady—go and peel some potatoes!' Billy was assisted to his feet by a firm though not unkind hand on the scruff of his neck.

'Oh, do not blame him—it was quite my fault!' Helena protested, handing her plate and mug to the boy. 'Thank you, Billy, that was very helpful.'

Adam strolled up, telescoping the spyglass which he handed to the mate. 'Watch out for the Wolf Rock.'

'Aye, my lord, though it's a good clear day and we'll hear the thing as soon as see it in any case. But I'll send a man aloft now, can't be too careful in these waters.' He touched his forelock and strode off.

'Wolf Rock? That sounds very alarming, my lord.' Navigation seemed a safe topic for conversation.

'My lord? It was Adam last night,' he teased gently. But, seeing her drop her eyes in confusion, he added, 'Did you sleep well? You look refreshed.' And, indeed,

Miss Wyatt with her creamy skin and clear violet eyes was looking fresh as a daisy despite her tangled hair and borrowed gown.

'I confess I slept like a log—' Helena laughed '—which I am sure shows I have no sensibility! But you are avoiding telling me about Wolf Rock—it sounds quite Gothic.' She spoke lightly, but felt everything she said was artificial. What was it that seemed to crackle between them like the air before a thunderstorm? Helena sounded to her own ears like the little ninnies who giggled and twittered at young men at dances and dinner parties. And she had never affected that style!

'It is very dangerous, that is for sure, although as for it being Gothic, you will judge for yourself for we will pass it at a safe distance. It gets its name from the howling of the wind and waves around it which the old seamen thought sounded like the baying of a wolf or the roaring of a lion. Once we passed it in the fog and the crew was convinced that all the hounds of Hell were calling them to their doom!'

'You sail this way often, then?' Helena was surprised by the shuttered expression that came across his features at this innocuous question.

'Occasionally,' Adam said shortly. 'We will arrive in the Scillies in about four hours. Look!' He pointed over the side. 'Porpoises chasing herring. See…' He took her hand and led her to the rail. Helena, entranced by the leaping, arcing creatures, was unconscious of his arm around her shoulders as he steadied her when she leaned out, the better to see them as they played in the bow wave of the *Moonspinner*.

For the rest of the morning Adam devoted himself entirely to Helena's entertainment, pointing out seabirds and another school of porpoise, spinning her yarns about mermaids and sea monsters and patiently answering her stream of questions about life at sea.

'...of course, my father used to tell us about life on a King's ship—at least everything that he considered fit for my ears!—but I am sure things must be very different on a ship like this. How John would love this! He is to go as a midshipman with his uncle the Commodore just as soon as he is old enough.'

'After the loss of your father, I wonder your mother allows her only son to go to sea.'

'Mother is a realist—and she comes from a naval family herself. She knows that John would run away to sea if she did not let him go; at least she knows he will be with my uncle.'

The time seemed to fly past and Helena wondered how she could ever have felt uncomfortable in Adam's company. Then there was a cry from the masthead.

'Land ho!'

All at once the deck became a bustle of activity with sailors climbing to the rigging and two men in the bows preparing the lead line for testing the depth. Adam's attention was no longer on her and for a few minutes Helena thought he was as preoccupied as his crew in navigating the rock-strewn waters.

But by the time she could make out the cluster of islands clearly and the leadsman was calling the sounding regularly, she realised that navigation was not what was preoccupying his lordship. The crew, it seemed, were more than capable of steering the winding course through the mass of islets and rocks; Adam himself was nowhere to be seen.

'Biggal Rock on the starboard bow, sir!' the lookout

shouted and the bosun ordered a change of course to the north-west.

'Billy, here, lad! Run and tell his lordship we're entering the Crow Channel now.'

The lad ran below and reappeared at Adam's heels, a leather pouch in his hands. Adam's expression was stern and distant, like that of a man about to give bad news to someone, and Helena puzzled over what could have caused this transformation from the relaxed and amiable man who had been at her side all morning.

Lord Darvell took the pouch from the boy and extracted a folded letter, opening the crackling folds in a scatter of scarlet sealing wax and conning the contents rapidly. If anything his expression darkened, as if whatever he read there gave him little pleasure.

Helena, seeing the falling wax, realised the letter could only recently have been opened, perhaps just now below decks. It was as if Adam was opening sealed orders, like a naval officer reaching a certain latitude before reading the Admiralty's directions. Which, of course, was ridiculous, for Adam was a civilian...

She drew back against the rail, well out of the way, and watched the weed-covered rocks as they drew towards the harbour of Hugh Town on St Mary's. The semicircular anchorage was fringed on the northern edge by rocky islets and the long, curving harbour wall jutted out, sheltering a handful of sailing vessels within its lee. The little town straggled up from the harbour to the walls of a small fort from whose topmost turret a standard flapped in the strong breeze.

'That's Star Castle, ma'am,' a sailor remarked chattily as he stood close by, coiling a thick rope in his hands. 'So called on account of its shape and built in the time of Good Queen Elizabeth to keep off the Spanish

scourge.' He spat over the side at the mention of the old
enemy.

They dropped anchor with a rattle and a splash and the
men began to swing out the skiff. Adam was obviously
about to descend the rope ladder—and without a word to
Helena. 'My lord!' she called and he paused astride the
rail. 'May I not come ashore with you?'

Adam looked at her with the expression of a man seeing her for the very first time. 'I had clean forgot you,'
he said without a trace of apology in his voice. 'No, I
am going on business; stay here, you will be safe with
the crew.'

Helena, stung, protested. 'My lord! I want to see the
town and feel dry land beneath my feet again. I promise
I will not impede your business.'

He smiled at her, but without humour. 'Indeed you will
not, for you will remain, as I ordered, on *Moonspinner*.'

'But…'

Adam appeared to relent slightly. 'I will take you
ashore this evening, Miss Wyatt. We can have dinner at
the Godolphin Arms. It is a respectable place and Mrs
Trewather keeps a decent table.' Seeing that she was
about to protest again, he added, 'Until then, I would be
obliged if you do as you are bid and *stay here*.' With
that he swung his leg over the rail and climbed down the
rope ladder into the waiting boat.

She stood glowering at his unresponsive back as the
skiff's crew dug the oars into the rippling water and
pulled for the quayside. Infuriating man! Why, what harm
could there be in her going ashore? If the Godolphin
Arms was a reputable hostelry with a respectable landlady, she could have requested a private room and a hot
bath. She pulled the sticky, tangled hair off her neck with

a grimace. The thought of dining with Adam looking such a fright was unendurable!

Her annoyance hardened into defiance. After all, Adam Darvell was neither her father nor her husband. He might be the master of this ship, but that did not give him any rights to command her! The sailor who had earlier spoken to her as they had entered port was just passing by and she arrested his progress with a devastating smile.

'I should very much like to take a walk ashore. Is there anyone who could row me across?'

The sailor, basking in the warmth of her smile, and the unfamiliar sensation of being addressed so pleasantly by a lady of quality, could see no reason not to hasten to oblige her. On previous voyages his lordship's other lady friends had always come and gone as they pleased and there seemed no reason why this one should not be able to stroll along the harbourside on this sunny afternoon.

'Of course, ma'am. I'll row you across directly myself if you're not minding the little rowboat.'

'You are very kind.' Helena completed his enslavement by bestowing on him yet another dazzling smile.

In no time at all, Helena was being handed out of the skiff onto the steps of the curve of the harbour wall which encircled the new port like a protective arm. For a few moments the stone pier seemed to move under her feet, so used was she to the movement of the waves, and her first few steps were uncertain until she regained the equilibrium of once more being on dry land.

The dark roofs of the houses and businesses of Hugh Town gleamed in the warm afternoon sun as Helena walked towards the main thoroughfare. It was surprisingly populous, with an air of bustling prosperity. Helena strolled past the Custom House, an ale shop, two butchers and a grocer's. Several neatly dressed women with the appearance of tradesmen's wives were walking with baskets over their arms, smiling and nodding pleasantly as they passed her.

The Godolphin Arms occupied a wide frontage on the main street and was indeed a fine-looking hostelry, with sparkling clean windows and flowers on the ledges. Certainly it was the sort of place she could enter alone without misgivings, Helena thought, as she pushed open the door into the wide, sawdust-strewn entryway.

She stood blinking in the cool gloom, her eyes not yet adjusted from the sunlight. Several doors led off the passage, but all were closed, and she was making up her mind which to try when the one at the end opened and a potboy with two tankards emerged. 'I'll be with you directly, ma'am,' he said before pushing open the entrance to a private parlour to one side and walking through.

Over his shoulder Helena saw two men sitting, heads together, at a small table. They were deep in talk but broke off immediately when the lad appeared. One of them, Helena saw, was Adam, and it was he who swiftly gathered up the litter of papers on the table and stuffed them back into the leather pouch she had earlier seen on board.

Instinctively she drew back into the shadows, not wanting to be ordered back to *Moonspinner*. But even as she did so, Helena realised that that was not the only reason she did not want to be seen. There was something in the way the men were talking, something in the set of their shoulders and the way they had fallen silent, which spoke of secrets, of intrigue.

'Yes, ma'am? Can I help you, ma'am?' the potboy was asking.

'Er...yes. I would like a word with the landlady, if

you please?' Helena asked. But her mind was still on that quiet room. What was Lord Darvell about, deep in secretive dialogue with a swarthy rogue who looked as though he would cut a throat for two pence?

Chapter Three

'Good day, ma'am! And how can I be of service?' A bright-eyed little woman stepped forward as the potboy opened the door through to a small parlour at the rear of the inn.

'Mrs Trewather?' Helena enquired, pulling her wandering thoughts together.

'Indeed, ma'am.' The landlady dropped a small curtsy.

'I have just come ashore from a ship and wonder if it would be possible to engage a room for an hour or so to take a hot bath and wash my hair?'

'Why, of course, ma'am. We have hot water a plenty on the range! Matt!' The potboy reappeared, only to be sent running to carry the bathtub up to number seven. 'And fill it up, boy! Don't keep the lady waiting.' She turned to Helena. 'If you'll just take a seat for a few minutes, ma'am, I'll get our Jinny to find soap and towels. Would you like some refreshment? A nice cup of tea and a drop scone with my best gooseberry jam?'

'That sounds heavenly. Thank you, Mrs Trewather.'

Half an hour later Helena was luxuriating in the streams of hot water Jinny was pouring over her soapy hair while she sat hugging her knees in the shallow tub.

Feeling clean again was bliss, she reflected, rubbing the lavender soap into a lather.

'Is there anything else I can do for you, ma'am?' Jinny enquired as she helped her out of the tub and into a smother of soft towels.

'A comb and a mirror, if you please! I must do something with my hair if I can!'

'I'll comb it out for you, ma'am,' the girl offered as Helena fastened her dress and pulled on her stockings.

It took their combined efforts, and much wincing on Helena's part, to tease out the tangles and leave the wet hair rippling down her back in waves.

'I cannot leave until it is dry—I will sit in the sunlight by the window,' Helena decided. Even in a town where she was not known, it would be hoydenish behaviour to walk on a public street with wet hair.

'I will ask Mrs Trewather if you could sit in her garden, ma'am. It is quite private.' The girl ran off to fetch the landlady, leaving Helena with the sudden recollection that she had not a penny piece to her name and an account to settle. She had just decided to explain all and ask for credit until they came ashore for their evening meal when a mischievous impulse overcame her.

'...so if you could just add it to his lordship's reckoning for this morning, Mrs Trewather,' she said calmly as she was ushered out into a pleasant enclosed garden, fragrant with herbs and pot marigolds and enclosed on all sides within the walls of the inn.

'I'll do that with pleasure, ma'am. His lordship always settles up on the spot, being a very thoughtful gentleman. He says, you never can tell when he might have to up-anchor sudden like, what with the weather and all.'

Helena sat and combed her fingers through her drying hair and smiled at the thought of Adam's feelings when confronted with the account for her bath! He would have known as soon as he saw her and she asked for the money that she had been ashore against his adamant instructions, but to be surprised with the bill and in a place where he would have to accept it with the appearance of equanimity would try his temper sorely. He would see Miss Wyatt was not a young lady to be ordered about with impunity!

She touched her hair, finding it still damp at the roots. The afternoon shadows were lengthening quickly within the walls of the inn and she shifted along the bench the better to catch the last of the sunshine. The action brought her closer to one of the thick-paned windows. She could not discern the room within with any clarity, but it was ajar and, through the crack, the sound of men's low voices just reached her.

Naturally Helena was too well-bred to eavesdrop but as she sat quietly in the warm garden the cadence of their speech caught her ear. It was not English, nor the local *patois*, but French, and spoken with the rapidity and ease of natives. She knew she ought not to listen, but Helena edged closer to the crack, straining to hear. Doubtless it had some natural explanation, but it was disturbing to hear the language of Napoleon, of her country's enemies, spoken in such a conspiratorial manner.

Her schooling—and the influence of her mother—had left Helena with a good command of French but, despite straining to the utmost, she could not catch any sentences complete. What she did catch, though, was Adam Darvell's unmistakable tones.

All scruples cast to the wind, Helena crouched under the window, concentrating hard. But what little she could hear was tantalisingly incomplete.

'...*la flotte française...provisiones...armements...*'

Adam's voice interrogatively.

'*...trois mois...*'

Helena half rose in her eagerness to hear more and, in doing so, dislodged the gravel under her feet. The scraping sounded loud in the still air and she froze, her heart in her mouth.

'What's that?' Adam rapped out sharply. Horrified, Helena heard footsteps approaching the window and crushed herself as tight to the wall as possible. Adam's voice seemed to come from directly over her head, 'Courtyard's empty, probably a cat.' Then the window shut with a snap.

Helena closed her eyes as a wave of relief washed over her, leaving her weak at the knees. Then the realisation of what she had been hearing struck her. *They were discussing the French fleet*—the navy of the tyrant Napoleon who, in the years since his great reverse at Trafalgar, had swept across Europe with his armies, occupying state after state in a seemingly unstoppable progress!

She tiptoed out of the courtyard and re-entered the gloom of the inn, bundling her hair up roughly as she did so. Mrs Trewather, emerging from a side room, dropped a curtsy. 'Was everything to your liking, ma'am?'

'Indeed, yes, I thank you, Mrs Trewather, I will be on my way now.' Suddenly she was eager to get away from the shadows of the inn, back to the windswept deck of the *Moonspinner*.

The crew must have been on the watch for her, for as soon as she reached the quayside and waved the rowing boat put out and she was soon back on board.

Pacing the deck, Helena turned over in her mind exactly what she had seen and heard. The scene in the inn had appeared suspicious and secretive, and Adam's companion certainly seemed a rogue. There seemed no doubt that Adam was gathering information—but on whose behalf? He was an English gentleman—obviously his loyalty would be squarely with his King and country. He patently enjoyed adventure; if that was leading him into dangerous association with smugglers, and that in turn meant he needed information about the French and their activities, well, that was none of her concern. After all, she owed him her life—the least she could do in return was to give him the benefit of the doubt.

Tucked away as she was on the leeward side of the ship, away from the wind, the first Helena knew of his lordship's return was the bump of the skiff against the side and his voice raised in anger demanding to know who had rowed Miss Wyatt ashore.

Helena hurried round the wheelhouse to find him tight-lipped and confronting the bosun, who was protesting that as his lordship had given no orders that the lady wasn't to go ashore; when she'd asked, of course, they had taken her.

'…and, after all, your lordship, it's not as if all your other ladies don't regularly disembark, is it?' the man added, fatally.

Adam's face darkened. 'Hold your tongue,' he barked at the sailor, 'and about your business. Look at the state of the rigging—and these decks!'

Helena reached his side, 'Adam, it really is most unjust…'

'And you, madam, can also hold your tongue!' He gripped her arm above the elbow none too gently, his eyes as blue as the sea—and as cold. 'Come below, I want a word with you.'

It would be undignified to struggle in public so Helena allowed herself to be virtually marched down to the cabin. Once inside, she shook Adam's arm off angrily. He closed the door with great deliberation and leaned against it, arms across his chest. In the small room he dominated the space and Helena found herself backing away until the edge of the bunk caught the back of her knees and she sat down with an undignified bump.

'Well?' he enquired, waving what was obviously the reckoning from the inn between his fingers. 'Why, Miss Wyatt, did you find it necessary to deliberately flout my orders?'

'Orders? I am not one of your crew to be ordered around, my lord.'

'While you are on this ship you do as I command, and I will not tolerate disobedience.' He straightened up and with one step was towering over her as she sat, straight-backed on the bunk.

'And if I chose not to, what then?'

There was a long silence. Then, 'I would suggest, Helena, that you do not provoke me.'

Her chin came up defiantly. Her heart was beating with apprehension, but also with a strange exhilaration and an excitement she had never felt before. 'Oh, really, my lord! You sound like the villain in some dreadful Gothic tale.' When this accusation elicited no more response than a further tightening of his lips she added, 'I shall do as I please. After all, what can you do about it?' It sounded petulant even to her own ears and she wondered at herself for behaving so badly.

His lordship raised one dark brow. 'As I keep trying to tell you, Helena, I can do precisely what I want on this ship.'

Before she knew it he stooped and took her in his arms, pushing her back onto the narrow bed, trapping her with his weight before claiming her lips in a kiss that was deep, insidious and a complete demonstration of his mastery.

Shockingly, through her fury, Helena realised she was enjoying it very much indeed. Her hands beat an angry tattoo on his back—such a very broad back—but it was like a moth beating against a window for all the effect it had. She tried to push against his chest, but her hands became trapped by the weight of him, and still the kiss, that sweet invasion, went on.

How could she be so angry with him—with herself—and yet thrill to the discovery of his strength, the alien quality of a man's body entwined with hers?

Adam's lips left her mouth and he began to nibble gently at her ear while his hand stroked down the column of her neck. It was a wonderful sensation, unlike anything she had ever experienced before—and it was quite outrageous that they were both behaving in this manner! Before she even thought about it she fastened her teeth on his earlobe, so conveniently close to her lips, and bit down.

'Ow!' He rolled off her and sat up rubbing his ear. 'You minx! What did you do that for?'

Helena scrambled up to kneel beside him, eye to eye. 'You know perfectly well why! Of all the outrageous, immoral things...'

He pushed the dark blond hair off his forehead and grinned at her ruefully. 'But you must admit it was fun.'

'Fun!' Then she caught the glint in his eye and found herself twinkling back. Yes, it had been fun. This was doubtless a terrible reflection on her moral character, but she very much feared she had enjoyed it as much as he. And she was far too honest to pretend otherwise. 'Well, that is as may be,' she conceded as stiffly as she could. 'But it must not happen again.'

'As you wish.' He sketched a bow, then spoiled it by

adding, 'Providing you promise to do exactly as I say in future.'

'I will do no such thing!'

Adam climbed off the bed and began tucking his shirt back into his trousers. 'Then, Helena, I can give no guarantees as to my future conduct.'

He looked down at her kneeling on the bed, violet eyes sparking, rich brown hair a tousled mass about her shoulders. Part of his irritation had been due to the knowledge that he had no choice but to marry this girl, as thoroughly compromised as she was. But he was becoming hourly more reconciled to the idea of Miss Wyatt as a bride. Not only was she lovely, but she was spirited, intelligent and very much her own woman at a time when young women schooled in social mores seemed to him to be cast from the same vapid, shallow mould. And she had a sense of humour which he now appealed to.

'If you solemnly promise not to steal one of my boats and row ashore, then I promise not to make love to you until at least after dinner.'

She opened her mouth indignantly, then saw the wicked gleam of mischief in his eyes. 'That seems a reasonable compromise my lord,' she replied with dignity. 'As I have secured my object in going ashore, I will have no trouble in obeying you.'

Adam put out a hand and helped her to her feet. 'Your object? Ah, yes, your bath. How did you know you could safely leave it for me to pay?' Suddenly his eyes were intent on her face.

'But you told me where we would be eating tonight,' Helena replied innocently, ducking under his arm to get through the door. 'Mrs Trewather seemed well used to accommodating your er…guests, in that way.' She whisked up on deck before he could retaliate.

It seemed politic to Helena to keep out of his lordship's path until evening. She was finding him altogether too attractive and difficult to resist. Leaning on the rail, she gazed unseeing at the bustling quayside peopled with fishermen, tradesmen and a few uniformed soldiers from the barracks on the hill. The standard was fluttering from the star-shaped castle in the onshore breeze and Helena shivered, but not from the warm wind.

Rather, it was the remembrance of how it had felt to be with Adam on the bunk, his mouth hot on hers. Helena shook her head in perplexity. What sea change had swept over her when she had been pulled from the waves by this man? Was it the proximity of death which had washed away all her upbringing, her own sense of right and wrong? Never before had she felt the slightest temptation to encourage even a mild flirtation to go further than a chaste salute on her gloved fingertips, however eligible or attractive the young man concerned might be. But this man…

Helena shook herself out of her reverie and turned her back to the sea, leaning on the rail to watch the work of the ship. A small group of men were sitting aft, a torn sail spread between them as they stitched. The bosun was standing with Adam, a chart spread out on a hatch cover. They appeared to be discussing a course and the bosun, an expression of doubt on his weatherbeaten features, was jabbing his forefinger at the chart and shaking his head.

Adam clapped him on the shoulder and his voice carried back to Helena on the breeze. 'I know what we agreed, my friend, but now my plans have changed. I must return as soon as possible.'

'Now, my lord?' The man still sounded inclined to argue.

'No, later this evening. I dine ashore. We will sail at half past ten.'

'It will be on a falling tide, my lord...'

'I have every confidence in your ability not to run us aground, Jenkins,' Adam assured him as he rolled up the chart and went below.

The bosun glanced at Helena with such an absence of expression on his face that she was convinced he had a very good idea of why Adam was dining ashore and with whom, and that he heartily disapproved.

The thought of food reminded her that she had had very little to eat since breakfast and that her stomach felt quite hollow. She would go in search of Billy, the cabin boy, and send him to find her some bread and cheese. In the event she found both Billy and the cook at work in the cramped galley below decks. The lad was sitting cross-legged in the corner, a bucket between his knees into which he was peeling potatoes. The cook, a hard-looking man, was stirring a large pan on the range on its brick hearth.

From tales her father and uncle had told her of shipboard life in His Majesty's navy, Helen had expected the galley to be a gloomy hole producing uneatable concoctions. She should have realised that his lordship, even if he had had to leave his French chef ashore, would not tolerate poor food.

The galley was certainly cramped and dark, but the smell emanating from the stew was appetising and copper pans glinted from the walls. 'How delicious that smells!' Helena exclaimed, giving the dour man a friendly smile. 'It must be well-nigh impossible to cook well in such cramped conditions.'

The man's face relaxed somewhat. 'Well, ma'am, you'd be right at that. It's what I tell 'em, but they do complain so. Let 'em eat navy rations, that's what I tell 'em! Knocking weevils out of hard biscuit, having to eat your meat in the dark so you can't see it moving about with the livestock in it. Sorry, ma'am—' he broke off. 'Shouldn't talk about things like that to a lady.'

'That is quite all right,' Helena assured him. 'I have heard much of this before from my father.'

'Is he a naval man, ma'am?'

'He was. He was killed at Trafalgar, along with many a good man—Admiral Wyatt.'

'Why, ma'am!' The cook's face lit up. 'I served under him at Copenhagen. He was a commodore then, of course. That's where I got this leg, ma'am.' He moved across the galley as he spoke, dragging his right leg as he went. 'I ended up ashore then, kept an inn for a bit, but that was a dull old life after the navy.' He shuffled back with a cleaver and began chopping onions. 'Then his lordship took me on, been with him two years.'

'But surely the inn must have been more interesting than just sailing about on a gentleman's yacht?' Helena smiled.

The man shot her an unreadable look. 'Wouldn't exactly say that, ma'am. It has its moments. Now, was it something to eat you was wanting?'

Given that she had none of the usual accoutrements of a lady's toilette, dressing for dinner should have been a straightforward matter of washing her face and pulling a comb through her hair. But half an hour after she had gone to her cabin, Helena was still in her petticoats, surrounded by every garment she had pulled out of the trunk and drawers in the room.

What she found certainly threw a lurid light on his lordship's social life. French silks and laces—doubtless smuggled—abounded. The quality of the sewing was exquisite—even the scandalous Indian muslin lingerie, diaphanous though it was, was adorned with minute pintucks and embroidery. Rubbing the fine fabric between her fingers, Helena mused that not only was his lordship unstinting in his generosity towards his lady friends, but that everything she had heard about his female companions was doubtless true.

Well, she had to have clean linen, so if this was all there was, she would just have to wear it, Helena thought defiantly. But at the back of her consciousness a little voice suggested that it would be very pleasant to be the recipient of such bounty…

By the time his lordship tapped on the door Helena had settled on a sea-green gown of silk and had managed to fashion a fichu from a gauze scarf which rendered the bodice, if not modest, at least not indecent. She pulled a dark cream ribbon off another gown and caught her hair up in knot on top of her head, allowing the curls to fall naturally, teasing ringlets to frame her face. In the absence of rice powder, scent or jewellery, there was little more she could do.

But it appeared that it was more than enough for Adam, judging by the look that crossed his face as she opened the door and stood haloed by candlelight on the threshold. He took her hand and kissed it decorously and when he looked up his expression showed only polite admiration. She might have been any debutante he was accompanying to Almack's instead of his companion for an intimate dinner *à deux*.

They exchanged few words as he wrapped a boat cloak around her shoulders and assisted her down into the rowing boat. The two sailors at the oars said nothing as they bent to their task, but Helena felt flustered that they would assume her relationship with their master was improper. She felt even more unsure of herself when they landed: it was as though being on the *Moonspinner* was fantasy and normal rules of conduct did not apply, but once more on land those rules returned with a vengeance!

Helena pulled the hood of the cloak up further and shrank back into its folds, feeling very exposed, expecting at any moment that one of the respectable citizens strolling past them would turn and point an accusing finger at his lordship's hussy.

Adam took her arm and she stiffened. 'What is wrong? Are you unwell?' Her hand was trembling on his arm and he realised that she was nervous. After all, despite the dramatic circumstances of her arrival and the enforced intimacy of life on board, now that they were ashore in the real world he, too, felt the weight of Society's rules and conventions once more descending. Perhaps she was still unsure that he would do the honourable thing by her: well, he would reassure her over dinner.

It was not until the door of the private parlour closed behind them that Helena would take off the cloak, and even then she blushed as Mrs Trewather greeted them.

'A pleasure to see you again, miss. A chilly evening, is it not? But you should be cosy enough in here with the fire.' Helena thanked her, moving across to the blaze to warm her hands while Adam ordered wine. She noticed that the landlady made no reference to having seen Adam earlier that day and once more wondered at the secrecy and at his purpose in meeting the Frenchman.

She felt more comfortable when they sat at the table and Mrs Trewather was bustling around, laying out the dishes. Helena noticed that the woman attended to them personally, taking trays and dishes from the potboy at the door. His lordship's desire for discretion was obviously well understood at the Godolphin Arms.

A tureen of soup was removed with a fricassee of chicken, a plate of salsify and a platter of tiny fish, floured and fried. Helena found herself surprisingly hungry, and food at least was a safe topic of conversation.

'May I help you to some fish, my lord? It is quite delightfully fresh, as is only to be expected. And this caper sauce is delicious.'

Adam accepted the platter and maintained the bland discussion of the merits of the food, watching Helena's face until he saw her expression relax. The rituals of formal dining, the necessity of maintaining a conversation, lulled her into a sense of familiarity. Adam filled her wine glass, waited and was rewarded by the time Mrs Trewather came in to remove the dishes, by seeing Helena smile.

He twisted his own glass between strong brown fingers, idly watching the ruby liquid catch fire in the candlelight as he tilted it. 'I do hope you are no longer worrying about your mama: despite appearances, the man I entrusted the message to is very reliable.'

'I am glad to hear it, my lord. I know it does no good to worry about it, but I cannot put from my mind the thought of how she must have felt when John reached home and told her how I was swept out to sea.' She sipped the wine, and asked, perhaps rather too innocently, 'Does that fisherman carry many messages for you?'

'Enough to judge his trustworthiness,' Adam responded levelly, only the quirk of one eyebrow revealing that he knew full well she was fishing. 'From what you have told me before, I gather Lady Wyatt is a woman of great strength of mind and not someone apt to give way to apprehensions and fears.'

'Indeed, she is,' Helena agreed warmly. 'She always used to say, when Papa was at sea, that she would not believe the worst had befallen him until a messenger came to the door with his sword. If she had believed Admiralty dispatches, she would have been widowed many times over!'

'Buttered crab?' Adam passed her the plate of local crabs and filled a clean glass with white wine. 'Try this, it will suit the dish better.'

Helena sipped it cautiously, and was pleasantly surprised at how light it was compared to the red. 'And, of course, Mama is a considerable scholar and always says that nothing takes one's mind off one's troubles like plunging into the wars of Sparta!'

Adam cracked open a crab claw and commented, 'Yes, I can see that it might! Although my own experiences of the Greek wars are of receiving regular beatings for failing in my translation at Eton.' He topped up the wine glasses.

'I must confess, my lord, although Mama is too kind to say so, that I would never make a classical scholar, try though she might to interest me. And as for John, the only time he pays any attention is if the Roman navy is mentioned.'

'Ah, yes, your brother. A keen interest in ships, as I recall.'

'Oh, dear, he was very naughty. But I had not told him he must not go aboard your yacht and so…he did.'

The room was really very warm and Helena was conscious that her face was glowing, although whether that was in recollection of her first encounter with Adam Darvell or because she had perhaps had one glass of wine too many, she was unsure.

'Natural enough in a boy of his age, I was just the same. Navy mad, I suppose?'

'Oh, yes! He thinks of nothing else, although he has still a year to go before my uncle will consider taking him. His main anxiety is that the war might end before then, little wretch!'

'Small chance of that, I fear,' Adam said sombrely, then shrugged off the darkness which seemed to enter the room with the thought. 'And your uncle?'

'Mama's brother, Commodore Sir Robert Breakey. He is with the Mediterranean fleet at present.'

By now Helena was quite comfortable. The wind sighed outside against the shutters, the candlelight flickered, but the wine was warm in her veins.

Mrs Trewather brought in a dish of nuts and a decanter of port which she placed firmly in front of his lordship. She raised her eyebrows slightly as Helena showed no sign of rising to leave his lordship alone. 'The private parlour's just the other side of the passage, miss,' she said with heavy emphasis.

'Oh? Thank you, Mrs Trewather,' Helena replied vaguely, giving the landlady a charming smile and staying precisely where she was. She suppressed a small hiccup and wondered if the buttered crab had been a little rich.

Thwarted, the landlady left, closing the door behind her with a click. In the darkness of the passageway she sniffed disapprovingly: it wasn't like his lordship to be having girls of that age on board. She'd seen some high-flying game pullets on his arm before now, but this one was far from that mode. Ah, well, not her concern—no doubt his lordship would find himself leg-shackled before long!

'May I have some, too?' the cause of the landlady's concern was asking. 'I have never had port before.'

Adam hesitated, looking at her narrowly. He had wanted her to have enough to drink to make the difficult conversation they were about to have run smoothly but, seeing her heightened colour and sparkling eyes, he wondered if he had overdone it. Not that it had impaired her complexion or her charm, both of which were quite captivating.

'There is a very good reason for that,' he remarked drily, pouring himself a glass and leaving the decanter well out of her reach. 'Now, there are things we must discuss...'

Helena wrinkled her nose in perplexity. 'Are there?'

He appeared not to hear her. 'Do I recall you saying you were intending to do the Season this year?'

'Yes—finally. Mama forgot last year. By the time she and her publisher had agreed on her treatise on the Punic Wars it was halfway through June and I had no gowns ordered.'

'Forgot! Forgive me, Helena, I do not seek to criticise Lady Wyatt, but I would have thought any mama with a marriageable daughter would have had that very much to the forefront of her mind.'

'Yes, but you see, she's not just any mama...' Helena discovered she was waving one finger at him to emphasise her point and folded her hands hastily. 'She was so shocked to discover the date that—with the exception of the poetry of Sappho, of course—she has devoted her energies to little else since. I do wish you could see my new gowns—and as for my riding habit...'

Adam sat back in his chair, cracking a walnut between his fingers. 'I shall look forward to it.'

'Oh, will you be doing the Season, too? How very

nice! Will you dance with me at Almack's? I have so many acquaintances in town that I am sure I will not want for partners, but I must confess it would be reassuring to know my dance card will not be quite empty!'

His lordship, aware that the conversation was slipping from his grasp, reached for his glass to refill it and found that Helena had picked it up and was dipping one finger experimentally in the remaining few drops of sweet wine.

'Miss Wyatt...Helena...'

'Oh, I am sorry, you want your glass back.' She handed it back with an apologetic smile that warmed her lovely violet eyes.

Adam gave himself a mental shake and said firmly, 'Helena, listen to me. I see no reason why your plans for the Season should be disrupted, and your new gowns will come in very useful and save much time...'

Helena broke in, utterly confused. 'My lord, what are you talking about?'

'Brideclothes, of course. Naturally, you may have whatever you wish, but time is of the essence and it would present a very odd impression if you did not have a suitable wardrobe.'

'*Brideclothes*? But I am not getting married! Sir, I am not yet out!' Indeed, I have had too much wine, she thought confusedly.

'I told you before, I will marry you. Indeed, I must.'

'What nonsense!' Helena declared stoutly, bringing one small fist down on the table to underline the point.

Adam took the clenched fist in his and patted it. 'Face the inescapable fact, my dear—you are ruined. You have no choice but to marry me.'

'I might be compromised, my lord, in the eyes of Society, but I am not ruined. I will return home with discretion and there the matter rests.' She snatched her hand away, suddenly very clear-headed. 'And do not call me your dear!'

'Lady Wyatt will insist.'

'Mama will believe what I tell her, and she would never force me to marry against my will.'

His lordship got to his feet and strode to the fireplace where he turned and regarded her coolly. 'My dear Miss Wyatt, what you want in this matter is neither here nor there. I have compromised you and I *will* marry you.'

Helena too was on her feet, sweeping around the table to face him with real anger in her eyes. 'I am not marrying you! There is no reason—I am not ruined!'

'Not yet,' Adam said, his voice silky. 'But there are still two days and nights before you reach home.'

The slap echoed round the room. Adam rubbed his cheek, his eyes never leaving hers. Before Helena could step back, his arms were imprisoning her and his lips were hot and hard against her mouth.

She wrenched herself free and confronted him. 'I would not marry you, sir, if you were the last man on earth!'

'In that case, madam,' he countered, his voice hard, 'we will remain at sea until you change your mind.'

Chapter Four

The walk back along the quayside was undertaken in icy silence on both their parts. Helena could only surmise that Adam's male pride was wounded by her refusal to fall gratefully into his arms like—if gossip was to be believed—any other woman who received his attentions.

As for herself, it was outrageous that he should assume she would welcome his offer of marriage, made under duress as it was! How dare he assume she would willingly—thankfully!—comply whether she loved him or not? Mama had not spent eighteen years schooling her to be of an independent cast of mind to see her throw herself at a man simply because that offered the easy way out of a difficulty.

As for being ruined, she was not, and she had no intention of being so, whatever his lordship's wiles or threats! The cool night air was beginning to clear the fumes of wine from her mind and Helena blushed to recall how easily she had almost capitulated to Adam's lovemaking on the *Moonspinner*. Well, never again would she allow him near enough to touch even a fingertip, even if it meant locking herself in her cabin for the entire voyage back!

The skiff was waiting for them, tied to the quayside, but with no crewmen aboard. Adam cast round, his face set and cold and, almost as if summoned by his silent fury, two sailors shot out of a nearby tavern and hurried to their side.

'Sorry, my lord!' the more senior apologised, scrubbing the back of his hand across his still-wet mouth. 'Just having a quick wet. Simeon! Move about, lad, get on those oars.'

Adam shot both men a look which boded ill for later and turned to offer Helena his hand. She turned her shoulder and reached down to Simeon who leapt to his feet, sending the skiff rocking, and took her hand in his rough grasp. He settled her respectfully in the stern, then swiftly bent to pick up the oars, conscious that he had done even more to incur his master's wrath. Cor! There'd be some gossip below decks tonight! It didn't look as if his lordship's usual luck was in...

'What are you waiting for men, bend to it!' Adam snapped as soon as his feet touched the bottom boards. In the starlight the sailors exchanged glances and did as they were bid. Still, one thing you could say for his lordship, he didn't bear grudges: with a bit of luck he'd be as right as rain in the morning.

During the short crossing, Helena's imagination ran wildly over what might happen next. By the time she was safely on deck she was prepared for anything from a raging row to his lordship sweeping her off her feet and down to the cabin and into his bed. It was a considerable anticlimax when Adam turned to the bosun and snapped, 'See Miss Wyatt below to her cabin—and see that she remains there.'

Standing glaring at his back as he stalked over to the wheelhouse, Helena was astounded. He could at least have been civil, have maintained a façade of politeness in front of his crew! She had been dismissed with little more ceremony than a naughty cabin boy.

'Good evening.' She smiled pleasantly at the bosun, determined not to show her chagrin. 'Please do not trouble to escort me. Is there a light in my cabin?'

'Yes, ma'am, I'll just help you down the companion-way, ma'am. Steps are very steep…'

Helena shut the door with a quiet 'goodnight', turning the large key with a determined twist of her wrist. She waited until she heard the man's footsteps retreating, then stormed over to the bunk, seized a pillow and pummelled it furiously until feathers began to leak from the seams and tickle her nose. Throwing it from her furiously, Helena sat down on the bed and concentrated on breathing calmly until she regained her composure.

How could she let herself be provoked so? But then, Adam Darvell was a provoking man. And she was honest enough with herself to admit that it was not just anger that he aroused in her. A little shiver ran down her spine at the memory of his touch, of the strength of him against her on this very bed…of that angry kiss in the inn.

She woke to the sound of the sea slapping against the sides of the ship and the pitch and toss of a vessel well out in open seas. Helena swiftly scrambled into her clothes, made a hasty toilette and went up on deck. She had no confidence that they were heading back to English shores: the mystery of the French agent, for he could have been nothing other, still nagged at the back of her mind.

But it was impossible to tell where they were, or where they were headed. Everywhere she looked the sea was grey, flecked with angry foam. Above them the clouds were dark and louring, heavy with unshed rain. Full sail was set despite the wind and the *Moonspinner* raced through the waters as if pursued.

The deck tilted and Helena grabbed at the side netting and clung on as the wind whipped her hair painfully past her cheeks. The crew were hurrying about their duties, bare feet confident on the damp planking. Adam and the bosun stood together by the wheelhouse, a chart flapping between them, their bodies bending instinctively with the motion of the ship.

Helena made her way nervously across to them, catching at every rope and spar she passed. She could quite see why the men wore no shoes, for her own leather soles were treacherous on the spray-drenched deck.

'Good morning. Where are we?' she gasped as she reached the wheelhouse, the words almost snatched away by the wind.

Adam thrust the chart into the bosun's hands and said to the man, 'I thought I had given orders that Miss Wyatt was to remain confined to her cabin.'

So that was how he wanted to play it! Helena smiled wanly at the petty officer and said, 'Please tell his lordship that if he wishes me to suffer the full effects of seasickness in what I believe is his *cabin*, he has only to say so. Otherwise I intend to remain in the fresh air.'

Adam saw the veriest hint of a twitch of amusement touch the seaman's lips. With an effort he controlled a strong desire to pick Helena Wyatt up, throw her over his shoulder, take her below decks and... Damn it, he did not know how to deal with this provoking female! But then, if she was one of those simpering little ninnies, or one of the sophisticated married ladies he knew so well, he would not find her half so interesting.

A gust hit them broadside and Helena staggered, clutching the bosun's arm for support.

'Tell Miss Wyatt that for her own safety she may either be lashed to the mainmast or sit in the wheelhouse and take her breakfast. The choice is, of course, her own.'

'Er…miss…'

'I heard his lordship, thank you. Some coffee and bread in the wheelhouse will be perfectly acceptable.'

Fulminating inwardly on the strange ways of the gentry, the bosun went in search of Billy the cabin boy.

Helena turned to look directly at Adam's expressionless countenance. 'I see your temper has not been improved by a night's rest, my lord. If you can bring yourself to address me, might I enquire where we are headed?'

A look of surprise crossed his face. 'Why, Siddlesham, of course. Where else?'

'France, perhaps?' The telltale words were out of her mouth before she could stop them.

Adam caught her arm none too gently and pulled her close. 'France?' His voice was low, so low no one even a step away could have overheard. 'And why might you assume such a destination?'

'I…er…a foolish thought, my lord. After all, we are so close and the weather bad. I wondered if we might be driven for shelter…' It sounded weak and unconvincing even to her own ears.

Adam pulled her even closer, his eyes narrowed slits as he watched her betraying countenance. 'This is a stiff blow, no-more—and you know it. No, Helena, I think the truth is that you have been spying upon me. Sneaking up to listen at windows at the inn. Hearing and seeing things you ought not. You should be careful, my dear, in these dangerous times, lest what you meddle in has unfortunate consequences.'

Helena wrested her arm free and flashed back, 'Such as being forcibly married off?'

'What a suspicious mind you have, Helena.' His smile was entirely without humour. 'Of course, a wife cannot testify against her husband—although I am not certain if that applies in cases of treason. And that is what we are talking of, is it not, Helena?'

She gasped at the effrontery of the man, to seize on her veiled accusation and throw it back in her face so openly. These were deep waters indeed. She did not, could not, believe him a traitor and would never have spoken of France if he had not provoked her so...

Helena was frightened, both by what she saw on Adam's face and by the enormity of what she had accused him of. He was an English gentleman, every dictate of honour was naturally for his King and country and for his place within that hierarchy. She had uttered the unthinkable: how could it ever be retracted?

'Sail on the starboard quarter!' The shout from the crow's nest rang out raggedly on the wind. It was enough to break their interlocked gaze apart. 'Coastguard cutter!' The second shout sent Adam striding to the rail, the danger of the tilting deck ignored, Helena forgotten.

The crew froze in their positions, eyes on the fast approaching cutter. Helena realized with a sudden insight that this was not a chance encounter, that this was something the crew of the *Moonspinner* both feared and were prepared for. She recalled her first suspicions that Adam was dabbling in a little smuggling—then she saw his face and knew it was much more momentous than that.

There was a puff of smoke on the side of the cutter, then, to Helena's utter horror, a splash just ahead of the yacht's bow and the sound of cannonfire. 'They are attacking us!' she gasped, unable to believe it.

'A warning shot only,' Adam said grimly. 'Get below. I cannot outrun them: if an officer boards, you must say we are betrothed. Nothing else will save your reputation.' He turned and shouted at the men in the rigging, 'Bring in sail, prepare to hove to.'

Helena tugged urgently at his sleeve. 'Adam! What did that Frenchman give you? If you have papers, I can hide them—they would never dare to search my person.'

'You would risk being thought a traitor?'

'Oh, don't be such an idiot!' Helena snapped. 'Just give me the papers!'

For a long moment Adam looked down into her earnest face, searching her eyes with his. Helena realized that it was not just her own instinctive leap of faith that he was not a traitor that was in question. Adam too had to invest all his trust that she would not betray him and his secret.

'*Moonspinner!* Hove to and prepare to be boarded by His Majesty's Excise!'

Even the hail did not make Adam look away. Helena saw something in his eyes change as though he had reached a decision. Abruptly he thrust his hand into the breast of his coat, pulled out a small parchment package with heavy red seals and pushed it into her shaking hands. Without another word he turned and faced the approaching vessel, shielding her from sight with his body.

Helena almost ran below, the package, still holding the warmth of Adam's body, clutched to her breast. Once in the cabin her first thought was to pin it securely into her undergarments, but then she paused, her fingers on the fastening of her gown.

Adam was right; if an officer—by definition a gentleman, with connections in Society—came on board, she would have no option but to admit to being betrothed to Adam. And even that would hardly do her reputation much good! It would save a scandal, but she would still be known as a flighty girl who would travel unchaperoned with a man. She would have no choice but to marry him. An idea half formed in her mind, then clarified. If she were not a *lady*, then no one would think twice either about her presence or her morals.

Urgently she began to put away all traces of her presence in the cabin, folding up the elegant gown and tucking the slippers into a trunk. Her old gown, the one she had been wearing when she drifted out to sea, had been returned to her and she tugged it over her head. It had been washed out but not pressed and the seawater had removed all lingering traces of respectability from it. A linen towel from the closet served to wrap her hair into a turban and her bare feet would soon become dirty on the decking.

Helena put her head cautiously out of the hatch at the top of the companionway. Everyone's attention was on the starboard side where, from the sound of voices, she guessed a rowing boat had just pulled to. She whisked out of the hatch and, half crouching, ran to the galley entrance, nearly tumbling down the steps in her haste.

The cook almost dropped the pan he was carrying as she literally fell into his tiny galley. 'Miss Wyatt! What's amiss?'

'I have no time to tell you now, but as you served my father, will you help me? I am sorry, I do not know your name.'

'It's Tom, miss, and of course I'll help you, only tell me how.'

'The excisemen are boarding us and I cannot be

found—or I will be ruined.' The man nodded in ready
understanding. 'I must pretend to be the cook—it will
seem just another of his lordship's eccentricities. Will
you fall in with my plan?'

The man grinned, obviously ready for any adventure.
'I will, ma'am, I will. I'll pretend to be cook's mate.' He
cast around the tiny galley for inspiration before snatch-
ing up a piece of sacking and limping over to her 'Here,
ma'am, wrap this round yourself for an apron.'

Helena did as she was bid, her fingers moving swiftly
to tie the rough hessian around her waist. As she did so,
her fingers encountered the bulge of the package pinned
in her petticoat and she bunched the cloth over to conceal
any sign of it.

'Your earrings!' the cook exclaimed as voices rang out
above them. Helena snatched off the filigree loops and
stood with them in her hand for a frozen moment. Tom
thrust the pestle and mortar along the bench towards her
and she dropped them in, pushing them under the peppercorns he had been grinding.

Feet were clattering on the companionway steps and
the light from above was cut off by the press of bodies
coming below decks. Even so, Tom realised, very few
people would be fooled into thinking Miss Wyatt was a
cook. A few days at sea had lightly coloured her skin,
but her complexion still had a perfection that spoke of
her status. With sudden inspiration he thrust his hand into
the flour barrel and tossed a handful of flour into Helena's
face.

She sneezed vigorously, batting at the cloud in a way
which spread it even more effectively over her clothes
and face. 'Tom!' But the minute the protest escaped her
lips she knew what he had been about and added to the
effect with a handful of soot from the range.

Tom had been gutting mackerel and Helena snatched up a fish and the knife and began to chop off its head and tail, her shoulder half turned to the entrance.

They were only just in time: the tiny space was suddenly filled with men in navy blue uniforms.

'Oh, get out of the light, do! Lummocking around in my galley!' Helena, calling on a childhood spent playing with the village children, fell into a broad Sussex accent. She stuck the gutting knife into the chopping board with some force and confronted the men, fists on hips, in a very good imitation of Mrs Charnock, the cook at home.

'Really, Darvell, I know you like to cultivate a reputation as an eccentric—but a female cook at sea?' There was a snigger from the group of excisemen at the speaker's shoulder. 'If...' the man's voice became an insolent drawl '...that is what she is.'

Before Adam could respond, Helena brought her chin up angrily and demanded in a shrill voice, ''Ere, what do you think you are? Calling me a trull, are you?'

Her eyes locked with those of the naval lieutenant who was obviously in command of the party. She had a fleeting second to think that, under any other circumstance, she would have thought him a handsome and presentable gentleman. The uniform sat easily across his broad shoulders; he was almost as tall as Adam, his dark hair grazing the deck beams overhead. His gaze flicked speculatively round the galley and when the brown eyes rested on her again they were hard and cold.

'What a very insubordinate crew you have, Darvell.' He snapped his fingers. 'Two of you, search in here. Every locker—and check the barrels too.'

The men shouldered past Helena and began to search. Tom, assuming an expression of vague stupidity, picked up a pail of potatoes which were soaking and slammed it down near one of the searchers, showering his white stockings with muddy droplets. 'Any more of that, you'll be scrubbing spuds on a King's ship,' the man snarled, pushing his face close to Tom's.

Everyone's eyes were drawn by the exchange and Helena snatched the opportunity to look at Adam. He was standing at the back of the group, apparently unconcerned, his arms crossed over his chest. But, knowing him, she could detect the tension in his tall, erect figure and see the tautness of his mouth. Yet when he saw her watching him, he raised one brow a fraction and his eyes were warm with amused admiration.

Helena felt instinctively that Mrs Charnock would not have stood idly by while this sort of disturbance went on in her kitchen. Grabbing a long-handled ladle by its bowl she poked the hook end into the ribs of the aggressive exciseman. 'Leave him be, you great lummock! He's worse than useless at the best of times without you making him all afeard!'

The lieutenant stepped forward and seized Helena by the wrist. 'Put that down, you harridan, I'll not have you assaulting one of my men.'

She did not try to resist, letting him take the ladle with his free hand, but she was conscious that his fingers tightened on the slim bones and his eyes dropped to look at her hands. 'You have very soft skin for a cook,' he remarked.

Helena almost gasped aloud. She did no physical work and her hands were indeed soft and pliable. She thought swiftly and rubbed her arm insinuatingly against the cloth of his jacket. 'Hold hands with many cooks do you, ducks?' she asked with a coy wink. 'Well, the secret of nice soft hands is lard, me love. That and the kneading…of the dough, that is.' And she winked again.

There was a hoot of laughter from one of the excise-man, hastily suppressed as the officer stepped abruptly from Helena's side with a look of disgusted fury on his face.

'Have you seen enough down here, Brookes?' Adam asked coolly. Helena could see the muscle at the corner of his mouth twitching and realised that he did not dare meet her eyes.

'In good time.' The lieutenant was making a point of not being hurried. He poked with his finger among the objects on the narrow shelf which ran along the bulkhead. He pushed aside packets of herbs, some broken sugar and the sugar tongs and stirred the peppercorns in the mortar with his forefinger.

'Oy! Get your hands out of there!' Helena protested. 'Do you know how much those cost?' It was enough to bring his attention from the peppercorns to her face and she held his gaze insolently, fearing a betraying glint of silver earring amongst the small black spheres.

'Enough!' Lieutenant Brookes raked her with a hard stare, then turned on his heel. 'Come, men, there is nothing here. Join the others in the hold.'

The boarding party pushed back up the companionway with Adam at the rear. He paused on the bottom step and looked back, a grin of unholy amusement on his face, then he was gone.

Helena's knees gave way and she sank down on to the flour barrel. 'Oh, Tom! That was a close call. What horrible men!'

'They're always like that, miss. And that Lieutenant Brookes is a mean piece of work. He hates his lordship— and finding nothing only makes his spite worse.'

'You sound as though this were a common occurrence.' Helena got up and pushed a floury lock of hair back under her makeshift turban. 'We had better keep working in case they come back and try and catch us out.' She picked another fish out of the tub and slit it open.

'Every voyage, almost.' Tom stirred the pot on the stove. 'At least, ever since the Admiralty started putting naval officers with the excise vessels to give them a bit of backbone. That Lieutenant Brookes thinks he's too good for chasing a few smugglers around. Wants to have his own frigate, I'll be bound. And,' he added musingly, 'I reckon its more than that. From the way he and his lordship talk to each other, they know each other ashore. Went to school together, the bosun says. One thing I do know—there's no love lost on either side. How are you doing with those mackerel?'

There was the sound of many feet on the deck overhead. Helena glanced upwards and the cook commented, 'Sounds like they're done. They won't have found anything—they never do.'

'Is that because there is nothing to find?' Helena asked tartly.

Tom winked at her. 'That'd be saying, ma'am.'

Helena was certain he was talking about smuggling; nothing more sinister. A private yacht like this would be an obvious target for the Excise for, even with England at war with France, the demand for French silks, lace and brandy was as keen as ever. And the Scillies were a known entrepôt.

But whoever Adam had been head to head with in the Godolphin Arms in St Mary's had not had the look of a wine merchant about him! She was suddenly very frightened for Adam: Lieutenant Brookes's cold eyes and hard mouth were those of a calculating hunter who would not easily give up until he had caught his prey.

The edge of the parchment bundle caught against her shift. What was it Adam was up to? And why should she trust him rather than a King's officer? And yet…and yet, she did. Whatever he was about, however illegal, she could not believe he meant harm to his country. She touched her lips, unaware that her eyes had a soft expression which did not go unnoticed by Tom.

She paced up and down the narrow galley. 'Why are they so long leaving?' she fretted. 'I must find out what is happening.' Ignoring the cook's protest that it would be better to stay below, Helena tiptoed up the companionway and gingerly peered over the edge of the hatch.

Most of the excisemen had climbed back over the side to their skiff, leaving Adam confronting their officer at the rail. Adam's voice was hard, and strong enough to carry both to the men in the boat and to Helena. 'I warn you, Brookes, if this harassment continues I will take the matter up with the Admiralty. I am not without influence.'

The two men were standing close together, eye to eye, the animosity crackling between them. 'I am aware that you have influence, my lord,' Brookes sneered back. 'It is the only way I can account for your charmed life. But I am watching you—sooner or later I will have the proof I need of your trafficking in these waters. Then see how much good your influence does you.'

With that final threat he clapped his hat back on his head, swung over the rail and disappeared.

Helena ran to Adam's side. 'Have they gone for good?'

'I hope so, for we must make more speed and for that I must take a risk.' He strode over to the wheelhouse where the bosun was picking up the sea charts which had been scattered in the search. 'Wait until they are hull down, then pull in the cargo.'

'But if they double back, my lord?'

'Then we throw it overboard. We can stand the loss, but I want to get Miss Wyatt home quickly now and with the drogues out we are losing speed.'

Helena watched in amazement as, half an hour later, two seamen began to fish over the stern with long boat-hooks. After a few minutes the men were pulling in chains, dripping with water and seaweed, then a heavy bundle bumped up on deck, water streaming from its tarpaulin cover.

'And what might that be, my lord?' Helena asked with dangerous calm. Had she been taken for a fool, throwing herself into danger simply to cover up smuggling?

'Silk and tobacco. A small quantity this time—I am sure His Majesty's exchequer will not notice the loss.'

Helena, with a glance at the bosun, asked in frozen tones, 'May I speak with you alone, my lord?'

Once in the cabin she turned on him furiously. 'How could you? How could you drag me off to Scilly, put me in danger of disgrace and discovery—all for a few guineas' worth of smuggled goods? Did you find it amusing that I was in dread that Lieutenant Brookes might discover your correspondence with your French supplier, or whatever it is I have tied up in my shift?'

'So that is where you put it.' Adam's eyes were teasing. 'I think you should hand it back now.' He moved towards her with obvious intent in his eyes.

Helena backed away, but found herself once more cornered in the tiny room. Adam reached up and untied the towel she had wrapped round her hair. The curls fell loose around her shoulders and he dabbed the flour from the end of her nose with one corner of the towel.

She batted irritably at his hand. 'Why do you do it,

Adam? You cannot need the money, for you are well known to be a wealthy man. Is it the excitement? Why not join the navy if that is what you seek and fight like an honest man?'

'As you observe, I am in no need of money,' he remarked, reaching around her waist to unfasten the sacking apron. 'And I am certainly in no need of any additional excitement in my life.' His voice was husky and his breath warm on her neck as he freed the coarse hessian. 'You cannot really have believed I wished to place you in danger, but you must know that smuggling brings the country much useful intelligence. Now, where did you put my notes?' His fingers caressed through the worn cotton covering her back.

Helena knew her breathing was ragged. The anger had changed into something else entirely, and she knew she desired nothing more than to melt into Adam's arms, which now encircled her completely. His fingers, with practised expertise, had freed the bodice of her gown which slipped from her shoulders.

With a gasp of shock Helena stepped back and Adam let her go, allowing the gown to fall unhindered to her feet. Left standing in her shift, Helena crossed her hands over her breasts instinctively and the parchment package crackled under the pressure.

'The classic hiding place.' The words were soft and teasing, but Adam's face was very intent as he watched her flushed face and his fingers were very gentle as he delicately eased the folded papers from the warmth of her bosom. Without a second glance he tossed them onto the chest and gathered Helena back into his arms. One palm spread firmly across the small of her back, while the other hand journeyed over the soft curve of her hips. Adam's mouth came down on hers with gentle certainty and Helena, all caution and common sense gone, kissed him back.

She found herself lifted and placed, with infinite care, on the narrow bed. Her eyes were closed, her heart beat wildly in her ears and she sensed rather than felt Adam smoothing the shift from her shoulders. The little voice of common sense tried to reassert itself, then died, lost in a wave of sensation as Adam's lips grazed their way down one breast to the taut nipple.

Helena whimpered complainingly as the sensation stopped, feeling the bed move as Adam shifted his weight, then there was the sudden shock of his hot, smooth flesh against her sensitive breast.

Adam groaned deep in his throat as his hands moved down over the plane of her stomach. Helena instinctively arched against him, her untutored body desperate for his touch. Her voice whispered against him, inciting him, 'Yes Adam, please, Adam…'

His hands stopped moving, his lips broke free and he lay still against her, holding her close.

'Adam?' she whispered again. 'What is wrong? Have I done something to displease you?'

He spoke into her hair softly, 'No, Helena, you have done nothing wrong. But I can wait…must wait, until we are married. I may have compromised you, but I cannot take advantage of your innocence.'

Helena lay next to him cradled in his arms, a growing sense of dismay spreading through her, driving out the wild, sensual excitement that had filled her. What had she been thinking of? How could she have allowed this to happen? Only Adam's scruples—the very scruples which were driving him to marry her—had saved her from absolute ruin. She would have had no option but to

marry him. And exciting, attractive, dangerously mysterious as Lord Darvell was, he did not love her.

She struggled up into a sitting position, averting her
eyes from him as she gathered the ruins of her chemise
modestly around her. And she had only known him a few
days, knew nothing of him except by reputation and what
she had observed—and none of that suggested a suitable
husband! Perhaps all girls, kissed for the first time as
expertly as she had been, felt stirrings of love. But it was
nonsense, of course, and he must be brought to realise it.

'Helena…' He was sitting up too, shrugging into his
shirt. 'The next time…after we are married…'

'Married?' Helena laughed brittlely. 'I commend you
for your restraint just now, my lord, I fear the fright of
the last few hours quite overturned my judgment. But I
say again, I cannot marry you—indeed, I will not marry
you. I would be obliged if you would leave me now so
I can get dressed.'

Adam stared at her, and for a long moment she feared
he might forget his restraint and push her back amongst
the pillows. Then he swung his legs to the floor and stood
up, towering above her.

'Then it seems I must be more frank with Lady Wyatt
than I had intended. For believe me, Helena, marry me
you must and will. However much you dislike the prospect.'

Chapter Five

Lady Wyatt set her after-dinner teacup down as the front doorbell sounded, shattering the silence of the house. Only the slightest rattle of china against china betrayed her strained nerves, although under the discreet trace of rouge her cheeks went white. As Scott's footsteps crossed the hall she stood up, smoothing the skirts of her heavy silk evening gown, her heart beating uncomfortably in her chest. She prayed that whoever was at the door had news—good news—about her darling girl.

The most rigid self-discipline, learned during years as a serving officer's wife, had enabled her to show a façade of calm self-control in front of the servants and to explain Helena's absence in Chichester plausibly to those neighbours who paid morning visits. And for John's sake she had made light of the matter, for the little boy was distraught with the knowledge that he had put his sister in danger.

But at night her hard-won composure gave way and her mind filled with dreadful possibilities. Even before the arrival of Lord Darvell's message she had not been able to bring herself to believe Helena had drowned; for a rational woman, she had the wholly irrational belief that if her daughter were to die she would immediately know it. But there were other possibilities which were almost as bad…and which had haunted her nights: what if she had been washed up on the coast of France?

Then the message had come, delivered by a man Scott had described as 'a shady cove, my lady'. Relief at knowing her daughter was alive was slowly eroded by nagging anxiety as day followed day and no further word came. They could have been boarded by the French, they might have been shipwrecked. But even if those disasters did not befall, Helena was alone on a ship crewed by rough sailors under the command of a man who was a local byword as a rake.

When she heard Helena's voice greeting the butler Anne Wyatt sat down suddenly, her knees giving way in reaction.

Her eyes were blurred with emotion and the next thing she knew Helena was kneeling beside her, her head buried in her lap, hot tears staining the elegant garnet silk of her gown.

Anne stroked her daughter's hair as she had done when she had been a little child and murmured, 'There, there, my love. You are home, you are safe now.' Helena hugged her convulsively back and it was some minutes before the affecting reunion was interrupted by the butler.

Scott cleared his throat discreetly and announced, 'Lord Darvell, my lady.'

The double doors closed behind Adam with some emphasis: below stairs the loyal staff were well aware of both Miss Helena's disappearance and this man's role in it and had come to the conclusion that, if such a rake was involved, no good would come of it.

Lady Wyatt gently extricated herself from her daughter's embrace and got to her feet, regarding his lordship with the calm hauteur natural to a granddaughter of the Earl of Portchester. Helena moved to the back of her mother's chair and stood holding the back, her fingers kneading the upholstery nervously.

'Lord Darvell, I understand I have you to thank for rescuing my daughter from the sea, and for that you have my eternal gratitude.' Adam met the cool, unsmiling gaze with equal calm, reflecting that Lady Wyatt was indeed an impressive woman. She was neither the vague bluestocking her reputation might suggest, nor a nervous widow thrown into disarray by the alarming circumstances of their meeting. 'I am grateful also that you sent word to me so promptly that my daughter was not drowned. As you may imagine, both her brother and I had feared that she was dead.'

Adam was acutely aware that he was being kept standing when the dictates of good manners should have meant that he would be seated and offered refreshment by now. The unspoken 'but' hovered heavy in the air as Lady Wyatt continued to regard him across the candlelit room. The French clock on the mantle chimed ten, and still the tall, striking woman watched him from under level brows.

'No doubt you are wondering, ma'am, why I did not restore Miss Wyatt to you immediately after plucking her from the sea.' Adam kept his temper, well aware that her ladyship had good cause for anger.

'I confess, my lord, that that question was uppermost in my mind, from the time I received your letter—and remains so now.' Lady Wyatt turned to Helena and patted her cheek with a smile. 'You must be exhausted, my dear. Go to your room and ring for Lucy to bring you some supper—she will be overjoyed to see you. I will come up presently.'

This was not at all what Helena had expected would happen. In her imagination this scene involved her calmly explaining to her mother that it was quite unnecessary for her to marry Adam and that all was well. But now this vital interview would take place without her and she was too exhausted, drained by the relief of being home, to do more than nod obediently and quietly leave the room.

As Helena closed the door behind herself she heard her mother say, at last, 'Please be seated, my lord.'

Her maid Lucy could hardly contain her joy at seeing her mistress alive and well. She ran across the room and threw her arms around Helena, with whom she had grown up since childhood, and for a few minutes the two girls clung together, shedding tears of relief.

'Oh, Miss Helena! We thought you'd drowned…and then we got word you'd been saved…but, ooh! miss…that man! The things they say about him—why, you might as well have been rescued by a ravening pirate!'

'Now, now Lucy, I am quite safe now. You must not say things like that about his lordship—he saved my life and looked after me very well.' Lucy looked dubious, but with another convulsive hug hurried out to fetch her mistress some supper.

Lucy had hardly brought Helena's hot water and glass of milk when the front door closed and they heard hooves on the gravel driveway beneath the window. He had scarcely been alone with Mama for fifteen minutes! Helena burned with curiosity, despite her fatigue.

Moments later her mother swept into the bedroom, dismissing Lucy with a smile and sat on the edge of the bed beside Helena. She pressed her cool fingers lightly against Helena's temple, then cupped her face between her hands and looked searchingly into her daughter's violet eyes.

'At least you do not appear to have caught a chill,' she murmured. 'You must go to sleep now; we will have a long talk in the morning before Lord Darvell returns.'

'Mama...'

'Enough!' Lady Wyatt held up her hand in reassurance. 'There is nothing to worry about, all will be done for the best. Now, drink your milk and go to sleep.'

Despite feeling the bed rocking as though she were still at sea, Helena fell asleep almost as soon as her head touched the pillow.

When she woke the light was pouring through the window, cascading across the foot of the bed, and the sounds of the household at work below reached her faintly.

Suddenly starving, Helena tugged the bellpull for her maid but, to her surprise, it was not Lucy but her mother who brought in her breakfast tray.

Anne Wyatt watched her daughter swiftly dispatch her coffee and bread and butter, waving Helena into silence whenever she tried to speak. It was not until Helena began to peel an apple that Lady Wyatt broached the subject that was uppermost in both their minds.

'Now, first of all, you must not be concerned that there has been any talk about your absence. The servants know, of course, but their loyalty is assured. As to our neighbours, they believe you to be in Chichester, staying with your Aunt Breakey. That is such a frequent occurrence it has given rise to no speculation whatsoever. It would be wise perhaps, if asked, to say you had a slight cold and therefore did not attend any functions. Your aunt and I have been corresponding regularly while you were missing; she knows what our story must be.'

Helena sank back against the pillows with a sigh of relief. 'Thank heavens! I had feared my absence would be the talk of the neighbourhood. I was heavily cloaked last night, and no one could have recognised me leaving the *Moonspinner*. And the crew are his lordship's men: they will say nothing.'

'Indeed, we have had a most fortunate escape from gossip. There will be no untoward speculation when your engagement to Lord Darvell is announced. After all, he is almost a neighbour.'

The apple fell unheeded from Helena's fingers and bounced onto the floor. 'Engagement! But, Mama...there is no need! We have just agreed that no one knows, that there will be no stain on my reputation.'

Lady Wyatt sat back and regarded her daughter in astonishment. 'My dear girl—think of the circumstances! You have been alone, unchaperoned, at sea with a man whose reputation as a rake is a byword, for the best part of a week! You are hopelessly compromised, dearest—there is no alternative for you but marriage.'

Helena, white-lipped, sat up and said with every ounce of conviction she could muster, 'I may be compromised—although no one knows but us and a handful of people who will keep quiet about it—but I am not ruined, Mama. I do not *have* to marry Lord Darvell, and I assure you I have no wish to!'

She rarely saw her mother taken aback, but she was now. Her jaw dropped and her brows raised as she asked disbelievingly, 'You do not *wish* to marry that man? My dear girl, what can you be thinking of!' Anne Wyatt stood up and began to pace the room, speaking as she did so with unusual emphasis. 'You know I do not advocate marriage as the only career for an intelligent girl of spirit and breeding. If you had received no eligible offers and had wished to continue your studies or your art, then I would have raised no objection.

'But only think!' She paused at the foot of the bed, and looked at her daughter. 'This is the most eligible of offers. Lord Darvell is son of the Earl of Shefford, heir to a large estate. He is wealthy and intelligent. And,' she added meditatively, 'quite one of the best-looking young men I have set eyes on for many a long year!'

'Mother!' Helena was aghast at this insight into her mother's character, never before glimpsed. 'As though I would allow considerations of rank and wealth—let alone good looks—to influence me!'

'Oh, fiddlesticks!' Lady Wyatt snapped. 'He would not have had to have asked me twice at your age—or, indeed, any young woman in Society, for many have thrown their caps at him.'

Helena threw back the covers and padded barefoot to her mother's side. 'Mama—' she took Lady Wyatt's hands in hers and looked imploringly into the anxious, handsome face '—I truly do not wish to marry him. I do not love him, he does not love me. You brought me up to think clearly, not to be bound by foolish conventions and other people's expectations. I do not have to marry Lord Darvell and I do not choose to do so—is that not enough?'

Lady Wyatt led her daughter to the chaise-longue in the window bay and pulled her down to sit beside her. 'My dear, I must ask you these questions, and you must answer them frankly. Are you telling me that not the slightest impropriety occurred between yourself and Lord Darvell?'

Helena could not control the hectic blush which rose to the roots of her hair. 'He did kiss me, Mama, and...I kissed him back.' And what had followed she could never confess to anyone, least of all her mother.

'And...then...?'

From being scarlet Helena felt the blood now leach from her face. No, she could not tell her mother what had happened, but at least she could truthfully reassure her on the one point that really mattered. 'You have my word, Mama, that I am still a...virgin.'

A short silence ensued, then Lady Wyatt broke it. 'I should tell you, my dear, that Lord Darvell is more than willing to marry you.'

'Why?' Helena asked baldly.

'Because he is very conscious that he has compromised you, of course! And, let us not mince words, you are a very good catch. Well-bred, well-connected, intelligent, beautiful—what more could he ask for?'

'I do not choose to marry a man whom circumstances have forced to make me an offer.' She could not speak to her mother of love; after all, few people of their social class married for love. They were allied fittingly according to rank and to consolidate estates and fortunes; if deep affection followed, that was an unexpected bonus. Even with a mother as unconventional as hers, one who had truly loved her husband and been loved in return, talk of a love-match would cut no ice.

Lady Wyatt stood up with a sigh. 'Well, Helena, I can see we are going to have a difficult conversation at eleven o'clock when Lord Darvell returns to discuss this at more length with both of us. Oh, dear,' she added with an air of distraction, 'I suppose this means you will be doing the Season after all...'

'Oh, Mother!' Helena laughed for what seemed like the first time in days. 'You know you will enjoy it when we get there! Aunt Breakey will enjoy going to parties with me and you can visit the libraries and museums and literary circles to your heart's content. And I cannot believe you are not looking forward to getting a fashionable new crop and ordering new gowns and bonnets.'

Helena's cheerful spirits ebbed as eleven o'clock approached. The servants all had a tendency to treat her as if she were ill and John, after a burst of tears, haunted her side, endlessly offering to run errands, plump up her cushions or close windows in case she were in a draught. In the end she had to beg him to go out and play with the Vicar's son. But when the door had banged behind him, it was all too quiet.

At the stroke of eleven the knocker sounded and Helena and her mother, seated side by side in the morning room, exchanged nervous glances. For the second time in twelve hours Scott announced his lordship.

It was the first time Helena had seen Adam in riding dress. His valet had obviously been up to the mark for such an important occasion: Adam's breeches were immaculate, his boots shone like burnished conkers and the fit of his coat displayed his muscular physique to perfection. For a moment he seemed a stranger, then Helena realised his hair had been trimmed, revealing the paler skin at the nape of his neck. Her colour rose as she remembered the feel of that hair as she twined her fingers in it on the bed such a short time ago. It was almost as if he read her thoughts, for across the room his deep blue eyes sent her a message that made her feel weak with longing.

'Lady Wyatt, I bid you good morning.' Adam bowed, then strode to take Lady Wyatt's hand, before turning to Helena. 'Miss Wyatt. I hope I find you well.'

Helena curtsied, her eyes dropped before his penetrating gaze, her cheeks warm. 'Thank you, sir, I feel much refreshed for a night's sleep.'

'Please, my lord, will you not sit and take refreshment?' Lady Wyatt made light social chitchat while the butler poured amontillado and bowed himself out.

Adam sipped his sherry and returned the pleasantries, outwardly relaxed, yet covertly watching Helena and every nuance of her expression. Her eyes were still downcast, they would not meet his after that first penetrating glance as he entered the room. He had never seen her in a fashionable and elegant morning dress suitable to an unmarried girl. The sprigged jonquil muslin and the modest row of pearls matched the spring weather outside; her skin was clear, only slightly touched by the sun at sea. Her hair was glossy and freshly curled and he remembered the spring of the fine tendrils round her ears as he had traced a line from her temple to her throat...

Her colour ebbed and flowed as he watched her. Doubtless her mother had questioned her rigorously about exactly what had occurred during her sojourn on the *Moonspinner*! She was so fresh and charming he found himself impatient to do what was, after all, his inescapable duty and marry her.

'My lord?' Lady Wyatt had obviously been waiting for a reply to a question.

'I do beg your pardon, Lady Wyatt, I must plead a certain fatigue. You were speaking of London, I believe?'

There was an awkward silence while Lady Wyatt fiddled with her rings. She had momentarily lost her self-assurance and found herself at a loss as to how to broach the subject they all had foremost in their mind.

Adam was suddenly impatient with these niceties. 'When Miss Wyatt and I are married I intend opening the town house. My parents rarely use it these days and

I am sure Helena will enjoy redecorating it. It will be a very suitable base for her to do her first Season.'

'Lord Darvell...' At the tone of Lady Wyatt's voice he was suddenly all attention. 'My lord, I believe you and I may have been a little premature last night in our discussion. It is not necessary for you to marry my daughter, although naturally she is sensible of the honour you do her.'

Adam could scarcely credit what he was hearing. 'Madam, it cannot have escaped your notice that Miss Wyatt was alone with me for several days—and nights. She is, in the eyes of Society, hopelessly compromised and it is my duty, as a man of honour, to marry her. And I may say, I would assume it would be your most urgent wish as her mother.' His voice was hard now, although still restrained.

'My lord, you must not take our refusal of your offer as a personal slight. I seek to impugn neither your honour nor your dignity. Given that no one in the neighbourhood knows of Helena's absence, I am correct, am I not, in saying that there is no compelling reason why she *must* marry you.'

Helena wished the floor would open up and she could disappear through it. This discussion was verging on the improper and it would only take Adam to throw all propriety to the winds and describe just one of the incidents in his cabin to her mother to make the question of their marriage a certainty.

She raised her eyes to Adam's and met his blue stare. Outwardly controlling his fury at this totally unexpected, inexplicable snub, he could not keep the anger out of his eyes. But equally, seeing the distress and pleading in Helena's eyes, he knew he could not pursue this course. Why she should find him so unacceptable he knew not, but he had too much pride to persist in the face of such flat rejection.

Adam got to his feet with grace and bowed to both ladies. 'Lady Wyatt, I must of course accept your decision in this matter as final. Rest assured, no word of Miss Wyatt's absence from her home will ever escape my lips. Miss Wyatt—' his expression as he regarded her, might have been that of a total stranger '—I wish you a…successful Season. Ladies, I bid you good morning.'

Even before Lady Wyatt had time to ring for Scott he was gone. They heard his voice in the hall, then the front door closed and they were alone together.

Her mama turned to Helena with an expressive lift of her eyebrows. 'I do not believe his lordship was best pleased by our decision, my dear, which is understandable. No man likes to be rejected. However, there we will let the matter rest; there should be no reason for your paths to cross again, for although the family has had that manor in West Itchenor for many years, he is rarely seen in local society. Now, let us go in to luncheon.'

It took the Wyatt household two weeks to prepare for their sojourn in London. The day before they planned to go up to town was a Sunday, but Helena found herself alone at matins in Selsea church, her mama having had one of her periodic fallings-out with the local vicar, this time concerning his interpretation of a Greek translation of St Paul's Epistle to the Ephesians which she felt was fundamentally flawed.

She had had no hesitation in telling him so and, although as a gentleman and a man of the cloth he had kept his temper, the atmosphere between Vicarage and Manor was decidedly cool. This state of affairs never lasted long, but in the meantime Lady Wyatt would attend church elsewhere.

'But Mama,' Helena had protested, pulling on her gloves and picking up her prayerbook, 'why did you have to tell him you disagreed in such strong terms? Poor man, he was quite taken aback—although I suppose,' she added thoughtfully, 'he must be used to it by now.'

'Well, that is as may be,' Lady Wyatt replied robustly. 'But I shall spare myself the annoyance of having to sit through a sermon based on an inaccurate reading of the text. Shall I take John with me to Pagham church or do you wish for his company?'

It was settled between them that John would stay with his sister, for Helena knew he would want to run away and play as soon as the service was over. And so it was: claimed by Harry, the Vicar's youngest son, he ran off towards the woods, happily ignoring his sister's warning to keep his Sunday suit clean at all costs.

The congregation dispersed quickly after the service and Helena, unwilling to return inside on such a beautiful spring morning, wandered through the churchyard to where the straggling hawthorn hedge separated the sacred ground and its tilting tombstones from a rough bank and the wide mudflats of Pagham harbour.

The hedgerow flowers were tossing in the sharp breeze, although the sun shone in cloudless blue sky. Helena pulled her pelisse more closely round her shoulders and climbed carefully through a gap in the hedge and down on to the edge of the mudflats, now fully exposed by low tide.

The bells of Pagham church, whose services started later than Selsea's, rang out over the water, mingling with the plaintive cries of seabirds on the flats. Oystercatchers, smart in their pied plumage, dug into the grey ouse and a few curlews stalked amongst the smaller waders, their curved bills probing delicately.

Helena took a deep lungful of the fresh, tangy air and reflected that, exciting though the prospect of doing the Season was, she would miss this wild corner of Sussex. Most of the packing and preparation was done, she could allow herself a last long walk. The shore was both muddy and stony, but her feet in their stout boots were sure and the brisk activity soon brought the colour to her cheeks.

As Helena rounded a bend in the path two retrievers bounded muddily towards her, tails wagging madly in eager anticipation of a game. As they danced round her feet Helena stooped, picked up a piece of driftwood and tossed it for them. They galloped off in hot pursuit across the mud and returned panting to lay it at her feet. Wondering how she was ever going to get rid of them now that she had begun, she threw it again with more force, sending them bounding through the shallow pools, scattering a flock of dunlin which flew off piping in panic.

Shielding her eyes from the sunlight with one gloved hand, Helena watched the dogs' antics with amusement, unaware she was not alone until a familiar voice rapped out, *'Come back here!'* The animals instantly responded, their romping high spirits turning to sheepish obedience as they trotted back to their master.

Helena wheeled round to face Lord Darvell, almost dropping her prayerbook in her surprise. They confronted one another across three yards of mud, he with an expression of considerable displeasure, she with dismay.

'Miss Wyatt, good morning.' He doffed his hat and Helena realised he must be out shooting, for a shotgun was cradled in the crook of his arm and he wore a shot-belt slung across his frieze jacket. 'Sit down, damn it,' he snapped at the dogs, who were spraying mud over his breeches and boots.

'My lord.' Helena struggled to restore her equilibrium. 'What are you doing here?' Her heart was beating uncomfortably and she was aware she must sound both peremptory and breathless.

There was a long pause while Adam surveyed her from her flushed cheeks to the mud-spattered hem of her gown and her unfashionable walking boots. 'Exercising my dogs—I believe this is a public right of way.' He raised one brow and Helena blushed in earnest.

'My lord, forgive me...I did not mean to imply you had no right to be here. I was just startled—I had thought myself alone.'

'Brooding, Miss Wyatt?' he asked abruptly.

Helena's shoulders went back, her chin up. 'Certainly not. I have nothing to brood upon, my lord. I believe I am as entitled as you to take the fresh air, which I was doing in perfect tranquillity until you accosted me.'

'Had you not been inciting my dogs to behave like ill-trained puppies, I would have had no reason to *accost* you. Sit, sir!' He turned irritably on one of the hounds, which had jumped eagerly to its feet at the sound of his voice, and pushed it back into a sitting position with the toe of his boot.

'I trust you will not beat your dogs, sir!' Helena's temper was rising dangerously.

'I do not beat any animal of mine, madam,' he retorted.

'I should not be surprised at anything you did, such is your temper, sir,' she responded frigidly.

Adam glared at her. 'I do not think you have any reason to complain of my temper, Miss Wyatt, despite considerable provocation on your part. I cannot recall the last time anyone flouted my orders or my wishes as you have done.'

They were both suddenly and inexplicably furious with each other. Helena was too angry to retreat in a dignified manner, even though she knew she should simply turn on her heel and leave him.

'As I told you at St Mary's port, my lord, you have no right to command me. You are neither my father, my brother nor my husband...' Helena saw the pit opening at her feet as soon as the fatal word was uttered.

A grim smile set Adam's mouth. 'Since you broach the subject, Helena, and as we are quite alone, perhaps you would do me the courtesy of explaining exactly why you find my offer of marriage so unacceptable.'

His eyes were as cold as the water behind him and Helena felt suddenly very alone and vulnerable. 'Sir, you are no gentleman to ask me such a question!'

'Madam,' he responded evenly, laying down the gun and taking one slow step towards her, 'you are no lady to cause me to ask it.'

Helena drew breath sharply, the cold air hitting the back of her throat. Without thinking she moved towards him, one hand raised to slap his insolent face, and found her wrist imprisoned in his hard grasp. Adam pulled her towards him until their faces were so close she could feel his breath on her lips.

'You struck me once, Helena; I will not permit you to do so again.'

They stood as if frozen, staring into each other's eyes. Helena felt all her anger ebb from her, and in its place was a terrible burning desire to be in this man's arms. Surely he would kiss her, his lips were so close now. The seconds slowed; still he made no move, no attempt to draw her closer, to answer the yearning in her eyes.

Unable to meet that hard blue stare any longer, yet equally unwilling to break free, Helena closed her eyes, feeling her strength ebbing from her. Why, oh why, would he not kiss her? Did he no longer desire her?

Her lips were forming the shaming word 'please' when his mouth found hers and his strength pulled her hard against his body, crushing her captive hand between his chest and her breast. As she clung to him he kissed her with passion, his mouth opening her willing lips, his tongue sweetly invading, inciting.

And Helena responded with answering passion, her free hand locked into the frieze of his jacket, holding his body against hers as if she would never let him go. He deepened the kiss, his hand tugging the strings of her bonnet free until he could cast it aside. His palm pressed against the exposed nape of her neck, before moving over her back, down into the curve of her waist, impelling her further into his hardness.

Helena was lost in a wave of sensation and longing, totally oblivious of her surroundings, totally oblivious of anything but the sensation of his skilled mouth on hers, as a little moan of supplication rose in her throat.

Adam opened his hands and stepped back, leaving her reeling from the unexpectedness of it.

'Yes...' he said thoughtfully '...no lady. I am sorry if you are regretting your decision to decline my offer, Miss Wyatt, but it will not be repeated.' He stooped to pick up the shotgun, whistled up the dogs and strode off across the saltmarsh without a backward glance.

Chapter Six

If anyone had told her that it were possible to feel such scalding humiliation as she was feeling now, Helena would never have believed them.

She hugged herself, suddenly shivering with cold and reaction despite her warm pelisse. How could she? How could she have thrown herself at him like that? How could she have incited him to kiss her, caress her in such a shameless way and, worse still, have responded to him as she had? She had behaved no better than...than...an opera dancer!

Of course Adam had taken advantage of her! He had been angry, provoked, goaded beyond the restraint of any man, even a gentleman such as he. 'And what must he think of me?' she wailed out loud to the empty marsh, startling a wader which had ventured close to her frozen figure.

She had turned down his honourable declaration of marriage without offering him an explanation—reasonable or otherwise. And then to behave with such shocking familiarity, to beg him to kiss her...and when he did, to respond to his advances in a way that only a married woman should to her husband!

Helena stooped and picked up her prayerbook where it had fallen unheeded to the ground, its black leather stained with mud. And on a Sunday, too! A day when she should have been thinking on higher things, resolving to be a dutiful daughter, to withstand the temptations and shallowness of Society to which she would shortly be exposed in London.

The sharp wind lifted the curls at the nape of her neck, reminding her she was bonnetless. The hat lay where Adam had tossed it, its feather bedraggled, one muddy paw print besmirching the fine cream straw. Helena picked it up, her eyes filling with tears which rolled unchecked down her cheeks as she trudged back to the house.

But, by the time she had wended her way home through the churchyard and narrow lanes, her contrition was replaced by an increasing sense of indignation. Yes, she had behaved badly, but so too had Adam! He was a man of the world, she an inexperienced girl. How much greater was his responsibility, therefore, for his behaviour. At any point he could have turned on his heel and left her! She scrubbed the traces of tears off her cheeks with her handkerchief, no longer feeling any inclination to penitence.

As she walked on, another thought slowly came to her. This was the second time Adam had started to make love to her, only to break off. This time he was doubtless motivated by the desire to punish her for her refusal of him. But before, on the ship... Why had he begun with such passion, only to stop so abruptly? The more she thought of it, the less she believed his protestation that he wanted to wait until they were married. If he truly believed that, he would never have gone so far past kisses and harmless caresses. The only result of that incident had been to drive all thought of that mysterious package she had hidden for him from her mind. And the tactic had been so effective that until this moment she had hardly given it another thought.

As she rounded the curve of the drive, these disturbing thoughts were overtaken by the sight of her aunt's carriage drawn up before the front door. Helena quickened her pace, a sense of unease growing in her mind. For her aunt to travel from Chichester on a Sunday was unprecedented; like all gentlefolk, she considered that to journey further than to church and back on the Sabbath was unfitting. The fear that was never very far from the minds of anyone with a loved one serving in the army or navy filled her and she broke into a run.

Unmindful of her muddy boots and bedraggled appearance, Helena pushed open the door and hurried across the hall towards the drawing room where voices could be heard. She swung open the panelled door and entered without ceremony. Lady Wyatt, from the couch where she was pouring wine for her visitors, regarded her daughter with dismay.

'My dear Helena, you look a perfect fright! You are so muddy—what have you been doing?'

The confusion this question would normally have provoked was overtaken by Helena's cry of joy and relief as she recognised not only her aunt, but also her uncle. Commodore Sir Robert Breakey had risen to his feet when his niece entered the room, but now strode across to embrace her.

'Uncle Breakey! We thought you were with the fleet off Toulon!' Helena hugged him convulsively, then stepped back to regard his bronzed face with concern. 'You are not wounded, are you?'

The Commodore smiled with indulgent affection at his

niece whom he had not seen for six months. During that time she had blossomed into a beautiful young woman, he thought, although, as her mother had remarked, strangely bedraggled for a Sunday. But nothing could detract from the sparkle of her violet eyes and the freshness of her complexion.

'My dear Helena, I am, as you see, in one piece. I landed at Portsmouth yesterday, and I will be going up to town with you tomorrow, for I have dispatches from the fleet for their lordships at the Admiralty. I expect to be able to remain in Brook Street for several weeks.'

And indeed the Commodore looked his normal self: not above average height, his relative youth was belied by a shock of iron-grey hair, which, set against his tanned skin, gave his normally serious features a look of distinction.

'Helena,' her mother reproved, 'luncheon will be served shortly. Can you not change your gown and shoes before you distribute any more mud on my new carpet?'

Glancing down at her bedraggled skirts, clinging muddily to her ankles, Helena could only agree with her mother's words of censure. 'Yes of course, Mama, I am very sorry—I was jumped at by some dogs on the marsh.' Well, it held some modicum of truth.

Hastening out, she encountered her brother John in the hall, returned from birds' nesting in even more of a messy state than she. Hurrying him upstairs with the promise of a great surprise if he would only make himself presentable, Helena pulled twigs from his hair and tutted over his torn stockings. 'John, you look as though you have been dragged through a hedge backwards!'

'I have,' he said cheerfully. 'Harry did it, 'cos I wouldn't give him my hedge sparrow's nest. Anyway, you don't look much better!'

At that moment Nurse emerged from the linen room, regarded her small charge with horror and, with the speed of long practice, whisked him off for a good wash. 'Do not tell him our surprise, Mrs Goody!' Helena called after them as she hastened to ring for her own maid.

The pleasure of her uncle's safe return and the excitement of the final preparations for the trip to town almost served to push the memory of her encounter with Lord Darvell to the back of Helena's mind. Whenever a wayward recollection surfaced, she thought determinedly of silk stockings or vouchers for Almack's or pressed her long-suffering uncle to recount more stories of life with the blockading fleet. And yet the memory of Adam's embraces haunted her, and the unanswerable suspicions about him would not leave her.

When the cavalcade of carriages finally set out from the Manor, the Commodore obligingly sat with the ladies instead of riding alongside, as was his usual habit. John, protesting vigorously, was dispatched to sit on the box with the coachman; normally a high treat, this was now torture to him, so eager was he to cajole his uncle into taking him back to sea with him.

It was an impressive procession for the quiet Sussex locality, for not only was there Lady Wyatt's carriage, and two coaches containing her baggage and servants, but the Breakeys' vehicle followed behind empty, ready to take up their servants and belongings at Chichester.

They took two days over the journey, for neither lady enjoyed travelling at speed and Sir Robert's dispatches were of no pressing urgency.

It was evening when they drew up outside the Breakeys' town house in Brook Street and, by then, they were all heartily glad to be out of the swaying conveyance and into the warmth and light of the tall house.

'I declare, I would rather be in the teeth of a gale in the Bay of Biscay, than spend another day in that vehicle,' Sir Robert grumbled as he helped the ladies to descend.

They enjoyed an excellent dinner, for Lady Breakey had taken the precaution of sending her French chef on ahead, and it was a happy, if tired, group who assembled in the salon afterwards. Sir Robert sat scanning the pile of letters his agent had left for him, muttering darkly about the amount of work he must fit in, as well as the time he would doubtless have to spend kicking his heels at the Admiralty in attendance on their lordships. 'For mark my words,' he grumbled, from long experience, 'they will keep me hanging around while they draft orders for half the Mediterranean fleet!'

The ladies, meanwhile, were entertaining themselves with an album of prints which he had brought back from his travels and paying little heed to the Commodore, who as usual, talked to himself as he scanned the papers.

'No need to increase those rents…of course I will not sell those fishing rights, the man's a fool! Hmm, I must see what I can do for old Hodgkinson's nephew…Lord Darvell…'

All three ladies started as though a shot had gone off and turned to regard him with, as Lady Wyatt said later to her sister-in-law, an expression of guilt and alarm on their faces.

'What on earth is the matter, my dears?' the Commodore enquired, understandably bemused by the reaction his innocent words had provoked. 'If you have such a fixed opposition to my acquiring more grazing land, Lady Breakey, I will of course proceed no further with

the offer, but you have never interested yourself in such
matters before.'

'Grazing land?' his wife repeated blankly.

'Yes, I have here a suggestion from my agent in Sussex that I buy some salt marsh grazing that Lord Darvell
is selling near his estate in West Itchenor. It seems sensible as the price of wool is rising, and the land marches
with my own down there. What is there to alarm you all
in that?'

'Nothing at all, Sir Robert,' Lady Breakey responded,
her cheeks somewhat flushed. 'It was merely that Lord
Darvell has…a…reputation, and I would not discuss him
in front of our niece…'

'Really, my dear, I think you refine upon it too much.
Unless the man has changed greatly since I was last in
the country, he is not such a rake that a young lady
should be alarmed to hear his name spoken! Why, he
spends his money much as he likes, and a good part of
that goes upon a string of fine mistresses, but what of
that? He can well afford it.' He waved aside his wife's
scandalised clucking. 'Do not be such a prude, my dear,
Lord Darvell is no danger to well brought-up young girls!
Half the young bucks in town set up a mistress, there's
no need to glare at me like that! The girl's no empty-
headed ninny—she knows what goes on, even if she pre-
tends not to.'

'I would be obliged if you would select another topic
of conversation, Sir Robert,' his wife retorted frostily.

Helena, doing her very best to look like the sort of
young girl to whom Lord Darvell posed no threat, kept
her head bent over the album of prints and wished with
all her heart that her aunt would say no more.

The thought of Adam being concerned with grazing
land and other problems of estate management was cu-

riously attractive and she indulged herself for a moment with the image of him striding around a well-managed estate, tenants respectfully doffing their caps, his dogs gambolling at his heels.

At that point she took a firm hold on these fantasies which were leading her into dangerous waters and got to her feet. 'Aunt, I think I will retire now, I feel very tired. Goodnight, Mama.'

'Of course, my dear.' Her aunt patted her hand, looking at her with such concern that Helena was only grateful that her uncle was once again immersed in his papers or he would soon be demanding to know what secret his female relatives were hiding from him.

At least, she thought, slipping thankfully between the sheets and blowing out the candle, Adam was safely down in Sussex. Strange as it was to imagine him as a country landowner, it was even more difficult to transpose her memories of his barefooted, windswept figure, braced against the wind on the deck of the *Moonspinner*, into the formal world of London Society. The whole painful episode could sink into the past, she would soon forget all about him, for assuredly, he would have forgotten her much sooner...

Why, with such sensible musings as she fell asleep, Helena should pass such a troubled night was a puzzle to her. She could not recall what had disturbed her dreams and left her tossing and turning, but whatever it was resulted in heavy eyes and a slight headache the following morning.

She was partaking listlessly of bread and butter and a cup of chocolate in the dining room when the sound of the knocker heralded the arrival of the post. The Breakeys paid extra for the early morning delivery and the letter which was now brought in by the butler sent her megrims flying.

'Mama—it is from Portia! You remember, Aunt—Mrs Rowlett, my old school friend. She is in town, after all; only last week she wrote to say she would have to remain in Bath for the entire Season, for old Lady St Clare was insisting her gout was too bad for her to be left—and you know the only companion she will tolerate then is Portia.

'But Portia writes that the waters seem to have quite revived her grandmother's spirits. She is content to remain with friends and she has told Portia she should re-join her husband.' Helena turned the closely written pages. 'The House of Commons is still sitting so Portia says she will have all the time in the world to go out and about with us.'

Lady Wyatt folded her newspaper and regarded her daughter down the length of the table. 'And is her husband in the Cabinet yet?'

'You forget, Mama, Mr Rowlett is still quite a young man. But I believe he has hopes of a secretaryship before long.'

'I must say,' Aunt Breakey observed, 'I am surprised that such an admirably sensible and hard-working man should have married such a frivolous woman—and one so young into the bargain!'

'Aunt, you are unfair,' Helena protested in defence of her oldest friend. 'I know she was only seventeen when she married Mr Rowlett, and we had only just left Miss Marsham's Academy, but she is totally devoted to him, his career, and, of course, the children.'

'Yes, dear, but you must admit she *bounces* so!'

'Portia has great energy, Aunt. She cannot curb it. I know, for Miss Marsham often tried to no avail.'

'I will concede she is a dear girl and has been a true

friend to you over the years,' Lady Wyatt said. 'I could only wish *you* were as happily and well married, Helena,' she added with heavy emphasis before picking up her *Times* once more.

With her mother in that mood Helena was only too glad to escape. She stood on no ceremony with Portia, and arrived at the unfashionably early hour of ten-thirty at the Rowletts' smart house in Grosvenor Square. Despite his very junior position with the Government, Mr Rowlett was alarmingly well-connected to virtually every great family in England and was extremely wealthy into the bargain.

Helena's school friend was therefore indulged in her every whim by her doting husband and wanted for nothing. Fortunately, she was also down to earth and commonsensical, with a well-developed sense of the ridiculous, and none of this had spoilt her natural *joie de vivre*, kindness or good humour.

'Helena! Darling!' Helena was hardly through the front door when she heard her friend calling from above. Dressed in a sumptuous Chinese silk wrapper that scarcely contained her voluptuous figure as she leaned over the banister, her blonde curls cascading round her shoulders, Mrs James Rowlett presented an outrageous sight. The butler, his eyes firmly fixed on Helena's face, enquired, 'Shall I show you up, Miss Wyatt?'

'Thank you, Simpson, I know my own way.' Helena handed over her tippet and parasol and ran up the curve of the stairs to be swept into her friend's warm embrace.

'Really, Portia,' she remonstrated as soon as the door was shut behind them. 'You will give poor Simpson a stroke, he scarcely knew where to look! Oh, my goodness, what have you done to this room?'

It was a scant year since Mr Rowlett had indulged his

wife by transforming her boudoir into a pink cavern reminiscent of the inside of a mother-of-pearl shell. Now it was a startling black-and-gold chamber, all Oriental lacquer, silks and brocade, with hand-painted papers on the walls.

'Do you like it?' Portia enquired, gazing round complacently. 'It is in the very latest mode. James engaged the services of an interior designer who has worked for the Prince at Brighton.'

Helena gazed in wonderment, before finally expressing the opinion that it must have cost a fortune. She tactfully failed to add that she thought the room perfectly hideous. 'And I am green with envy! How very much Mr Rowlett does indulge you.'

Portia twinkled naughtily. 'Mr Rowlett is very well rewarded for his indulgence.'

'Portia!'

'And you—an unmarried girl—should not have caught that allusion, my dear! I cannot tell you what fun it is being married—you should try it. I am quite determined that this Season we will catch you a husband. You are quite at your last prayers!' she teased. 'I will take you in hand, for I know all the charming and eligible young men in town.'

'Just because Mama forgot about last Season until it was too late, it does not mean I am at my last prayers at nineteen,' Helena protested. 'And how are the children?' she said, neatly turning the subject, for Portia was a devoted mama.

'They are divine—and do not try to make me feel guilty about being here enjoying myself. They are in the country with their grandmama Rowlett and not missing me in the slightest—she spoils them to death. Pull the bell, darling, and have some chocolate while I dress.'

* * *

It was a good hour later when the young ladies were handed into Portia's extremely fashionable barouche. 'Now, what shall we do first?' Portia enquired while the groom stood patiently at the horses' heads. 'What are you reading at the moment?'

'A Greek history that a friend of Mama's has just published.'

'My dear! Fatal! If you do not die of boredom, you will be taken for a blue-stocking in which case you may as well be dead anyway. We will go to Hookham's and borrow some scandalous new novels, a book or two of poetry and the latest fashion plates. Then a drive in the Park to see who is in town and, after luncheon, some really serious shopping. And you must have your hair cropped.' She regarded Helena's brown curls critically. 'And then I must think carefully on the most advantageous hostesses of my acquaintance for introductions— for although I know there will be no shortage of eligible young men, it will do no harm to waste no time in making you known!'

Helena could not imagine finding much consolation in the company of Portia's 'young men', but she could not afford to let her bruised heart show, even to her friend. Still, she could play the game of fashionable flirtation that was permitted to unmarried girls as well as the next debutante...

The first part of Portia's agreeable programme was readily accomplished and they were just emerging from the subscription library, followed by the footman with a pile of volumes, when Portia's sweeping exit caused a gentleman passing by to step off the kerb onto the road.

'My dear sir, I do apologise, I fear I never look where I am going.' Portia dimpled prettily at the tall, rangy, gentleman who was doffing his hat. It was Adam Darvell.

Helena just managed to bite back a gasp of sheer surprise
and edged backwards behind the broad figure of the footman who observed these antics with well-trained composure.

'Madam,' Adam was replying gallantly, 'the fault was
all mine. Allow me to help you to your carriage.' He
held out his gloved hand and Portia, with a gracious
smile, placed her little one in his and stepped forward to
where her fashionable conveyance awaited.

The footman paced forward in her wake, leaving Helena exposed, and feeling very foolish, in the library
doorway. Portia glanced round for her companion and
stared in surprise at the sight of Helena, pink-cheeked
and apparently rooted to the spot. 'Helena, dear! Do
make haste.'

His lordship turned with a start of surprise which Helena had not the slightest doubt was contrived. The
wretched man had seen her from the beginning and, from
the dark glint of amusement in his eyes, she knew he was
enjoying her discomfiture!

'Miss Wyatt, what an unexpected pleasure. I did not
see you there, nor indeed hope to see you again so soon.'

He was mocking her, enjoying this little revenge. 'Lord
Darvell! I...er...good morning. You are in London!'

'As you see.' Adam sounded dry, as well he might in
the face of this gauche response. Immaculately dressed
in a coat of dark blue superfine, cream pantaloons and
highly polished Hessians, he stood waiting patiently for
her to come forward to the carriage.

Helena pulled herself together with an effort, despite
the fact that her heart seemed to have lodged in her
throat, and remembered her social obligations. She managed an appearance of reasonable composure as she said,

'Mrs Rowlett, may I present Lord Darvell. Lord Darvell, Mrs James Rowlett.'

'Enchanted, Mrs Rowlett.' His bow was as immaculate as his composure and Helena eyed her companion with some trepidation. Lord Darvell was also contemplating Portia; indeed, she was well worth his attention. Her blonde curls peeped charmingly from a bonnet of dark pink velvet which exactly matched the deep raspberry pink of her pelisse. From the curling ostrich feather in her hat to the tip of her fine kid boots, Mrs Rowlett was the epitome of fashion and beauty, and quite well aware of the fact.

Helena, more than happy to have her elegant new outfit of fine grass-green wool eclipsed by her friend, was appalled to hear Portia say gaily, 'And how fortunate to have encountered you Lord Darvell! Miss Wyatt and I were just saying—were we not, Helena?—that it was a pity we have no gentleman to escort us to Tessier's. I have a necklace to collect.'

'But we should not trouble Lord Darvell...' Helena began, glaring at her friend.

'It is no trouble,' he rejoined smoothly. 'I am going in that direction. It will be my pleasure to accompany you— may I offer you my arm, ladies?'

With Portia on his right, Helena had no option but to rest her fingertips on his left sleeve and listen to Portia's charming chatter as they strolled along to the jewellers. Adam answered her easily, with a ready charm, but other than steering them both carefully through the passersby, he paid no attention to Helena at all.

The warmth of his arm seemed to burn her fingers through the fine cloth. Helena kept her eyes firmly ahead, yet her mind was in a turmoil of memories, of recollected sensation, of the pressure of his lips on hers, of the weight of his body on hers on the feather mattress.

By the time they reached the entrance to the fashionable jewellers her breathing felt ragged, she knew her cheeks were flushed and she could only thank her mother's rigorous social training which kept her standing there with an expression of polite interest on her face.

Adam doffed his hat once more, smilingly agreed to Portia's pressing invitation to call on her at Grosvenor Square at the earliest opportunity, and took his leave.

Both ladies gazed after the tall figure disappearing down Bond Street, very different thoughts filling their minds as they did so. The manager emerged beaming from his office and hurried to the doorway. 'Mrs Rowlett, good day, ma'am. How may I be of service?'

Portia, who had fabricated the story of the necklace on the spur of the moment, was temporarily at a loss. 'Oh, a wedding present. I need something...ah, that salver looks just the thing.'

As they emerged twenty minute later and the package was handed into the barouche, Helena hissed, 'That serves you right!'

'Oh, one can always use a salver,' Portia replied airily, settling back against the cushions. 'But, my dear, why did you not tell me you were acquainted with Lord Darvell? He is absolutely gorgeous! And such a rake, if one is to believe half of the stories one hears about him! What is your mama about, permitting you to know him? Perhaps she thinks there is safety in numbers if she brings you to town!' She broke off to wave at a passing phaeton. 'Oh, do look, there's Anne Gregson in such a quiz of a hat.'

Receiving no response, Portia glanced back at her friend and, seeing Helena's far-from-happy expression, leapt to the wrong conclusion. 'Why, never tell me he is not declaring an interest?'

'I do not know what you are talking about,' Helena protested feebly. 'I hardly know the man.'

Portia treated this with the contempt it deserved; taking Helena's hand, she patted it briskly. 'You must not despair, dearest: rich, handsome rakes only exist to be reformed and married. We must put our heads together; just because he has eluded matrimony so far, it does not mean he can escape forever.' She leant over and patted Helena's cheek. 'And especially not with a lure as lovely as you.'

Helena hardly paid any attention as Portia chatted on. She could only be grateful that she was sitting down, for her legs felt weak with reaction. Why she had never imagined him coming to town she could not comprehend. Of course someone of his social standing would be in London for the Season. And to be treated like that, with such cold civility, cut like a knife! It would have been easier to bear if he had turned on his heel and strode off. Well, it was plain his lordship felt no pangs of conscience for what had transpired last time they met.

'Oh, do pay attention, Helena!' Portia demanded. 'Do not think to gull me with this unconvincing indifference! If you hardly know the man, why did you go so pale when you encountered him, and why were the two of you so careful to exchange only the most commonplace remarks?'

Helena glared at her. 'Shush! The servants will overhear.' Although the coachman was intent on making his way through the now thronged streets back to Grosvenor Square, the footman sitting up behind them, with his arms folded, was well placed to hear every indiscretion.

* * *

James Rowlett was in the hallway when they arrived back at Portia's house, taking his hat and cane from the butler. Portia rushed over to kiss her husband directly on the lips, ignoring the effect this had on her bonnet, and then stepped back, pouting. 'Darling, you are not off to the stuffy old House already? I told you Helena would be here for luncheon.'

Punctiliously Mr Rowlett bowed to Helena. 'Please forgive me, Miss Wyatt, I am summoned to the Admiralty. I dare say you will both enjoy a good gossip over luncheon without me.'

'Darling! I never gossip!' Portia protested. Her loving husband, who was as dark as she was fair, and whom even his best friend would not describe as a handsome man, allowed a pained expression to cross his homely features. However, he said nothing, merely twinkling at Helena with brown eyes which did much to show his kindly, affectionate nature.

Portia whisked Helena into the dining room, flapping her hands dismissively at the butler. 'Thank you, Simpson, if everything is laid out, that will be all. We will wait on ourselves.' As the door shut behind his rigidly disapproving back, Portia sighed. 'Poor James works so hard! Never mind, without him here we can talk about Lord Darvell immediately. Now help yourself to the salmon and let me pour some wine.'

Helena obediently filled her plate from the delicious cold collation that was set out and took the glass of white wine Portia poured. The food looked wonderful, but she knew it would taste like ashes in her mouth, so she simply sat, waiting for the expected stream of questions from her friend.

Portia looked at her shrewdly. 'Come on! There is some secret here.'

Half an hour later, the salmon was still untouched on Mrs Rowlett's plate as she hung agog on every thrilling word. Never in her wildest dreams could she have imagined the exploits that were being recounted. Helena expunged the more intimate details of her encounters with Adam, and no word of her suspicions about the possible French agent passed her lips, but there was enough in her tale to astound Portia.

'And this lieutenant never guessed you were a lady?' she demanded.

'No, I believe he did not.'

'And then what happened? Oh, Helena! This is more exciting than any serial novel I have ever read!' But when the tale turned to Helena's return home, Portia's common sense reasserted itself. 'But, Helena—why are you not marrying Lord Darvell? You were alone with the man on his ship in conditions of the most extreme intimacy for several days and nights! I know your mama has er… advanced…ideas, but surely she will have insisted that he marry you?'

Helena stopped pushing her food around the plate and put down her fork. 'Naturally, Lord Darvell felt honour bound to make me a declaration. But I turned him down.'

'What!' Portia just gazed open-mouthed at her friend. 'What possible reason could you have for doing such a quixotic thing?'

'I may have been compromised,' Helena said stiffly, 'although no one who would say anything knows of it. But I am not ruined—and there is no reason why I *have* to marry him.'

'But why not? He is handsome, eligible, well bred—and very rich with great expectations. My dear, what a figure of a man—that mouth, those eyes, those shoulders…I may love my darling James, but that does not make me blind to the attractions of a man like Lord Darvell.'

Helena stood and walked up and down the room, finally coming to rest in front of the long window giving out on to the rear garden. 'I would not wish to figure as a woman who entrapped a man against his will.'

'Oh, fiddlesticks! You are eminently eligible—and he has to marry somebody, when all's said and done. He may as well marry you as anyone else—for you are well bred, intelligent, beautiful and well-dowered.'

Helena could well imagine that Portia was already considering the guest list, the wedding flowers and the composition of the wedding breakfast. She swung round, holding up an admonishing finger. 'Portia, stop planning! I know you too well. Just believe me when I tell you that I do not wish to marry a man who does not…does not love me.'

Portia regarded her friend through narrowed eyes, a deep suspicion forming in her mind. 'He may, or may not love you, but you are in love with him, are you not? And do not try and deny it,' she added hastily as Helena opened her mouth indignantly. 'I saw how you acted this morning. It is not like you to be so gauche. But now I see it all: you love him, and he has piqued you because he has offered you no word of love. Is that not so?'

Helena stared back at Portia, the angry words of denial dying on her lips. It was as if a large hand were squeezing her heart painfully, so sharp was the longing for Adam in that moment, so bitter was the realisation that Portia was right.

She loved Adam, loved him body and soul despite everything and, if it were not for her stupid obstinacy, she would already be his affianced bride.

Chapter Seven

The clocks at Almack's Assembly Rooms struck eleven in unison, signalling that the time for admission had passed. As Helena was swept down the set, her mind half on the intricate figure of the cotillion, the double inner doors into the ballroom swung open.

Several heads turned to see who the latecomer was, but only Helena faltered in her step. Lord Darvell paused on the threshold, smoothing the cuffs of his immaculate evening coat, his eyes moving, with little apparent interest, over the assembled debutantes thronging the room.

In the candlelight his tanned skin gave him an air of rakish danger, a hint of the unconventional despite the rigorously correct evening attire without which no gentleman, however exalted, could gain admission to Almack's. Several debutantes watched him, despite their mamas' disapproval, and several of the more dashing young matrons became suddenly more alert.

Helena's partner for the dance had been introduced to her by Portia, who seemed to have an inexhaustible supply of young men at her beck and call, and as the last chords struck he escorted her gallantly back to the cluster of gilt chairs where the party from Sussex sat.

'May I hope for the honour of another dance later this evening, Miss Wyatt?'

'Thank you, Mr Seymour, but I fear my card is full.' She bestowed a smile of consolation at the tall young man who bowed over her hand and retired with good grace.

Aunt Breakey began saying, 'My dear, you are having a success this evening...' then broke off, stiffening to attention as she saw who had entered. Rapidly opening her fan, she turned to her sister-in-law.

'Sister! See who has just come in! I had no idea he was in town. Of all the ill luck—Helena, you must not—' She broke off, eyeing her niece's expressionless face. 'You knew he was in London!'

'Yes, Aunt, Portia and I encountered Lord Darvell yesterday in Bond Street. He was good enough to give us his escort to Tessier's.'

James Rowlett could be heard moaning gently at the thought of his extravagant wife loose in a fashionable silversmith's. 'It was only a salver, Mr Rowlett,' Helena reassured him, although she did not add that the purpose for its purchase was a complete ruse. She refused to respond to her aunt's agitated whisperings and concentrated on keeping as calm an expression as possible.

The indulgent husband mopped his brow with his handkerchief and watched his wife, who was being waltzed around the floor by Commodore Breakey, an unexpectedly enthusiastic dancer.

'I do wish one of the Patronesses would approve my dancing the waltz,' Helena said wistfully.

'Do not seek to change the subject, Helena,' her mother reproved, low-voiced, one eye firmly on Mr Rowlett to make sure his attention was engaged elsewhere. 'We must decide what to do if his lordship comes over.'

Helena unfurled her fan with a defiant flourish. 'There is no reason why he should do more than make a passing acknowledgment to our party. I intend behaving as if I hardly know his lordship, Mama. He made me an offer and I declined it: as a gentleman he will make no reference to it.' Thank heavens Mama had no idea what had transpired on the beach at Selsea!

She swept her fan elegantly, cooling cheeks made suddenly warm by the remembrance of Adam's lips on hers. She inclined her head graciously to a passing gentleman who had partnered her earlier in the evening and took the opportunity to look for Adam. He was strolling in their direction around the edge of the dance floor, stopping to greet acquaintances and bow over hands. Several parties detained him, but he made no attempt to ask any of the young ladies to dance, to the ill-concealed chagrin of both debutantes and their ambitious mamas.

Helena looked around the room, in every direction but at Lord Darvell, smiling and nodding at acquaintances, bending to listen to her aunt, her every sense aware of Adam, her skin tingling with his nearness. Her back was straight in her gown of fine cream muslin, but she found her fingers fiddling with the trailing moss-green ribbons which fell from the high waistline and controlled herself with an effort.

Both the older ladies were very tense under their outward appearance of social ease and Helena could sense their relief when the waltz came to an end and both the Commodore and Portia rejoined the party. Mrs Rowlett arrived back with all her usual verve and, in the ensuing flurry of finding chairs and discussing the dance, Helena hoped that Adam would merely nod and pass by as he reached them.

It was not to be: Portia, settling down like the Queen

of the Night in a gown of dark blue gauze spangled with gold stars, gave a little cry of pleased recognition. 'My lord! Lord Darvell, please, do join us.' She managed to sound as though she had only just seen him, but Helena knew her friend had had him in her sights from the moment he walked through the door, and whatever the stage of the dance, would have been back with their party at the moment he reached it.

Several heads turned at her raised voice and one of the more severe Patronesses, Mrs Drummond Burrell, raised her lorgnette and viewed Mrs Rowlett with air of disapprobation.

Adam was bowing with great aplomb over Portia's outstretched hand. 'Madam, you outshine the night sky.' He turned to greet Lady Wyatt, who bowed slightly. 'My lord, may I make known to you Lady Breakey, my brother Commodore Sir Robert Breakey, Mr Rowlett. I believe you are acquainted with my daughter.' Not by the twitching of a brow did his lordship betray that he was very well acquainted indeed with Miss Helena Wyatt. Bows and curtsies were exchanged all round and his lordship took a seat as a country dance struck up.

'I believe I must thank you for escorting my wife and Miss Wyatt yesterday, my lord,' Mr Rowlett remarked.

'A small service, but a great pleasure,' Adam responded smoothly while Portia threw her friend a meaningful glance and received a sharp tap on the ankle for her pains.

'Helena! You caught my ankle—do be careful, dearest!' Helena found herself glaring, then caught Adam's eye and turned her gaze to the dancers. If Portia was set on teasing, the only defence was to feign indifference. She knew there was no malice in it; her friend was matchmaking with her usual unsubtle enthusiasm.

Adam, a faint smile on his lips, consulted his dance card. 'Will you do me the honour of the next dance, Miss Wyatt?'

'I fear I cannot, my lord,' Helena replied demurely, consulting her own card on its silk ribbon. 'It is a waltz.' Like all debutantes, she had to secure the approval of one of the Patronesses before participating for the first time in this daring dance, and this had so far not been forthcoming.

Adam rose gracefully to his feet. 'In that case, may I fetch refreshment for the ladies?' Receiving a request from Portia for orgeat and for lemonade from Lady Wyatt, he strolled away in the direction of the refreshment room, leaving four rather thoughtful ladies behind him.

When he reappeared five minutes later, it was with a waiter in his wake and Lady Jersey on his arm. The Patroness, known by the unkind as Silence, was in typically voluble form, chattering animatedly to her dashing escort.

'Miss Wyatt, may I present Lord Darvell to you as a partner for the next waltz.'

Helena curtsied gracefully to her ladyship, hoping she was effectively masking her dismay. 'Lady Jersey, Lord Darvell, how kind! But you put me in a quandary; I had promised my uncle my very first waltz at Almack's.' Behind her she heard a little sigh of relief escape the compressed lips of both the older ladies at her quick thinking. But they had all reckoned without the Commodore, gallantly rushing in and completely oblivious to the glares of his wife and sister.

'I would not dream of it, my dear! You do not want to dance with your old uncle when you can have a dashing partner. Besides—' he placed his hand on his chest theatrically '—I am quite exhausted and must rest.' He broke off, looking at his wife with a puzzled expression.

'My dear, what is amiss? You are positively frowning at me—do you have a headache?'

Lady Breakey was thrown into confusion. 'Sir Robert, I do not know what you can mean! I do not frown at you, nor do I have a headache... Why, it is a little warm, to be sure...'

Helena, furious with them all, met Adam's eyes defiantly. They were brimming over with amusement; he could hardly contain his laughter and was perfectly aware of the anxiety he was arousing. The orchestra struck up and Helena put her gloved hand in his and allowed herself to be led out onto the dance floor.

To be so close to him, to feel the warmth of his hand through the flimsy fabric of her gown, to be swept along to the rhythm of the dance following Adam's lead, was intoxicating. Unwilling to meet his eyes, fearful of what he would read in hers, Helena fixed her gaze on his shirt button and concentrated on her steps.

'It is normal in these circumstances to make conversation, Miss Wyatt,' he said, breaking the awkward silence.

'What would you have me discuss, sir?' Helena riposted, relaxing into the rhythm of the dance despite herself.

Adam's hand tightened at her waist: the message of the pressure was unmistakable and Helena felt her colour rise. Since admitting to herself how much she loved him, she had dreamt of a moment like this. Now, in his arms, watched by dozens of pairs of eyes, she realised what a dilemma she found herself in.

If she betrayed what she felt for him, she was risking cruel rejection again. Yet, if he were disposed to forgive her, she did not want to discourage him by coldness.

There was nothing in her experience that equipped her to cope with this, she would have to rely on her instinct.

Helena looked up and managed a calm, friendly smile. 'It would be foolish to allow what has passed between us to colour our behaviour. If we are seen to be at odds, it can only cause comment and speculation, which I am sure you are as anxious to avoid as I.'

The look his lordship returned was enigmatic and it was probably as well for Helena's pride that she did not know the thoughts that were passing through his mind. Without undue arrogance, Adam Darvell was well aware that almost any young woman in the room would jump at an offer from him. He was also quite aware that many of the married ones would happily take him to their bed if the opportunity arose. So why did he find himself dancing with Miss Wyatt, who had made it all too plain that she would not have him, however much she appeared to want him?

'Avoiding comment and speculation has never been one of my talents,' he said with irony. 'However, I agree it would be better to forget the past. As to the future...'

The promise of this phrase went unfulfilled as the music ceased. They applauded politely, then Adam began to escort her back, not to her friends, but towards an unoccupied alcove. Helena's heart began to beat faster, then with disconcerting abruptness he changed direction and she found herself back with her party. Adam bowed and turned on his heel, striding swiftly to the door.

Helena sat down, feeling humiliated. She had anticipated a tête à tête and instead found herself deposited with the barest civility. Once again he had toyed with her emotions and let her down painfully. Her uncomfortable thoughts were interrupted by Portia exclaiming, 'Mr

Rowlett, do look—is that not that nice Lieutenant Brookes we met at Lady Oxford's rout party last week?'

'So it is.' Mr Rowlett was making welcoming gestures to the tall man who had just emerged from the card room. If Helena had been disconcerted to see Adam Darvell, that was as nothing to the sensation which filled her now. Walking towards her was the man she had last seen wearing the uniform of a first lieutenant and ruthlessly searching the galley of the *Moonspinner*—for contraband, or worse.

Her first instinct, swiftly suppressed, was to run. Her first thought was, how could Adam have abandoned her in the face of this danger, leaving her to the mercies of the one man who could ensure her utter ruin? If this man with his sharp, observing eyes recognised her as the 'cook' from Adam's yacht, then she was quite undone.

With a huge effort Helena pulled herself together to find James Rowlett was making introductions round the small circle. 'Lady Wyatt, Lady Breakey, Miss Wyatt: may I present Lieutenant Brookes, of His Majesty's navy. Sir Robert, Lieutenant Brookes; Lieutenant, Commodore Sir Robert Breakey.'

Bows were exchanged, and the Lieutenant greeted his superior officer with considerable deference, inwardly delighted at the introduction to such a well-connected naval family. Reflecting fleetingly that it was a pity that the uncommonly handsome daughter was such a shy debutante, he turned to Lady Wyatt. 'May I ask, madam, if I have the honour of addressing the widow of Rear Admiral Sir Gresley Wyatt?'

'Yes, sir, Sir Gresley was my husband.'

'A great loss to the country, madam, and a true hero,' Mr Brookes opined sincerely. Lady Wyatt nodded gravely, but Helena knew she was pleased by the tribute to her late husband, lost at Trafalgar.

Helena began to edge her chair further back, hoping to escape the further attention of Mr Brookes. She tried to tell herself that he had only seen her in the gloom between decks, and in the character of a brazen hussy covered in soot and flour, but none the less she had no intention of putting herself forward in any way.

Aunt Breakey, observing her niece's uncharacteristic shyness, drew the wrong conclusions. If the sight of the handsome Lieutenant Brookes had rendered Helena so bashful, then this was a hopeful sign. Lady Breakey did not hold with her sister-in-law's advanced views: she believed young girls should be married, and married well. Helena had seemed politely attentive but indifferent to the half-dozen or so young men she had thrown in her way. Well, whatever had prompted Helena's wilful behaviour over Lord Darvell, this man could be a very acceptable substitute. What other purpose could a debutante have in pursuing the Season but to catch herself a good husband?

She pounced. 'Helena dear, pass me my reticule.' Having thus ensured Lieutenant Brookes's attention was on her niece, she asked, 'May I enquire, sir, if you are related to Lord Brookes of Eaton Bray?'

'Why, yes, madam, he is my uncle,' Daniel supplied easily. 'Do you know him?'

'He is my second cousin twice removed on his mother's side. You recall, Helena, they once paid a visit when you were staying with me at Chichester.'

'Yes, ma'am,' Helena replied colourlessly, eyes fixed on her gloved hands which rested demurely in her lap.

Lady Breakey was not to be deterred. 'My dear niece is often with me. The Commodore and I having no chil-

dren of our own, she is almost like a daughter to us.'
Helena groaned inwardly: her aunt had as good as ad-
vertised the fact that she was her uncle's heiress.

Mr Brookes's attention being thus forcefully drawn to
Miss Wyatt, he attempted to engage her in conversation.
'Do you live in Chichester, Miss Wyatt? A most con-
genial city, is it not?'

'Indeed, yes sir, I have always found it to be so, but I
do not live in the city.' She spoke so quietly, her face
still downturned, that he had to lean close to hear her
over the hum of chatter in the room.

'But you live near by,' he prompted.

Helena, realising she would have to take a more active
part in this conversation, looked up and found herself
gazing into a pair of dark eyes set in a skin taut and
tanned by time at sea. She realised with a jolt of alarm
that she was piquing his interest: the expression in those
eyes was sharp and interested, but not, thank heaven,
touched by any recognition.

'On the coast sir, with my mother and young brother.'
She was prepared to parry his questions with willing, but
anodyne, replies until he lost interest, but once again her
uncle was the unwitting instrument of her discomfiture.

'What say we move to the refreshment room?' he enquired of the party at large. 'You would welcome a cup
of tea, would you not, my dear? Will you not join us
Lieutenant?'

They moved off as a group, the Lieutenant offering his
arm to Helena as far as the buffet before bowing himself
out. 'I hope I may be permitted to call upon you, Lady
Breakey?'

'Of course, Mr Brookes. We are much out and about,
as you may imagine with a debutante in the house, but
we would be delighted to see you.' As the Lieutenant

vanished back towards the card room, she remarked complacently to her sister-in-law, 'There is no harm in letting that young man know how much in demand Helena is.'

'Are you sure you will not accompany us to Lady Fanshawe's, Helena?' Lady Wyatt enquired as she pulled on her gloves the following afternoon. 'You are not sickening for anything, are you, dear? You look a little pale.'

Her ladyship regarded her daughter as she sat on the sofa, her embroidery neglected beside her. Helena was curiously lacklustre, but then perhaps it was not to be wondered at after her tribulations of the past weeks and the excitements of coming up to town.

Helena smiled. 'Merely a little tired, Mama, I will soon be used to town hours.'

'In that case I will send John out to Green Park with his nurse—you will not want him racketing about the house. Meanwhile, do not strain over your needlework. Your aunt and I will return about five: we will make an early dinner as we do not expect your uncle to join us this evening.'

The house seemed very quiet when they had all gone and the salon felt stuffy. The day had been unpromising when she had dressed—an overcast and chilly morning for late spring so she had donned a walking dress in pale dove grey wool. But now she felt overwarm. Helena crossed to throw open the doors into the conservatory and was immediately attracted by the thought of sitting for a while in its cool and fragrant freshness.

Her sketchbook was lying on the pianoforte in the salon and she took it and found a seat amongst the burgeoning greenery. It seemed a long time since she had picked up her pencil. She recalled the last occasion when she had planned a sketch, sitting on the quayside at Siddlesham Mill, trying to fix the image of the man on the deck of the yacht in her memory. The man who had come to mean so much to her…

With a flick of the page she abandoned the outline of a fern she had just begun and paused for a moment, nibbling the end of her pencil. Then, as if with a will of its own, her hand moved over the paper and the shape of a pair of strong bare feet began to appear.

Her memory gave her every detail of Adam's feet, the taut tendons, the curve of his toes as they flexed against the deck to give him balance, the arch of the foot, the sharpness of the ankle bone, the suggestion of the strong legs on the verge of movement. The sketch grew rapidly and she realised with delight that it was perhaps the best thing she had ever done.

Helena knew it was so good because she was putting all her emotion, all the love she could not express out loud, into the drawing. Her art had always been admired, and she knew she had talent for an amateur; but it had always been academic, never from the heart…until now. She laid in a few more details, then put aside her pencil and held the sketchpad tight against her breast, as if by doing so she could hold Adam himself.

The sound of a throat being cleared recalled her to her senses. Fishe, the Breakeys' butler, was standing just inside the salon doors. 'Are you At Home, Miss Wyatt? Lord Darvell has called. Shall I call your maid?'

Helena jumped to her feet with a gasp, scattering pencils over the tiled floor. Fishe glided forward and retrieved them. 'Thank you, Fishe, no, I am not at home.'

'Yes, Miss Wyatt. May I enquire if you are At Home to anyone this afternoon?'

'No…yes…only if Mrs Rowlett were to call.'

'Very good, Miss Wyatt.'

Fishe bowed himself out, managing to imply the very faintest disapproval that any young lady should deny an audience to such an eligible caller.

Helena stayed on her feet when he had gone, pacing agitatedly up and down between the high benches laden with ferns and the Commodore's prized orchids. The nerve of the man! He had walked out last night, abandoning her to Lieutenant Brookes and all that would have followed had she been recognised: loving Adam as she did she felt that betrayal keenly. And it was even more cruel, coming after that waltz, coming at the moment when she had sensed he was taking her aside to be alone with her. And then there was the promise of that unfinished sentence... 'As to the future,' he had said. What future could there possibly be for them?

After a few minutes Helena sat down and picked up her sketchpad once more, but the drawing was complete, there was nothing she could add to it. And, where before it had given her satisfaction, she now felt only a great sadness.

Somewhere there was a click and a faint breeze touched her cheek and stirred the ferns. Helena supposed the door into the garden had come unlatched, but the fresh air was pleasant and she made no move to get up and close it.

'Helena.'

She jumped violently and swung round, knocking over a tier of pots, sending orchids scattering across the benching. Adam sprang forward and deftly caught a tumbling pot, setting it back in its place with only a fallen petal to show for its mishap.

Helena could hardly squeeze the words out past her tight throat, but finally gasped, 'What are you doing here! How long have you been watching me?'

He propped his shoulder against the door jamb, crossing his booted feet at the ankle, and contemplated her. 'Forgive me, I did not intend to alarm you so, but you made such a pretty picture lost in thought among the flowers.'

His insouciance was stunning! 'I told Fishe to deny me—how did you get in here?'

'Fishe! What a wonderful name for a butler…' He saw she was becoming seriously annoyed and stopped teasing. 'I climbed over the wall.'

'*Over the wall?* Why, it must be quite seven foot high!'

'I stood on the saddle and shinned over. Fortunately I had my groom with me, so he is holding Samson by the back gate.'

'Which is locked.'

'Exactly. Why do you think I had to climb over?'

Helena shook her head as if to clear it, sending the brown curls bouncing at her neck. 'Enough of walls and Samson and Fishe! How dare you break in here? And after last night…'

Adam was suddenly deadly serious. He pushed himself away from the wall and came and took her hands, pulling her down to sit beside him on a rustic bench. 'Yes, last night. That is why I am here.'

'You deserted me…' Helena tried to tug her hands free, but with no real effort. She hated the tremor that was in her voice but she could no more control it than the sudden rapid beating of her heart.

'I was afraid that was how you would interpret it.' His gaze was open and clear on her face, his voice rueful.

'How else should I interpret it?' she demanded, finally freeing her hands with a jerk. 'I never thought you would run away from that man.'

'Think, Helena! It is most unlikely he would recognise you, an elegantly gowned young lady, accompanied by friends of the utmost respectability, as the befloured harridan in my galley. But you know as well as I what a strange thing memory is. He may feel he has met you somewhere before: but he would never be able to place you unless something triggers the association. If Brookes sees us together, that is all it might take. And be in no doubt, Helena, Brookes hates me enough to think nothing of ruining you if that would bring me down too.'

'But why does he hate you so?' Helena asked. 'What have you ever done to him to earn his enmity?'

Adam stretched out his long legs in front of him and seemed to be looking back into the past. 'We were at Eton together and it seemed to me we disliked each other on sight. And for some reason I always managed to be the one who beat Brookes to things he wanted: even as a boy he was overweeningly ambitious. He would do anything to win, however trivial the prize.

'And then I found he had done something so scurrilous…I cannot tell you more, it is not fit for your ears.'

'Oh, do not be so mealy-mouthed, my lord! Are you telling me he got some girl into trouble?'

'Very well, if you must have it. He seduced the daughter of a respectable tradesman, then abandoned her when she told him she was with child. I happened to find out and discovered her living in utter penury, turned out of the house by her father. I secured her a position as a dairymaid with an honest tenant of my father and now she runs the dairy and her son is a fine strapping lad who believes his father was killed in the army.'

Helena suspected there was more to the tale than Adam was telling her, but she did not probe deeper except to ask, 'And did Brookes know what you did for the girl?'

'Yes, I told him, for I felt he should have another opportunity to right the wrong he had done and support them both. But I believe he thought I had done it for no other reason than to put him in my power and hold the shabby story over his head.'

A short silence ensued, then Helena said, 'It is very shocking, but not, I fear, an uncommon story. I am amazed it still rankles, that he is such an implacable enemy to you.'

'It is not just that. As I said, Brookes is fiercely ambitious. In the past my father, the Earl of Shefford, had some influence at the Admiralty and Brookes believes he was influential in denying him some crucial posting. The fact that he is presently seconded to the Excise only serves to increase his anger and frustration: he would dearly love to catch me smuggling.'

Helena was suddenly fearful and clutched Adam's hand. 'You will be careful—for you are smuggling, are you not?'

'You know I am.' He grinned at her suddenly. 'It is a sport, something to add spice to the sailing. And how else do ladies get their silks and lace now we are at war?'

Helena blushed at the thought of the garments she had worn which had been fashioned from those silks and laces. She started to say, 'Is that all you are doing...?' But Adam did not notice her confusion or her words: his attention had been caught by the upturned sketchbook lying where it had fallen from her startled grasp. He bent and retrieved it, turning the pages slowly.

Helena caught the edge and tried to tug it from his grasp. 'Please, my lord, they are only foolish scribblings.'

He said, almost absently, 'You were used to call me Adam when we were alone. This is good.' He had come to a portrait of John, sound asleep and curled up on the sofa, one grubby hand clutching a toy boat.

'Adam…may I have my book back?' He was up to the page with the half-finished fern on it.

'In a moment—do not be so modest, Helena. These are really excellent. Do you paint also?'

'Yes!' Helena replied eagerly. 'Let me show you some of my watercolours—leave that, they are only sketches.'

Too late. He had turned the page to the study of the bare feet. There was a long silence, then Adam's startling blue gaze settled on her hectic complexion. 'Good,' he drawled, 'very, very good. You have an excellent visual memory, but you had better not let Lady Wyatt see this.'

'What do you mean?' Helena blustered. 'It is merely a study from a statue in the British Museum. I had intended working it up into a pastel for Mama.'

'A classical statue standing on a deck? Most unusual. You have caught the caulking between the planks to perfection.' Adam's eyes were dancing with amusement. 'Come now, Helena, stop blushing. I am very flattered that you should recall details about me with such clarity. May I have the sketch?'

Helena was totally at a loss to know how to respond, but finally blurted out what was uppermost in her mind. 'I am surprised, my lord, after the way we parted at Selsea, that you should want anything that reminded you of our association.'

She swallowed. 'I realise that you had to put on a social façade last night, but the way we parted on the beach, the words that were exchanged—' She broke off, then ventured, 'Last night you said something about the future…'

His expression was so gentle that her breath caught. 'I was going to say that it was obvious that we would be thrown together in London and that we should start again as mere acquaintances.' Adam patted her arm, then got to his feet. 'We were thrown together by extraordinary circumstances. There was a degree of attraction that I now see was inevitable, however regrettable, given the conditions. I admit my pride was hurt that you should reject my offer of marriage, but now I can see it was for the best.' He stood up, the sketchbook still in his hand, ready to take his leave.

'Thank heaven that, while I was driven by convention, you had the courage to reject those social constraints. Now at least neither of us are in a position we would have swiftly come to regret: I believe that a marriage, to be successful, should be based on mutual affection as well as on considerations of rank and fortune.'

Between frozen lips Helena heard herself say, 'I am glad you have come to see we have both been saved from a most unfortunate misalliance.' She took the sketchbook from him and ripped the study out, handing it to him dismissively. 'You may as well take it, my lord, for it is of no consequence to me.'

Adam rolled it carefully, tucking it into the bosom of his riding coat. 'Thank you. It may be of no consequence to you, but to me it is a souvenir of a most…surprising voyage. Good day, Helena. No, do not trouble to ring, I will let myself out.'

Chapter Eight

Portia dug her spoon into one of Gunter's famous ices and regarded the approaching cake trolley with a wicked smile of anticipation. 'Is this not heaven, Helena my dear? A whole morning shopping and now the prospect of the very best Gunter's can afford!'

'Mmm,' Helena responded doubtfully, crumbling a wafer over her vanilla ice. 'Do you realise, Portia, that I have probably spent my entire quarter's allowance and we have only been in London a week?'

'Oh, do not fret!' Portia responded with all the unconcern of a woman with a doting husband and unlimited pin money at her disposal. 'By the time Madame Haye sends in her reckoning for those hats, it will be nearly next quarter and, of course, you would not dream of settling at once.'

'Well, if it were only the hats...but I paid cash in the Pantheon Bazaar for those gloves, and the silk stockings, and that reticule. And then there was the Burlington Arcade...'

'But that was on account and in any case it would have been criminal not to have bought that spangled scarf...'

'…or that muff. I do agree, but even so, I fear Mama may be displeased.'

'Lady Wyatt will not be displeased when she sees how charmingly you look. And, after all, why have you come up to London if not to look your best and catch yourself a husband? Just wait until Lord Darvell sees you in the satin straw bonnet!' Portia broke off and eyed the array of sweetmeats, the very tip of her tongue showing between her teeth. 'Do you think it would be greedy to have just one madelaine with cream?'

'It may not be greedy, but it would certainly have an effect on your waistline and think of that new gown you have just bespoken at Miss Martin's!'

Portia pouted, but reluctantly waved the cake away. 'Oh I suppose you are right. I do wish you would expend as much energy attaching Lord Darvell as you do nagging me!'

Yesterday's bland rejection was too raw to conceal. Stiffly Helena replied, 'Please do not speak of an attachment between myself and Lord Darvell. We have agree we would not suit.'

'You told me all about it, but that was ages ago. Look at the way he singled you out at Almack's! And I know you would not tell me what you felt for him—but I am not blind! When you were dancing together, it was as plain as the nose on your face that there is a strong attraction between you both. And,' she added tartly, 'I was not the only one to remark upon it.'

'But that is appalling!' Helena almost wailed. 'I would not be talked of so for anything! But there is no hope…I mean, possibility, of an alliance between us. We agreed so only three days ago.'

Portia dropped her spoon into her saucer with a clatter. 'An assignation! My dear Helena, I would never have thought it of you! I met your mama and Lady Breakey that afternoon and they said you had stayed home with a headache—so where did you meet him, you cunning thing?' She was frankly agog, leaning across the table, her eyes sparkling.

'Shh! People are looking at us!' Helena glanced round at the other ladies in the room, seated around the little marble-topped tables and exchanging delightful tidbits of gossip with their companions. 'And it was not an assignation, he came to Brook Street.'

'You cannot tell me Fishe let him in while you were there unchaperoned! Why, he's the stuffiest old thing in creation.'

Helena felt the colour mounting hectically to her cheeks. 'Fishe did not let him in. He...he got in by other means.' As soon as she said it she realised it was a mistake.

Portia gasped with delighted horror. 'You do not mean to tell me he climbed over the garden wall? *Helena!*'

'Oh, shush!' Helena dropped her own voice to a whisper, wishing she was anywhere but in the middle of the fashionable refreshment rooms in Berkeley Square. 'Yes, he climbed over the wall and came in through the conservatory.'

'Did he make love to you?' Portia demanded.

'Certainly not! He came to apologise for leaving somewhat abruptly at Almack's and to agree with me that we should not suit. Doubtless we will meet again, but I trust it will be on a basis of acquaintanceship and nothing more.' Helena was rather proud of that dignified assertion.

Portia, however, was completely unimpressed. 'Frankly, darling, I find it very difficult to believe that taradiddle. If that was all he had come to say, he could

have left a note with Fishe, not gone shinning over walls
like some character in a novel! There is something you
are not telling me.' Portia's blue eyes were narrowed in
speculation.

'There is nothing to tell you—and even if there were,
I wouldn't,' Helena stated with more spirit than clarity.
Portia regarded her friend's heightened colour, the flush
on her creamy skin, the spark in her violet eyes and recognised defeat.

'Oh, very well, but do not say I did not tell you so.'

By the time Portia's barouche had travelled the short
distance up Davies Street from Berkeley Square to Brook
Street the two friends were again on speaking terms,
united in their attempts to smuggle in Helena's numerous
parcels and hatboxes before Lady Wyatt saw them.

Helena's maid Lucy had just scuttled upstairs with the
last of the shopping when the salon door opened and
Lady Wyatt emerged, pince-nez in one hand and Greek
lexicon in the other.

'Ah, there you are, Helena. Good afternoon, Portia.
You both look exceedingly well—have you enjoyed your
expedition into Bond Street?'

'Yes, Mama, thank you.'

'And do you have any of your allowance left, my
dear?' Lady Wyatt enquired wryly.

'No, Mama,' Helena responded truthfully. It was hopeless trying to hide anything from the acute eye of her
mother.

'Never mind, dear,' Lady Wyatt replied mildly, 'another banker's draft will soon put that right.' Helena was
left speechless by this unexpected streak of frivolity, but
her mother swept on through the hall, saying to Portia in
passing, 'Now, you will not forget our "At Home" tomorrow afternoon, will you, Portia?'

'No, indeed, Lady Wyatt, I thank you. But I fear Mr Rowlett will not be able to accompany me, he is engaged with a very tedious bill in the House.'

Lady Wyatt paused on the threshold of the library. 'By the by, Helena, Lord Hilton called and left his card, as did Mr Seymour.'

As soon as the door shut Portia exclaimed, 'Excellent tactics, my dear! These admirers will soon make Lord Darvell jealous!'

'I have no wish to make him jealous!' It was the truth but, in saying it, it occurred to Helena that if she had more than one admirer then Lady Breakey might not be so fixed on encouraging Mr Brookes.

After Portia had left, Helena took up her sketchbook and retreated into the conservatory to finish the sketch of an orchid which she had promised her uncle. The flower with its exotic, almost decadent, bloom was at its peak, its heavy scent drugging in the warm room. A lone bee was buzzing drowsily in the ranks of blossoms and a slight breeze made the fern leaves whisper.

Helena struggled with the intricate whorls and curves of the flower, but her mind would not focus. Suddenly she flipped the page over and her pencil seemed to fly across the page of its own volition.

Rigging spanned the sheet, the bold curve of the ship's rail arched below it and the figure of Adam in his canvas trousers and linen shirt, hands on hips, head thrown back, dominated the foreground.

Without any effort Helena's pencil recaptured the crisp curl of the over-long hair at his neck, the stretched tendons of his throat, the suppressed energy of the taut figure.

Casting down the pencil at last, Helena held out the

sketchbook at arm's length and was almost scared by what she had created. It was Adam in loving detail, caught by a lover's hand, all the emotion she could not express in words poured out onto the page.

Caution sent her hand out to rip the page, to crumple and discard it for fear of what it would betray to any observer. If her mama saw it, she would be dismayed; if anyone else saw it, then all the careful subterfuges would be as nothing. She could surround herself with a hundred eligible men and deceive no one.

But she could not do it: it would be like throwing away all her memories of Adam; and that was all that she had, all she would ever have, he had made that plain enough the other day.

With infinite care Helena took up a fruit knife and scored along the paper, excising the sheet. No, no one else would ever see this picture of the man she loved, but she could not destroy it. She was still holding it, wondering where the safest place to keep it would be, when Fishe appeared at the conservatory door.

'Lady Wyatt's compliments, Miss Helena, and do you intend accompanying her to Lady Faulkener's?'

Lady Breakey's rooms were gratifyingly full for her At Home and the conservatory was also being pressed into use as a reception room.

Sir Robert was doing his duty by chatting to a group of elderly dowagers, his ready charm and hearty manner keeping them enthralled. As one was heard to remark to his confusion, 'It is so reassuring to know that the Tyrant Bonaparte is being held at bay by such British heroes!'

Helena, observing him, smiled to herself. She had no doubt that her uncle, an enthusiastic but harmless flirt, would soon reward himself for his devotion to the dowagers with a little light conversation with the younger, more comely, matrons.

Lady Wyatt came up behind her daughter and laid her hand on her shoulder. 'Are you enjoying yourself, my dear? I must say, you are looking very well in that gown. You should wear blue more often, it becomes you so.'

'Thank you, ma'am. And you, too, look very fine, if I may say so. That new crop suits you—I told you it would.'

Lady Wyatt put up one hand to pat her fashionably styled hair. 'Yes, I surprised myself, but there is no persuading your aunt, she prefers never to cut her hair. Now, who is that arriving?'

She moved across to the door to join her sister-in-law in greeting their new guest. 'Lord Darvell, good afternoon.'

Helena stepped back behind a potted palm, her heart thudding painfully, telling herself she had to take a grip on her emotions. She had known he had been invited and it was inevitable they would constantly meet in Society. She must stop behaving like a gauche schoolgirl.

Consequently she squared her shoulders and greeted Adam with calm civility when she found him before her. Her resolve was shaken by the gleam of admiration in his eyes as he took in her stylish afternoon gown which showed off her figure to admiration. After an exchange of the merest pleasantries he enquired wickedly, 'Will you not show me your uncle's conservatory, Miss Wyatt? I hear he has a fine collection of orchids.'

Adam offered his arm and, without appearing rude, Helena could do nothing but place her fingers lightly on the dark blue superfine cloth and allow herself to be conducted to the conservatory.

Helena was painfully conscious of his nearness, the

faint tang of his cologne touching her nostrils. She glanced at him, seeing the laughter lines at the corner of his eyes, paler against his still-tanned skin. The fashion for closely tailored trousers and coats suited his lean, rangy figure to perfection and Helena was sensitive to the envious glances from several other women in the room.

As they reached the scented glasshouse he remarked, 'What a pleasant structure. Does it open out direct on to the garden?'

'You know full well it does,' she hissed under her breath. 'Do not tease me, Adam!' At her use of his Christian name, his head turned and he smiled at her.

'You blush so charmingly, I could not resist it. Forgive me.'

'Certainly not. Come, I believe you have not met the Misses Turner. Miss Turner, Miss Anne Turner, may I make known to you Lord Darvell. Lord Darvell is very interested in orchids.'

The two earnest young ladies, thus addressed, pounced on his lordship with exclamations of delight. 'My lord, do come and see the cymbidiums. Do you not agree they are the most magnificent specimens outside Kew Gardens? There is to be the most interesting lecture at the Royal Society on Wednesday on the newest Oriental strains, will you be there? We find cultivation from the dormant bulbs a problem...'

Satisfied with her revenge and ignoring the anguished glances Adam was sending her above the heads of the two blue-stockings, Helena turned to go back into the salon.

But her way was barred by a tall figure in naval uniform. 'Miss Wyatt, I do beg your pardon.'

Helena, aware of the need to turn him from the conservatory, greeted Lieutenant Brookes with considerably more warmth than she should properly exhibit towards a man she had met only once socially. 'Lieutenant Brookes, what an unexpected pleasure. Mrs Rowlett had given me to understand that you were engaged at the Admiralty.'

The Lieutenant, somewhat taken aback by his reception after Miss Wyatt's lacklustre response to him at Almack's, was more than willing to return to the salon.

Mr Brookes could scarcely believe this was the same rather vapid young woman who had mumbled monosyllabic replies to his questions at Almack's. Miss Wyatt outshone any other young woman in the house: her violet eyes were sparkling, her face was alight with animated interest in him. Her slender figure, clad in a periwinkle blue gown, was delightful and her glossy brown curls gleamed in the afternoon sunlight streaming through the long west-facing windows of the salon.

Daniel Brookes was a very careful man: at the start of his career in His Majesty's navy he had drawn up a plan of campaign designed to steer him from midshipman to admiral in the shortest possible time. His connections and social standing were good, but none of his relatives had naval ties or—more importantly—influence at the Admiralty. The right marriage into a naval family would make good this deficit.

Securing an introduction to the Wyatt-Breakey clan had been a coup he was very anxious to consolidate. At Almack's he had reconciled himself to paying court to a pretty but colourless debutante as a means to achieving his ends: now necessity would be a positive pleasure.

'May I pour you a cup of tea, Lieutenant?' Miss Wyatt asked charmingly. 'And then you must tell me all about your ship—are you with the Channel fleet?'

'Thank you.' He accepted the proffered cup and sat beside her on the sofa. He was very ready to talk of his

career and impress her with his achievements, but his
discourse was slightly distracted by the little glances she
kept casting over his shoulder as if she were anxious to
avoid someone. Perhaps her mama, a strong-minded
woman by all accounts, would not approve of her daughter setting up a tête à tête in this way.

Helena realised she must be sounding particularly
vapid. She was prattling, she knew. In her nervousness
she was in danger of overplaying her hand and giving
Lieutenant Brookes entirely the wrong idea. She wanted
to distract him from Adam, but she had no desire to cast
him any lures.

'…at the moment I am seconded to the Excise,' he
was saying. Helena jerked her eyes back from the conservatory door, wondering when Adam would escape the
Misses Turner and what she should do if the two men
came face to face.

Without thinking, she said, 'That must be so exciting,
boarding smuggling vessels!' Oh, no! Why had she said
that instead of turning the conversation to more neutral
matters?

There was a slight, uncomfortable pause. 'More dis-
piriting than exciting, ma'am. You would be amazed how
many so-called gentlemen support this infamous trade in
defiance of His Majesty's laws.'

'I am sure the loss of revenue is very shocking…'

'It is not the revenue, it is the intelligence that passes
that is the danger.'

'Intelligence, Mr Brookes?' A slight flush rose to Helena's cheeks and her heart began to thud uncomfortably.
Her conscience was still uneasy about the part she had
played and she could not exorcise from her mind Adam's
meeting with the Frenchman in the Godolphin Arms or
his evasion in the face of her questioning.

'In many cases no harm is meant, but smuggling crews landing in French ports are free to come and go as they please by direct order of the Emperor Napoleon. He knows how much is let slip over a bumper too many of brandy. And then,' he added evenly, 'there are those who trade in secrets. They are the true traitors, Miss Wyatt, for they know exactly what they are doing and who they are betraying.' In her present state of guilt it seemed as though he were making a direct reference to Adam.

'But from what motives, sir?' Helena asked with such concern Daniel's attention was caught.

'In a few cases they espouse the French cause. In most it is for money and a few—most often idle gentlemen— do it for devilment.'

Her face had gone so pale he was fearful he had said too much and alarmed her delicate feminine sensibilities.

'Do not worry yourself, Miss Wyatt; these villains will not prevail. Very soon we will overcome the tyrant. I am sorry, I did not seek to alarm you.'

'Oh, no, Mr Brookes, you have not alarmed me,' she hastened to reassure him. 'It is just that the day has turned out unaccountably warm—do you not think so?'

Daniel Brookes was watching the play of emotions on her face. 'Forgive me, Miss Wyatt, but I have suddenly had the most unaccountable notion. Have we ever encountered one another before? Perhaps at some reception or ball where we had not been introduced...'

For one awful moment Helena feared he knew the truth and was playing with her. Then she saw the puzzlement in his eyes and knew he was genuinely baffled. 'Perhaps, sir. My aunt and uncle have a very wide circle of friends and acquaintances, many of them connected with His Majesty's navy. Doubtless it is as you say and you have seen me at some gathering. Will you take more tea?'

The Lieutenant, satisfied for the moment by her response, accepted the offer of another cup. Helena began to relax again, then from behind where they were sitting she heard her mother's voice and that of the person to whom she was speaking.

'A delightful afternoon, ma'am. I thank you for your hospitality.'

At the sound of Adam's voice Brookes's back stiffened. He put down his cup with some emphasis and rose to his feet. 'Good day, Lord Darvell.'

'Lieutenant Brookes: good day to you, sir. I see the Admiralty has been able to spare you this afternoon.' It was perfectly pleasant; perhaps only Helena's sensitive ear caught the underlying dislike.

'Indeed, my lord, as you say. I shall be glad to get back to sea to do my duty, however: there are many rogues to be apprehended. And they appear in the most unlikely settings.' His neutral tone masked the barb which Helena knew was aimed straight at Adam.

His lordship bowed slightly. 'Your vigilance reassures me, Lieutenant. I am sure we may all sleep easier in our beds for knowing that every bottle of brandy and every yard of lace has its full duty paid.'

Brookes's face tightened at this palpable hit, but only Helena caught the glimpse of pure hatred that blazed briefly in the hard eyes. 'I do my humble best to serve my country, my lord,' he responded stiffly. 'I could not endure a life of selfish pleasure spent idling in ladies' drawing rooms—however delightful the company. Nor do I take any pleasure in mischief-making at the expense of those who are only trying to do their duty.'

Helena realised that she was clenching her fists so tightly that her nails cut into the palms. She forced herself to relax her hands, but she could not bring herself to look up. Her mother with her usual tact walked towards the door, continuing to talk to Adam and thus obliging him to follow her.

Lieutenant Brookes, white to the lips, bowed to Helena. 'Excuse me, Miss Wyatt, I had promised myself a glimpse of your uncle's famous orchids.'

She made no attempt to accompany him but sank back on the sofa, legs weak with reaction. The hostility between the two men had almost flared into the open. That, combined with Daniel Brookes's feeling that he knew her from somewhere, left Helena feeling quite sick.

It was a few moments before the giddiness passed and she could cast round to see where the Lieutenant had gone. He was just inside the door to the conservatory, his pocket book in his hand, an expression she could not read on his face. He stood, as though deep in thought for several seconds, then decisively snapped shut the book and thrust it into the breast of his coat. As though he had just recalled an appointment, he made his way over to his hostesses and bowed his leave of them without a backward glance at Helena.

This abrupt departure, however, did not mark the end of Lieutenant Brookes's interest in Helena. Quite the contrary, as Lady Breakey observed over luncheon a week later.

'Mr Brookes is becoming most attentive to Helena, is he not, my dear? Quite the most persistent of her young men.'

Her sister-in-law, thus addressed, gave the matter some thought. 'Well, I believe you are correct, Celia. Now you come to mention it, scarcely a day has passed when he has not called upon us here.' She turned to her daughter and enquired, 'Is he taking you riding again this after-noon, Helena?'

'Yes, Mama,' Helena replied colourlessly.

Lady Breakey was unexpectedly sharp. She put down her cup with some emphasis. 'I am beginning to lose patience with these languishing airs, Helena. Lieutenant Brookes is an entirely acceptable young man: good connections, a fine career which your uncle would be in a position to advance, and most personable. The other young men of your acquaintance are all well connected, but none, I fancy, are quite as suitable.'

'I go riding with him, and receive him when he calls,' Helena protested.

'Yes, and show him about as much distinguishing attention as you do the curate! I had great hopes that he was just the man to take your mind off that unfortunate connection with Lord Darvell.'

'Well, he at least is no longer calling,' Lady Wyatt remarked. 'Which is doubtless a good thing.'

'Yes, Mama,' Helena concurred meekly. And common sense told her her mother was right: seeing Adam only hurt her broken heart the more, reminding her of what she had willfully rejected. How bitterly she regretted that now! And yet, how humiliating to be married to a man who had offered for her merely out of duty!

And it was safer for Adam not to be seen with her. Daniel Brookes was a shrewd and intelligent man—it would not take him long to make the connection between Helena and Adam Darvell if he saw them together. The memory of the blazing hatred in his eyes when he looked at Adam kept her awake at night. She had no doubt that if he could have done he would have run Adam through, so goaded was he.

By continuing to encourage the other young men who

squired her to galleries or receptions—Mr Seymour, Lord Hilton, even Mr Yates the curate—she hoped to obscure the close attention she paid to every nuance of Mr Brookes's behaviour.

Helena knew she only had two options: she could tell Daniel she no longer wished to see him or she could allow his visits to continue with her family's active encouragement. Seeing him was a constant danger in case he recognised her, yet instinct told her to keep him under her eye, engage his attention. And if Daniel was feeling welcome and flattered he would not be brooding on ways to get even with Adam.

But it was a fine line she was treading: she had to keep him close enough to watch him, yet not encourage him to the point where he made a declaration. Surely Daniel would receive his orders and go back to sea soon? Every day she expected him to call and say he was about to depart.

She had even resorted to asking her uncle. 'I am surprised that Lieutenant Brookes is still in London,' she had remarked with a feigned degree of unconcern one evening when they found themselves alone.

'Eh? What?' Sir Robert had put down his paper and twinkled at her, misinterpreting her interest. 'Anxious in case your beau ups and leaves you?'

Helena blushed. 'No, of course not; he is not my beau.'

'Well, you need not fear, I cannot say too much, but I believe our friend will be in London for a few more weeks yet. You will not mention this to anyone, of course, but his experience with the Excise has led the Admiralty to think about what possibilities for gathering intelligence that branch of the service might have.'

Her kindly uncle, in his attempt to please her with news of the young man's possible advancement, could not have said anything worse. Helena, unable to sit still, crossed to refill the Commodore's glass. 'I will not say a word, naturally, but do you mean that the Lieutenant is to become an intelligence officer?' Her hand shook as she poured the port, the edge of the decanter clinking against the rim of his glass.

'Careful, my child, you will spill it! Thank you.' He took a sip and regarded her sombrely over the top of the glass. 'Yes, that is what I meant. But do not fear for his safety, he is an experienced officer and intelligence work is not necessarily more dangerous than any other branch of the Service. I must confess I am pleased with that young man, he is living up to my expectations.'

Helena almost missed it, then the significance of what he was saying struck her. 'You have drawn the Admiralty's attention to him!'

'Well, one is always on the look out, don't you know.' Her uncle sat back, stretching his legs out in front of him comfortably. 'I had a word with one or two people and there was no difficulty in finding him useful occupation which will keep him in town for a little longer.'

It was all Helena could do to keep her temper in the face of her uncle's benevolent belief that he was giving her the best of news. It had to be Aunt Breakey's doing: she could not resist matchmaking. And she had so taken against Adam that she would regard any stratagem to detach Helena as fair.

But the anger soon turned to dismay, edged with fear. She had counted on Daniel going back to sea very soon. Going out and about with him, she hoped, would ensure that his memories of her were all of the here and now. There had been no repetition of that uncomfortable moment when it had seemed to Helena that he was within an ace of recognising her.

Familiarity was breeding another danger, however: Helena was uncomfortably aware that Lieutenant Brookes's manner towards her was verging on the proprietorial, despite her best efforts to behave with cool decorum towards him, and never to dance more than once of an evening with him, however much he pressed her.

The uncomfortable memories of that conversation with her uncle were still troubling her as she dressed for riding that afternoon. Lucy, tugging the hem of the tight-fitting jacket, remarked, 'This new habit is very dashing, miss!'

Helena twirled in front of the long pier glass and was inclined to agree. The style was extreme, and very daring for an unmarried lady, but Portia had persuaded her that it was the first kick of fashion.

The broadcloth was dark raspberry pink with fir green frogging in the military style and epaulettes, cut tightly to show off her slender figure. An equally daring hat was tipped provocatively over one eye and wreathed in dark green veiling, and as a final flourish Helena had invested in a pair of gauntletted gloves.

For once she was early, and, feeling a little warm in the house, went to wait in the conservatory for the Lieutenant to arrive at half past two as arranged.

Helena drifted aimlessly around the cool glasshouse, touching and sniffing the exquisite blooms. Lying on a side table where the servants must have placed it for safe-keeping was her sketchbook. Idly she flicked through the pages until she came to the cut edge of the portrait of Adam she had removed just before the reception. Her brow furrowed—what had she done with that incriminating picture?

She could recall standing with it in her hand when Fishe had come in to enquire whether she was accompanying her mother and aunt to Lady Faulkener's At

Home but, rack her brains as she might, Helena had no recollection of what she had done with it thereafter....

Perhaps she had pushed it back into the sketchbook. Helena rifled rapidly through the pages, then began again, turning them more carefully and finally, pointlessly, holding it by the spine and shaking it. No leaf fluttered out; the portrait was not there. The sketchbook had lain untouched by her ever since that day—it must have been there when the reception was taking place. But none of the guests would have touched it without invitation, surely.

She tugged the bellpull and waited impatiently until Fishe appeared.

'You rang, Miss Wyatt?'

'Yes Fishe. Do you recall finding one of my sketches lying around here?'

'The sketchbook, Miss Wyatt, is on the table in the conservatory where I believe you left it over a week ago.'

'No, not the sketchbook, Fishe. This was a loose leaf I had cut from the book.'

'Not to my knowledge, Miss Wyatt. I am sure that if one of the servants had found such a thing they would have placed it with the sketchbook or handed it to yourself. I will, of course, make enquiries.'

'I would be glad if you could do so at once, please.'

If the butler was surprised by the emphasis in her tone he did not show it, but bowed impassively and left the room. He was back within a short space of time with the intelligence that none of the upper servants had any recollection of such an article. 'I have, of course, issued instructions that should it be found it must be handed to you immediately, Miss Wyatt.'

Helena was thanking him as the front-door knocker sounded and a footman came in to announce both the arrival of Lieutenant Brookes and that her horse had been brought round from the mews.

Helena's stunning new habit was not lost on the naval officer. He bowed over her hand and said gallantly, 'Miss Wyatt, I declare you will outshine everything in Green Park this afternoon,' before assisting her to mount her horse.

Sir Robert, with his usual generosity, had supplied his niece with a pretty grey mare, dappled on its quarters like a rocking horse and with a long, dark mane and tail. Mr Seymour, on one of their morning rides had assured her that 'Miss Wyatt and her grey' were becoming quite the talk of the town, so dashing a figure did she cut. Helena dismissed most of this as exaggeration, but was pleasantly aware that she did make quite an impact in her new habit.

However, this afternoon, her thoughts were distracted, dwelling as she did on the missing sketch. No one seeing that drawing would have any doubt that it was done with a lover's eye for every detail. Nor was there any hope that anyone who knew him could possibly fail to recognise Adam Darvell.

Helena was grateful that they were on horseback: threading between the traffic hazards as David Street crossed Grosvenor Street, there was no opportunity for conversation.

The Lieutenant had learnt that Miss Wyatt was a more than capable horsewoman who resisted any attempts to take her horse's reins when such crises occurred as a brewer's dray unloading kegs with a crash, or a sedan chair emerging from Mount Row right under their noses. The grey curvetted about prettily, but there was no malice or danger in its skittishness, and Helena kept a firm, but instinctive hand on the reins.

It was quieter in Berkeley Square and the Lieutenant drew his chestnut alongside Helena to trot with her as they turned east to skirt the central garden. 'Is that not Lady Jersey's residence?' he enquired as they passed one particularly fine mansion.

Helena was agreeing as they drew level with number forty-four, where a groom stood at the head of a powerful black gelding which fidgeted restlessly at the kerb. The front door swung open and a gentleman emerged, pulling on his riding gloves, his whip tucked under one arm.

The Lieutenant who, as Helena was fast discovering, could never leave well enough alone as far as Adam was concerned, reined in and doffed his hat with over-elaborate courtesy.

'My lord. I trust I find you well this fine afternoon.'

Lord Darvell, thus addressed, narrowed his eyes against the spring sunshine and regarded the two riders coolly. He pulled on the remaining glove and sketched a bow to Helena. 'Miss Wyatt: how you do illuminate our dull neighbourhood.'

Helena, left with the uncomfortable suspicion that he found her habit a touch gaudy, inclined her head stiffly. 'My lord.'

Adam swung up into the saddle with ready grace, waving aside his groom's offer of a leg up. He gathered up the reins, turning his horse to face in the opposite direction to Helena and Lieutenant Brookes. 'I had not realised you were a rider, Miss Wyatt.'

Piqued, Helena forced a brilliant smile. 'Oh, yes, I love to ride and Lieutenant Brookes has been good enough to offer me his escort *very* frequently. He has shown me all the most picturesque rides in all the parks.'

She was conscious that beside her Daniel was looking very pleased with himself and felt a sudden qualm at encouraging him in such a way. Her heart ached at the sight of Adam, yet she had yielded to the temptation to make him jealous, make him suffer as she was now doing.

'Then I will delay you no longer from your jaunt,' Adam replied, without the slightest sign of pique, or even, to her chagrin, interest. 'Good day, Miss Wyatt, Lieutenant.'

Chapter Nine

All her pleasure in the ride, in the beautiful fresh spring afternoon and in her new habit dissolved like mist in warm sunshine. Helena was conscious that she had behaved very badly with Adam, and without even the satisfaction of seeing him rise to her bait. And now all her earlier concerns about the whereabouts of the portrait of him sprang fresh in her mind.

Encouraged by her comments in Berkeley Square, Daniel rode close beside her, assiduously pointing out particularly pretty greenery or drawing her attention to notables who were also taking the air in Green Park.

The harder he tried, the more irritated Helena became, both with him and herself. She forced herself to make polite but neutral conversation, determined not to be drawn into any show of intimacy or warmth.

What had happened to that picture? Surely if her mama or Lady Breakey had it in their possession they would have confronted her with it at once? She supposed it was just possible that her mama had found it and destroyed it without a word, but it was unlikely that such a forthright woman would do such a thing.

Could Fishe be wrong? Could one of the servants have

found it and read its meaning aright? She had heard cases of perfidious servants blackmailing their masters with compromising letters, but it was hard to imagine any of her aunt's faithful and long-serving staff behaving so.

Riding with furrowed brow, answering Lieutenant Brookes automatically without really listening to what he was saying, Helena worked methodically through everyone who might have found the drawing. She must have tucked it back into the sketchbook, and that book had lain in full view throughout her aunt's reception. But none of the guests would have been so ill-bred to open it without her leave, and certainly not the very staid Misses Turner, who had been in occupation of the conservatory throughout the afternoon, rapt in contemplation of the orchids.

But there was one guest who had already had her permission to look through her sketchbook—and Adam had been in the conservatory for an extraordinary length of time.

He could have taken the picture—he had already asked for and received one of her sketches. And if Adam did have it, she would be safe: Lord Darvell was a gentleman, there was no question of his betraying her. And yet, a little worm of disquiet still remained. What if Adam was not the possessor of the sketch...?

Helena came out of her brown study to discover that they had come to a halt and that the Lieutenant was obviously expecting her to dismount.

Helena looked at him blankly and he laughed wryly. 'Miss Wyatt, I do not believe you have been listening to a word I have said these past ten minutes.'

'Oh, dear!' Helena blushed to realise just how unmannerly she must seem. 'I do apologise, Mr Brookes, what is it you were saying?'

'I had just observed what a fine new shrubbery has been planted here, and you had agreed to dismount and walk through it with me.' He smiled, showing even white teeth in his suntanned face. She was amazed how tolerant he was with her moods.

But Helena was reluctant to get off her horse: the last thing she wanted was to find herself in such close proximity to him. No one else was in sight enjoying the winding newly graveled path, but to refuse to walk with him in a public place would imply that she could not trust him to behave as a gentleman.

Daniel Brookes dismounted and, with his reins looped over his arm, reached up to take her round the waist, lifting her down from the saddle easily. Her mind filled with thoughts of Adam, Helena had never realised what a big, strong man the Lieutenant was, and she found herself flustered to be, even for a moment, helpless in his arms.

She blushed, unconsciously making an even prettier picture for the Lieutenant who was reflecting that doing the sensible thing to advance his own self-interest had never been so pleasurable. It would be no hardship to make love to Miss Wyatt, and now, alone in the Park so soon after she had clearly expressed her preference for his company, would be a good time to start.

Was it only her imagination, or did the Lieutenant's hand linger over-long at her waist? Helena glanced down, but Mr Brookes had released his hold and was tossing the reins over the horses' heads, the better to lead them. She could hardly refuse to take his arm when it was offered, but Helena merely rested her fingertips on the sleeve of his riding coat.

For several minutes they strolled through the shrubbery, exchanging observations on the planting and the rapid progress of spring. Helena relaxed slightly, reassured by his decorum.

'Shall we sit awhile on that bench?' he asked, already turning across the turf to the rustic seat.

Without seeming foolish she could scarcely say no so Helena allowed herself to be seated under the greening branches of a young lime. Daniel threw the reins of both horses over a nearby bush and came to sit beside her.

He half turned towards her, one arm along the back of the seat. Helena felt hemmed in, a feeling which increased when he gently took her hand and enclosed it in his own.

'Lieutenant Brookes!' Her tone was outraged—at any moment someone could come around the corner and see them. She should never have allowed herself to be led into this secluded spot.

'Forgive me, but I have waited so long to be alone with you. You cannot be unaware, Miss Wyatt, of my regard for you.' So saying, he raised her hand to his lips and pressed a kiss on her kid-covered knuckles.

'I assure you, sir, I am quite unconscious that you have any particular feeling for me! Please release my hand— anyone might come along and see us.' She tugged her hand back, but Daniel still held it and the gesture only served to pull him closer to her. He brought up his arm that had lain on the back of the bench and encircled her shoulders.

Helena found herself so close that she could see her own startled face reflected in the pupils of his dark eyes. 'Sir! This is most improper! I am in no mood for flirting!'

'Nor I,' he said huskily. 'You must know it is not flirtation I seek, Helena.' Daniel smiled down at her.

'No, no, Mr Brookes...' She shrank from him.

'Daniel, call me Daniel, Helena.' His breath was warm on her cheek, stirring the little curls at her temple.

'Mr Brookes,' she began again, firmly. 'Please, I must ask you to release me. This is not proper, and you have come to quite the wrong conclusion as to my sentiments.'

'Come, Helena, I know it is necessary to play the game and to make a token protest of maidenly ignorance, but we both know it is a charade.'

Helena gave a little gasp and met his knowing brown eyes. 'A charade? Sir, what do you mean?' Her stomach cramped painfully and her frightened mind echoed the words, *he knows, he knows, he knows...*

'Why,' he said easily, smiling down into her widened eyes, 'I mean that it is customary on these occasions for the young lady to pretend she has no idea what the gentleman is talking about. But we both know, do we not, Helena?'

Helena's mind raced. This might all be perfectly innocent, be exactly what it appeared on the surface. And, being ruthlessly honest with herself, she acknowledged that she may have seemed to give him more encouragement than her other beaux. And it would be in no way presumptuous of him to make her a proposal of marriage: he was in her family's profession, well-connected and a very personable young man.

She decided to take the bull by the horns. 'Sir...am I to understand that you are making me a declaration?'

There was a pause, just fractionally too long for her comfort. 'Why, my dear Miss Wyatt—what else could I be referring to?' One dark brow quirked interrogatively, but his eyes were sharp and watchful.

'Well, I...you must understand, sir, I have no experience of such matters...this is my first Season...surely you should address yourself to my uncle the Commodore…'

Daniel ran one finger down her cheek almost assessingly as though taking stock of something he was about to buy. 'Oh, I do not think that the fact this is your first Season necessarily has anything to do with…experience.'

Helena batted his hand away with anger, her cheeks flaming. The effrontery of the man! Everything that Adam had told her about him came to her mind and she believed every word. Why, he was treating her like a doxy from the Vauxhall Pleasure Gardens! Either he was so confident that she would fall into his arms that he had no use for subtlety, or he knew the truth and believed her to be no better than she should be.

With a jerk she freed her trapped hand and pushed with both hands at Daniel's broad chest, feeling the resistance of hard muscle under the broadcloth. She might as well have been pushing at the side of a ship.

'Oh, enough of this playacting!' He sounded amused, but there was a distinct edge, the irritation of a man not used to being denied. Daniel gathered her firmly in his arms, bent his head and kissed Helena with hard lips. Shocked, she resisted him, clamping her mouth closed and her lips tight, but it was hopeless. Ruthlessly his tongue pushed against her lips, shockingly invading, hard and intrusive.

Instinctively Helena bit down, tasting the salty tang of blood as he recoiled, cursing. 'Why, you little…' His face was livid and for one mad moment Helena believed he was going to strike her.

'Now, look 'ere, guvnor! Your 'orses is eating that new shrub what we only planted last week!'

Rescue had come in the most unlikely form of a pair of gardeners. Wrapped in great baize aprons and holding rakes, the men looked almost comical, but there was no disguising their annoyance at the wreck this gentleman's horses had done to the planting.

Daniel leapt to his feet, and one look at his face told Helena that the two men were about to get the rough edge of his tongue. He was obviously incandescent with fury, an anger at her that he would visit on these two insolent labourers.

Helena whisked round Daniel's rigid figure and hurried down the lawn towards her two unlikely chevaliers. 'Oh, I am so sorry! Such a pretty bush and you have worked so hard on this lovely shrubbery! If there is any recompense to be paid you must tell the Head Gardener to address my uncle, Sir Robert Breakey in Brook Street. Here...' she fished in the pocket of her riding habit '...this is for your trouble. I really am so very sorry.'

The bemused men, finding a generous tip pressed into their grubby palms, were completely won over by the brilliance of the beautiful young lady's smile. Helena unhooked the reins of her grey from the damaged bush and turned to the men. 'Would one of you be very kind and give me a leg up?'

Poleaxed by this encounter with the gentry, they happily complied, the smaller of the two holding the horse's head while the senior tossed Helena into the saddle with clumsy care. Without looking back at Daniel, she kicked her horse into a canter and set off for the North gate.

The two men, conscious of the furious young man they had been left with, picked up their rakes and vanished rapidly into the undergrowth.

Helena spurred on through the park until the sight of the startled faces of fashionable strollers and the increased traffic of carriages brought her to herself. Green Park was not the place where anyone went to indulge in fast riding under any circumstances, and the sight of an unchaperoned lady cantering across the well-scythed grass was little short of scandalous.

Two landaus were pulled up side by side while their occupants exchanged pleasantries and Helena was appalled to see Lady Faulkener's haughty profile. Pulling on the reins, she urged the grey towards a clump of trees and pulled up under their dipping branches to recover herself.

Her heart was thudding madly in her chest, and her mouth felt swollen after Daniel's invasion. He had recognised her from the *Moonspinner*, she had no doubt about that now! It was the only explanation for his conduct—he assumed she had been Adam's mistress and, seeing the *froideur* between them now, had decided to step in. Presumably his ambition was such that he had no qualms in marrying 'damaged goods' if she brought him the influence and connections he so desperately craved.

Helena let the reins go slack, allowing the horse to dip its head to graze. Through the screen of branches she was hazily aware of polite Society going about its social round in the Park. A small boy chased a hoop, screaming with delight, while a lapdog ran after him barking madly. It all seemed as remote as a dream.

She forced herself to think what Daniel Brookes might do with his knowledge. Not only was he an ambitious man, but a proud one, and she had humiliated him in front of the lower orders, spurned his suit and fought off his advances in a manner which could only anger him. He frightened her; she had no doubt that everything Adam had told her about his character was true.

What would he do now? How would he use his knowledge to his advantage, for she doubted he ever did anything that was not to his gain. Presumably he would come and be more explicit, tell her in no uncertain terms that he knew she had been at sea with Adam and expect her to agree to marry him in exchange for his silence. And if she refused? Well, then she had no doubt that he would threaten to tell her uncle.

He would tell the story as though he had a moral duty to rescue her from the consequences of her fall from virtue. He would pose as a man in love who was prepared to forgive all, to accept her despite her past and give her a respectable name. Her aunt would do everything in her power to promote the match and her mother, even with her well-known eccentricity, could not permit her daughter to be ruined.

The horse extended its neck, jerking her in the saddle. Helena peered out between the leaves but the two landaus were still there, the dowagers chatting animatedly and showing no inclination to tell their coachmen to drive on. Helena knew she must take the North gate—any other exit from the Park would leave her with a far longer journey through the streets to negotiate.

She could hardly stay where she was until it got dark—being out on the streets at night would be even more scandalous. Finally the carriages rolled away. Helena pulled down her veil and, for the first time regretting that she had chosen such a distinctive horse, trotted circumspectly towards the gate.

Crossing Piccadilly, she attracted many curious stares and quite a few blatantly admiring glances from passing men. Looking to neither right nor left, Helena made her way through the traffic. The streets were thronged with deliveries and with carriages returning from afternoon calls and drives in the parks. Hoping that it would be assumed that her groom was behind her, Helena rode grimly on, her cheeks flaming under the veil.

The footman was startled to find her on the doorstep unaccompanied by the escort she had departed with, but received no explanation. Helena ran upstairs, whisked into her bedchamber, pulling urgently at the bell.

Lucy found her mistress breaking her fingernails in her effort to undo the tight buttons down the front of her jacket. Her hat and whip were thrown onto the chaise-longue and the face she turned to the girl was set and miserable. 'Help me out of this habit, then take it away and burn it!'

'But, Miss Helena, it's brand new!' Lucy protested, her hands stroking across the rich cloth. Goodness knows what was amiss: when she had hurried past Edward in answer to the peremptory peel of the bell, he had warned her that the young mistress was in a right taking. 'Never seen the like before,' he had muttered. 'And her gentleman wasn't with her—riding alone in the street, goodness knows what the master'll say when he finds out!'

Helena spun round, 'Just take it away and do as I tell you, Lucy! And please tell my aunt I will lie down until dinner. I have a headache.'

And that was nothing but the truth. Shutting the door firmly behind the maid, Helena turned the key and dropped onto the bed. The room spun as she lay back against the pillows, massaging her throbbing temples. She was in a complete state of turmoil and, what was worse, could see no way out.

Try as she might, Helena could not suppress the memories of Daniel's mouth ruthlessly plundering hers, his tongue invading and demanding. She shuddered, rubbing her hand across her swollen lips as though she could erase the imprint. How very different it had been from

Adam's caresses, even though Adam too had been demanding. But she had welcomed Adam's kisses, had revelled in his passion and given herself up to their mutual arousal...

She had begun by trying to make Adam jealous: now she had made an enemy of Daniel Brookes and had put her own reputation in jeopardy by riding unescorted through the streets of Mayfair.

Thankfully no one came to enquire after her, although she knew her aunt and uncle and mother were in the house. Doubtless it would not be long before they came up to change for dinner. She would just close her eyes, rest and try and regain some composure before she had to face them.

The sound of the door knocker made her eyes fly open in surprise. It was a strange time for a caller. With a growing sense of unease, Helena got up from the bed and tried to see if there was a carriage below. Most likely it would be Lady Faulkener, losing no time in reporting Miss Wyatt's outrageous behaviour to her shocked relatives.

It was a full ten minutes later when Lucy entered Helena's chamber and bobbed a curtsy to her mistress who was pacing anxiously up and down. 'Lady Wyatt's compliments, Miss Helena, and she says, will you please join her in the drawing room. And, miss, she says you're to wear the jonquil silk.'

Oh, dear—it must be Lady Faulkener, and Mama wanted her to look as demure as possible in the most understated of her evening gowns. Helena had still to think of any convincing excuse for her behaviour other than that she had lost control of her horse—not that any of her family would believe that for a moment!

Fifteen minutes later she took a deep breath on the

threshold of the drawing room and pushed open the doors, fully expecting to be confronted by Lady Faulkener, resplendent as usual in purple. But in place of a censorious dowager there was Lieutenant Brookes, darkly handsome in full dress uniform, standing with her uncle before the hearth.

The Commodore was beaming with delight. At the sight of Helena he crossed the floor and took both her hands in his. 'Helena, my dear, there you are! You look as fresh as a daisy—that yellow becomes you very well, very well indeed. Now, see who has called! Make your curtsy, my dear.'

Utterly off balance, Helena still had time to notice the expression on the faces of her mother and aunt as they sat side by side on the sofa. Lady Breakey looked particularly triumphant, her normally pale features animated and a broad smile curving her lips. Even Lady Wyatt was looking as near smug as that well-bred lady would ever permit.

Bobbing a curtsy, Helena fought with her confusion. Why were they all looking so pleased? And Daniel— why, he could not have wasted a moment from when she had fled from him in Green Park before repairing to his lodgings and changing for this visit.

Her uncle took her by the hand and led her to Daniel's side. Helena kept her eyes averted from his face. She knew she had gone pale and she could not trust her voice to speak.

But Sir Robert was doing all the talking. 'Now, my dear, Lieutenant Brookes has called particularly to speak to you, Helena. And I must say, we are all very pleased about the nature of his…er…' he cleared his throat and twinkled at her '…subject matter.'

Lady Breakey rose to her feet with a gracious smile.

'My goodness, look at the time: we must dress for dinner. Come, Sir Robert, come, Sister. Helena, you will entertain the Lieutenant in our absence.' It was a command, not a request. Helena watched helplessly as her relatives withdrew, leaving her with her adversary. What could they be about, to leave her so unchaperoned?

She stepped towards the bellpull hanging beside the fireplace but, before she could ring for her maid, Daniel's hand closed round hers, arresting the action. 'No, Helena, we do not need your maid. Why do you think I am here?'

Helena snatched her hand free and stepped back away from his looming height. 'To apologise, sir, I sincerely hope.' In the dark uniform he dominated the room, exuding the confidence and self-satisfaction of a cat.

'Apologise?' He smiled, but it did not reach his eyes. 'Apologise for sampling what you were offering?'

'Offering!' Helena was outraged. 'I would not offer you the time of day, sir! And if you know so little about women to believe I was compliant, then you have made a serious error of judgment.'

Daniel rested one elbow on the mantleshelf and smiled into her furious face. 'I have considerable experience of women…'

'So I have heard, but it would appear you have learned little from it,' she flashed back and saw the anger stir deep in his eyes as he realised that Adam must have told her something of his history.

'Considerable experience, as is only to be expected of a man of the world,' he continued smoothly. 'But young ladies are not expected to have *any* experience, are they, Helena? Certainly not as much as you have.'

'Sir, you are impertinent. I do not have to stay here and listen to your innuendoes.' Helena turned in a swirl of skirts and stepped towards the door.

Brookes moved swiftly, blocking her escape. 'Not so fast. No one will interrupt us, I am here with your family's blessing to make you a declaration.'

'*A declaration!* Have you taken leave of your senses? I would not marry you, sir, if you were the last man in Christendom!' So that was why her family were looking so smug. Daniel must have secured her uncle's permission to address her, and they had abandoned her, thinking no doubt that the privacy would be welcome to both.

And after what had passed between them in the park, she could not conceive that even this man, with his overweening confidence and transparent ambition, could believe his attentions would be welcome to her. 'You assault me and insult me, and now you have the effrontery to propose marriage to me. I can scarce believe my ears—but you, Lieutenant Brookes, had better believe yours, for I will tell you this plainly, I will never consent to marry you.' She faced up to him, her chin high with defiance, eyes sparking angry fire.

The Lieutenant was not in the least discommoded by her defiance, regarding her flushed and furious figure with amusement. By God! He had started this pursuit to advance his naval career and to get one over on Darvell. He would have married the plainest spinster in the kingdom if that would have served his purpose; but this woman was stirring his blood as no other had before!

'You really are magnificent when you are roused, Helena,' he drawled. 'I am becoming more and more reconciled to this course of action.'

Helena clenched her fists by her side in an effort not to strike out at him, puncture his self-assurance and arrogance. 'Oh, come, sir, since we are being frank, let us say it plainly. The only reason you want to marry me is to form an alliance with a family which has much influence in your profession.'

'That is very true, and I believe I would have offered for you even if you had been plain and at your last prayers.' Daniel Brookes was not going to admit just how much he desired her, he could not afford to give her any weapon against him. 'Your looks and your spirit are an added bonus. But you ask me to speak plainly, and I will do so. If you were not your uncle's heiress, then your attractions would not be enough to induce me to take used goods.' His face was hard, with every line of the hate and ruthlessness it had held on board the *Moonspinner*.

Helena felt as though all the breath had been squeezed from her lungs. With an enormous struggle for composure she managed to whisper, '*Used goods*! You insult me; I will call my uncle and have you thrown from the house.'

Daniel seized her quite roughly by the shoulders. His broad palms burned hot through the flimsy silk and she shivered with fear and loathing. 'Come, madam, stop playing the outraged virgin. Both you and I know you were on Darvell's yacht as his mistress, and that you acted the trollop to deceive my men and myself when we were about His Majesty's lawful business. So enough of this, unless you wish me to tell your family all.'

He knew! Daniel Brookes really knew that it was she on the *Moonspinner*! There was no point in continuing to deny it. 'They know what happened.' Helena twisted out of his grasp and took refuge behind the sofa. 'And they know nothing untoward or improper occurred. Lord Darvell rescued me when I was washed out to sea, and returned me as soon as possible to my mother, who was most grateful to him.'

'Poppycock. You forget, my dear Miss Wyatt, the length of my…acquaintanceship with Darvell. You expect me to believe that you were on his yacht and that you were not in his bed?' He sneered at the betraying colour on her cheeks. 'Oh, no, you may have gulled your dear mama and your aunt, but, Helena, I do not believe that if you had mentioned one word of this to your uncle the Commodore you would not have been married to Darvell within the week.'

'Then I will tell him now,' she defied him. 'He will be very angry, but he will believe me…'

'What, believe you have had no intimate relations with that man when he sees this?' Daniel Brookes removed his pocket book from the breast of his uniform jacket and unfolded a sheet of paper.

With a sinking heart Helena realised that he was the one who had found that treacherous drawing. She remembered seeing him stoop, then put his pocket book away at her aunt's reception, and it all fell into place. Frozen she watched his tanned fingers smooth the paper and hold up the sheet.

Even at that distance it was shockingly intimate, every line etched with a knowledge she should not have had. Her love and longing was writ large for the most insensitive viewer to read: her family would have no difficulty interpreting it.

He was too far away from her and the sofa was between them: she had no chance of seizing it. With deliberate care Daniel folded the paper and replaced it safely within his jacket.

'You would not, you could not be such a blackguard as to use that against me,' Helena gasped.

'Oh, I would. As I will explain to your uncle, my love for you has overcome my natural scruples and I am prepared to hazard my honour to save yours.' He grinned mockingly, his eyes roving impudently over her slender form molded by the silk gown.

The room swayed and Helena grasped the back of the sofa, holding on to it as she unsteadily worked her way round until she could sit on it. 'Sit there,' she commanded shakily, gesturing towards a chair opposite. 'Do not come near me—I must have time to think.'

'Very well.' Lieutenant Brookes dropped his long form into the chair and regarded her like a big tom cat who had caught a mouse and was tormenting it by letting it free between its paws.

Helena dropped her head into her hands, feeling her fingers cold against her hot cheeks. It steadied her and she fought to regain her composure and find a way out. If by her defiance she forced Daniel Brookes to show the drawing to her uncle, she was lost. The Commodore would not hesitate to insist on the marriage between them. If Sir Robert did not see the drawing but she told him the truth, he would insist that Adam married her—and she had no doubt that he would.

Tears filled her eyes. Adam would do the honourable thing the minute he knew she was compromised, as he had offered before. But loving him as she did, she could not bear to be married to him, knowing that he had been compelled to take her.

Helena could faintly see some glimmer of a solution, a thread of hope through the maze. She raised her tear-stained face and said, 'Very well, then, I agree to tell my family we are betrothed.'

Daniel got to his feet and came to make her an ironic bow. 'Madam, your warmth overwhelms me.'

He made as though to take her hand and Helena drew

back. 'If you try and kiss me, I swear I will claw out your eyes,' she said evenly.

'Oh, I intend to do rather more than kiss you, my dear, but that can wait. Anticipation adds spice, I have always found. Now, dry your cheeks and I will ring for your family to rejoin us and hear our *happy news.*'

Chapter Ten

The ordeal of Helena's family's congratulations and pleasure in her betrothal was difficult to bear. Her silence and flushed cheeks were regarded by her aunt and uncle as the bashfulness only to be expected from a well-bred young girl newly affianced. Lady Wyatt, however, observed her daughter with unease.

Something was not right, Helena was not happy. Lady Wyatt assumed that Helena's heart was still with that wretched rake Adam Darvell, but that her superior sense had guided her to a more suitable match. Ah, well, time and the respectful attentions of such a handsome and successful young man as the Lieutenant would soon put that right.

Her future son-in-law was responding with manly modesty to the hearty congratulations of his superior officer, but turned as soon as he could to her, paying Lady Wyatt every attention. 'Lady Wyatt, may I call later this week to discuss a date for the wedding? I am fortunate in being attached to the Admiralty at the moment—' he cast a warm glance towards the Commodore, who was sitting next to Helena on the sofa '—but I expect to return to my ship by the end of next month.'

Lady Wyatt raised a brow. 'If you intend to marry before then, we must certainly apply ourselves to the arrangements with some speed.'

Her sister-in-law appeared at her side, brimful of excitement. 'Now, you need not concern yourself, Sister, Helena will be married from Brook Street. St George's in Hanover Square, of course, is the only possible church, do you not agree, Lieutenant Brookes?'

He turned to her, instantly attentive. 'I bow to your judgment on all these matters, madam.'

With awful inevitability Sir Robert pressed Daniel to stay for dinner. The meal seemed endless to Helena, but by the time the desserts were set before them she had at least recovered enough composure to make small talk with her fiancé. But behind the façade of social chitchat Helena's mind was working furiously. She had a plan, but her first concern must be to do nothing to alert her aunt and uncle, and particularly her mother, who was very acute and attuned to her daughter's mood.

When the ladies withdrew, leaving the gentlemen to their port she forced herself to respond appropriately to the plans both older ladies were making for the wedding.

'Dear Portia as Matron of Honour, of course,' Lady Wyatt was saying as the gentlemen rejoined them.

To Helena's enormous relief Daniel did not linger, taking his leave just after ten, saying with a charmingly rueful smile that he must tear himself away and, besides, he knew Helena would want to be alone with her family.

No one was surprised when Helena retired to her room soon after. When at last the door was shut on her aunt's kisses and congratulations and her mother's loving good wishes, she leaned against the panels and closed her eyes for a long moment. When Lucy came and tapped she sent her away, calling out that she had already undressed and gone to bed and did not wish to be disturbed.

When she felt secure from interruption, Helena sat on the edge of the bed and worked through the plan that had been forming in her mind all the way through the evening.

She would go to Adam, tell him what had happened and ask him to come with her to her uncle. The two of them would explain to the Commodore what had happened aboard the *Moonspinner*, assure him that there was no reason why Helena *had* to marry, and that they had agreed that they did not wish to marry each other. Once they had convinced him, as they had her mother, then Helena would tell him of Daniel's blackmail.

With the full story before him she had no doubt her uncle would prevent the marriage; her only fear was that he would break Daniel professionally and in doing so intensify the hatred between Adam and the naval officer. Her uncle might even call him out, despite the rules about serving officers duelling.

After fumbling with the fastenings, Helena scrambled out of the silk gown and into a dark wool walking dress. Fortunately she had packed her heavy winter cloak with its concealing hood: Helena stood with it over her arm and thought. Would it be safer to walk to Adam's house or to find a cab? It was not a great distance, but at that time of night it would be prudent to drive. She checked her reticule had sufficient coin and, on a sudden thought, plucked her masquerade mask from the dressing table where it dangled by its silken ribbons from the glass.

Helena could hear the footmen moving about closing the shutters in the salon and dining room, but no one had yet secured the bolts on the front door. Her heart in her mouth, she gained the street without being seen and, drawing the cloak closely round her, walked swiftly to the corner just as a cab was passing.

If the cabby was surprised to be taking a young lady of the Quality to the house of a well-known bachelor, he made no comment. 'Do you want me to wait, miss?' he enquired, opening the cab door for her.

Helena glanced up at the candlelit windows of the first floor with relief: it seemed Adam was at home. 'No, there is no need to wait. Thank you.'

She had been congratulating herself on how smoothly this escapade was proceeding until the moment Adam's butler opened the front door. The vision of a cloaked, masked young woman standing on his master's doorstep at half past midnight appeared, momentarily, to take him aback, but he soon recovered his sang-froid.

'If you would care to take a seat in the Small Salon, madam, I will ascertain whether his lordship is At Home. What name should I say?'

Helena hesitated. She could scarcely give the servants her real name. 'Say…say, an acquaintance from the Isles of Scilly.' The butler bowed and withdrew, leaving Helena to warm her chilly hands at the small fire flickering in the grate.

Adam appeared within minutes, closing the door firmly behind him and crossing the room to her side, concern etched on every line of his face. 'Helena? What on earth brings you here at this hour? Are you mad? If anyone should see you, your reputation would be in tatters!'

Helena pushed back the heavy hood and tried to untie the strings of her mask, but the knots had tightened and she fumbled nervously.

'Let me,' Adam said gently, and seconds later his fingers gently teased out the ribbons and freed the mask. He stood very close, looking down into the troubled eyes turned up to his in supplication. Without hesitation he bent and kissed her, full and long on the lips, drawing her chilled body close against the warmth of his.

Instantly she responded with the innocent ardour he had come to know on the *Moonspinner*, and once again, as he caressed the tumble of dark curls spilling over his hands, he wondered what it was about him that made her so adamant in her rejection of him.

The long kiss ended as she pushed him away with a little shake of her head. 'No, Adam, that was not why I came here.' It was so hard to leave the arms she had dreamed about, had longed to be held by, but she knew she had to be strong or Adam would surely guess the depth of her true feelings.

'Is it not?' he asked ruefully, stroking the side of her cheek with a long, warm finger.

Helena shivered, wanting to coil her arms around his neck, pull his mouth down to hers again. Instead she stepped back, putting a safer distance between them. 'No, it is not,' she said sharply, more sharply than she had intended.

Adam pushed her gently towards a chair by the fireside. 'Here, sit down, you are chilled.' He poured a glass of sherry from the decanter on the sideboard and watched as she sipped it and a little colour came back into her cheek. 'I take it no one else knows you are here?'

Helena shook her head mutely, unable to look at him. All of a sudden this was an ordeal, not the sanctuary she had expected. His nearness and the depth of her longing for him was overturning the sensible little plan she had devised. With an effort she forced herself to begin.

'It is Daniel Brookes…'

'Ah, yes. Your new beau.' Adam sounded chilly.

'From our encounter this morning I see you did not pay any heed to my warnings about that…gentleman.'

'Of course I paid attention to what you said!' Helena turned in her chair to look at Adam. 'But I thought it would be safer to keep an eye on him. And I could hardly raise his suspicions by snubbing him: my family has encouraged him so.'

'Well, no doubt his reputation has not preceded him to London, whereas mine most certainly has,' he remarked bitterly.

Helena swallowed a retort about rakes and pressed on. 'My uncle the Commodore has used his influence at the Admiralty on Lieutenant Brookes's behalf—that is why he is still in town.'

Adam bowed ironically. 'I congratulate you. No doubt I shall soon see an announcement in *The Times*.'

'He has already made a declaration,' Helena almost wailed, pleating the heavy folds of her cloak between her fingers.

'So now I begin to understand why you are here.' Adam's face as he stepped into the circle of firelight was saturnine. He towered over her, darkly elegant in full evening dress, the flames flickering, harshening the planes of his face. 'No doubt you wish me to promise to keep silence about our little voyage. I am disappointed.' Helena's heart leapt at what he might be about to say, then fell as he went on, 'I should have thought you would have trusted my word as a gentleman to say nothing of that. I would do nothing to prevent your impending nuptials.'

Helena jumped to her feet, the cloak pooling around her feet. 'You cannot imagine for one moment that I want to marry him! He is odious!'

'So you have rejected him, then?' Was it her imagination or did he look relieved? It was so difficult to tell in the candlelight.

'*No!* I have accepted him.'

Adam's eyebrows rose. 'Helena, I confess I am deeply puzzled.' He pinched the bridge of his nose between finger and thumb as though grappling with a conundrum. 'You turn down my offer of marriage, despite never having, to my knowledge, described me as odious. And yet you agree to marry Daniel Brookes, even though his suit is clearly abhorrent to you.'

Helena slumped back into the chair, wondering where to begin. 'He knows I was on the yacht. He found a picture—a portrait, I had drawn of you.'

'That is hardly incriminating evidence. It is well-known that I have visited your aunt's house. I am sure you draw many acquaintances.'

Helena cast down her eyes, feeling the tide of hot colour flood up her neck. 'Er…not like that.'

To her fury, Adam seemed amused rather than alarmed. 'I am flattered. Do tell me—was I wearing *anything* in your portrait?'

'Of course you were! As if I would! And it is not as though I had ever…I mean, we had not…' Conscious she was tying herself in betraying knots she subsided, still flushed.

'Tell him to publish and be damned, as the Duke of Wellington said. Break off the engagement.'

'But if he shows that picture about town?'

'Who is to say you drew it? You did not sign it, did you?'

'Yes,' Helena admitted dismally. 'I always do. My drawing master taught me to.'

'Hell and damnation! Here's a coil.' Adam took three long strides across the room, then turned to face her.

'Like it or not, you must marry me. It is the lesser of two evils.'

It was hardly a flattering declaration, but for several seconds Helena felt herself weakening. She could have him; did it matter that he did not love her? Might he not grow to love her as many couples did? After all, a few months together…affection must surely follow.

'It would not be so bad,' he said placatingly, fatally. 'I would make few demands of you, once an heir was born. You could continue to live your life as you pleased, as I would live mine. You could stay down in Sussex, you do not have to come up to town.'

No, Helena thought bitterly, that might interfere with his pleasures. She felt a scalding humiliation that she had come so close to accepting his declaration. She should have learned by now that all men seemed to want was physical pleasure and material gain whether it was a place with the Admiralty or an heir to a title. Affection, love—these words were alien to them!

Sarcastically she retorted, 'I am overwhelmed by the warmth of your offer, sir, but that was not why I came here tonight. I have a solution that will not require such self-sacrifice from you.'

If Adam was surprised by the bitterness of her words he did not show it. The clock on the mantle chimed one and he cursed under his breath. 'Hell's teeth! I have a meeting in half an hour. This cannot wait, either—we must talk in the carriage.'

Helena stood, tying her cloak cords. 'Thank you, sir, but I will make my own way home back to Brook Street,' she said shortly.

'Now, do not be silly, Helena.' Adam took her elbow and steered her towards the door. 'I cannot allow you to caper about London unaccompanied; you have risked too much already coming here at this time of night.'

'Then drop me at my door!' Helena found herself being propelled out of the front door and up the steps into his waiting carriage.

'We have too much to talk about. You cannot take risks with the likes of Daniel Brookes.' Adam stuck his head out of the carriage window. 'Vauxhall Gardens.'

'I cannot go with you to Vauxhall Gardens,' Helena protested. 'Why, I would be ruined indeed if I was seen with you there.'

'You will wait in the carriage, masked and with my driver for protection. There is no reason why you should be seen. My business should take no more than half an hour.'

Helena subsided mutinously, glaring at him in the dark carriage. It was impossible to see his face except in brief flashes as they passed the torchères placed outside houses to light the footway.

'Now, Helena. You will not marry me, you declare you will jilt Brookes—so how do you intend to escape from this mess?'

'If you come with me to see my uncle and explain that nothing happened on the yacht…'

Adam snorted. 'If being in my bed counts as nothing, Helena…'

'Oh, nothing that means we *must* marry! Do not interrupt, Adam. If we explain, then Daniel's threats will be hollow. My uncle will be angry, but he will see that the Lieutenant is nothing but a blackmailer bent on furthering his own career through an alliance with my family.'

'And the drawing?'

'Uncle will pretend to be going along with him and

ask to see the drawing. Then, once it is in his hands, he will tear it up, or throw it on the fire.'

'You have worked it all out well, my dear,' Adam drawled. 'You must forgive me for asking how you intend to prevent the Commodore marching the two of us to the altar at gunpoint.'

'I will talk him round. He will not insist when I explain I do not wish to marry you.'

'You have great faith in your powers of persuasion, Helena.' The sound of the carriage wheels changed as they crossed the bridge and Helena realised they must be nearly at the pleasure grounds. 'How do you intend to persuade your uncle not to call Brookes out himself?'

'Naval officers are not permitted to duel,' Helena said. 'He could not, could he?' Her voice wavered.

'He will have no need, for I can assure you I will have already called Brookes out myself,' Adam replied grimly.

'Adam, you cannot risk your life for me!' Helena clutched his arm in horror.

'You flatter yourself, my dear,' he responded shortly. 'Do you expect me to sit by while that scoundrel compromises my honour by implicating me in his blackmail plots?'

'But he could kill you,' Helena gasped as the carriage slowed and wheeled to a halt in front of wide ornamental gates surrounded by brightly coloured lamps.

'Not as long as we use pistols,' Adam replied with some amusement in his voice. 'He never could hit a barn door. But he is an excellent swordsman, so let us hope he does not chose the rapier.' The door swung open and she saw his face clearly.

He was, Helena realised, greatly stimulated by the thought of a fight with the Lieutenant, by having an excuse at last to confront a man he loathed so deeply.

'Now, stay there,' he commanded, jumping down. 'I will not be long.'

Helena flung herself back against the cushions with a snort of fury. Men! If they were not pursuing some female, they were looking for an excuse to fight each other! Adam was obviously delighted to have an excuse to fight Daniel, never mind how she felt about it!

She leaned out to watch his back vanish into the throng around the gates. She had been to Vauxhall before in a large family party and had strolled among the groves and eaten in the pavilions while listening to the band. But great care had been taken to ensure that the young ladies did not come into contact with the parties of young bucks, the ladies of pleasure and the numerous cits out to mingle with the Quality.

The coachman hastily came to put up the window. 'Now, ma'am, don't you be leaning out, we don't want one of those young blades ogling you! His lordship left strict instructions you was to stay inside.' Without waiting for any response he fastened the leather strap that held up the glass and shut the door, but not before Helena saw a familiar figure, fully illuminated by a lamp by the entrance gate.

It was the Frenchman from the Godolphin Arms! She would recognise him anywhere, and here he was in the middle of London as bold as brass. He had to be there to meet Adam—anything else would be an unbelievable coincidence. All her worries, all her unease about what Adam was about on the Scilly Isles, resurfaced with a vengeance. She had trusted him then, and she still did, but with England at war he was flirting with danger indeed.

Without thinking why she was doing it, Helena drew up the hood of her cloak and gingerly opened the carriage door. Another carriage drew up, disgorging a large and very riotous party of young men and women. Adam's coachman swore, grabbing at his reins as the horses shied and whinnied at the sudden eruption of colour and sound. Taking full advantage of the distraction, Helena slipped out of the door and melted into the shadows beside the gate.

As the party entered the pleasure grounds, she detached herself from the shade and followed them through. For a few seconds she cast round, despairing of finding Adam in the throng, then she saw the Frenchman silhouetted against a brightly lit kiosk.

He seemed to be consulting a note in his hand, for he glanced down, then around, an odd figure in his sombre clothing among the flock of brightly clad, chattering partygoers. After a minute he appeared to have found his bearings for he walked off, weaving past a group of young men who were engaged in noisy dalliance with three young women wearing paint and spangled gowns.

Helena slipped after him, trying not to be distracted by her first close sight of the notorious 'barques of frailty' who haunted the pleasure grounds and the young men who were there, determined to yield to every temptation on offer.

Vauxhall Gardens were a maze of paths winding amidst the shrubberies, some ending at a little temple or grotto, others connecting together to lead back to the dance floors or dining kiosks. The Frenchman, with the occasional glance at the note in his hand, moved swiftly on, leading her deeper into the centre away from the gates and away from the main hustle and bustle.

Helena found herself almost running to keep the man's figure within sight. She gathered up her skirt and kept to the side of the path, starting nervously at rustlings in the bushes, the odd snatch of laughter.

Just when she thought she would run out of breath the man stopped and turned sharply left through a gap in the shrubs. Helena tiptoed after him and peeped round the corner to see a clearing with a miniature temple at the end.

Adam was waiting inside, his face lit by the lanterns which hung from the dome within. He looked up sharply at the sound of the Frenchman's footsteps on the gravel and greeted him in French.

The two men shook hands and drew back into the temple. Helena slipped into the clearing and inched her way around the edge until she was as close as she dared, but it was as frustrating as her attempt to overhear at the inn. Helena crept into the cover of a clipped box hedge. It was as close as she dared get so she crouched there, wrinkling her nose at the unpleasant odour of cats the box was giving off.

Not a word reached her; only by the rhythm of their speech could she tell that they were speaking French. Cramped, frightened, Helena huddled down, biting her knuckles in anxiety and frustration. Once again she found herself trying to eavesdrop on Adam, and yet on the yacht she had sworn that she trusted him—indeed, had put her own reputation in dire peril to demonstrate that trust.

And she did still trust him! If only she knew what he was about… If Daniel was right and Adam was indulging in smuggling for the pure excitement of it, was that leading him into danger now? She had heard tell that Lord Darvell was easily bored, sought the thrill of adventure. Had that led him into deeper waters than even Adam was skillful enough to navigate? Helena had no idea how she might help him, she only knew that instinct told her to be there, to watch his back.

Helena grew chilly as she crouched there, although it could not have been for more than ten minutes. Something tickled her nose: she blew at it and the tickling ceased. Then the men shook hands again and the Frenchman strode off out of the glade without a backward glance. Adam waited until he had vanished, then ran lightly down the steps of the temple and strolled across the clipped grass.

Conscious that she had to get back to the carriage before Adam reached it, Helena jumped to her feet. She would have to hurry, for Adam, although not in any haste, had a long stride.

As she stood, she realised that her left leg, which had been tucked beneath her as she knelt, had lost all feeling. At her first step it gave way and she stumbled backwards into the box hedge with a small cry.

Adam spun round, one hand on the dress sword at his side. Under any other circumstances the range of expressions which crossed his face in the light of the lantern would have entertained her, but Helena felt no temptation to laugh now.

Adam's first look of wariness gave way to one of astonishment, rapidly followed by exasperation. He strode over, seized Helena by the arm and hauled her to her feet none too gently.

'Ow!' she protested plaintively.

'That is no more than you deserve, Miss Wyatt,' he growled, giving her a little shake. 'Why are you creeping about like a thief in the night? Spying on me, I assume?'

'No! Well, yes, but... Let go of my arm, you are hurting me, Adam!' His grip was strong but not as painful as her tone implied: but Helena was desperate for a breathing space to think of some reason, any reason, she could give to account for her behaviour.

'Then stand still! I ask you again, madam—what are you about?'

Even in the subdued light she could clearly see the anger in his eyes. 'I was worried about you—I recognised that man going into the gardens. He is the Frenchman from the inn at St Mary's, is he not?'

'So it *was* you outside the window that day. I warn you, Helena, I do not brook interference in my affairs. This is more dangerous than you know.'

He sounded so grim it was all she could do to answer him. 'I know it is dangerous! I am so worried for you, Adam!'

Something in her tone arrested his attention, diverting his anger briefly. His face softened and his hand released its hard grip and moved up to rest on her shoulder. With his other hand he tipped up her chin and for a few long seconds he scanned her face. 'I thought—I believed—you trusted me, Helena Wyatt.'

'I do trust you! I would never have done what I did with those papers on the *Moonspinner* had I not trusted you. But, Adam...' She faltered suddenly under the intensity of his gaze. 'Why will you not trust *me* and tell me what you are about?'

For a long moment Adam hesitated, as though on the edge of speech, then he said, 'I cannot, Helena, it would put you in danger.'

'I am not afraid!'

'Then you should be,' Adam replied grimly. 'There are people involved who would not hesitate to cut my throat—and yours, too—' He broke off abruptly as two people, closely entwined, stumbled drunkenly into the grove.

Over Adam's shoulder Helena saw a young buck, his face flushed with wine and desire, fumbling with the low-cut bodice of a gaudily dressed young woman, who in her turn was groping with the waistband of his knee breeches.

With a swift action Adam pulled Helena close to him and called over his shoulder, 'Find another nest, my friend, I was here first and I like my privacy!' He turned his shoulder and bent to kiss Helena hard on the mouth.

'Oh, hell!' the other man swore amiably. 'The place is heaving tonight—can't find anywhere quiet to get my leg over. Come on, darling. Carry on, friend...' The young man waved a hand airily, almost losing his balance in the process. His doxy pulled his arm over her shoulder and they made their unsteady way back down the path.

Helena freed her mouth and whispered, 'They have gone now, Adam.'

'So?' He began to nuzzle her neck, sending *frissons* of quivering delight through her.

'Adam...' She was not certain herself whether it was a protest or an invitation.

His lordship chose to construe it as the latter. His hands moved inside the sheltering cloak, expecting to encounter the sensual slither of silk under his palms, the warmth of bare shoulders beneath his questing fingers. 'What have you got on?' he demanded against her hair. 'A nun's habit?'

'My best walking dress. I could hardly come out wearing my evening gown.' She was feeling increasingly lightheaded, but underneath the tide of sensation a little voice of reason cautioned her. He was trying to distract her, as he knew only too well how to do. Well, she was not so easily deflected. A sudden recollection of that painted doxy filled her mind. She was not going to be fumbled in the shrubbery like a lightskirt; this was not how she wanted to be with Adam, with the man she loved.

'No!' She wrenched away. 'Stop it!' The suddenness of it took him by surprise and Helena was running across the glade and out into the main walk before he could stop her. She did not stop to look back, only slackening her pace when she found herself in one of the more crowded thoroughfares.

The smell of hot alcohol filled her nostrils and she stopped beside a stall selling rack punch to catch her breath and get her bearings. Her heart was thudding, her breath short in her throat; Helena put up her hand to push the damp curls back from her forehead and realised to her dismay that not only was she unmasked, but that her hood hung down her back, leaving her face fully exposed.

She was frantically reaching for her hood when an unseen hand came to her assistance and she found the hood put into her grasp. Helena spun round, expecting to find Adam at her side, but instead encountered the hard, level gaze of Lieutenant Daniel Brookes.

Helena almost swooned with the shock of it. 'Mr Brookes!'

He was obviously furious, his face dark and set with anger. 'Perhaps you would be so good, madam, as to tell me what my affianced bride is doing unescorted in this place and at this hour?'

Without waiting for a response, Daniel took her by her arm none too gently and marched her away from the punch stall.

'Daniel, you are hurting me!' Her arm was already tender from Adam's angry grasp; the Lieutenant's grip brought tears to her eyes.

One of the little dining kiosks was empty and he pulled

her into it, not releasing her until the door was closed behind them. Helena could see out over the low frontage to the brightly lit crowd beyond, but inside it was shaded, private.

A party had obviously not long left it, perhaps for the dance floor, for a fan lay beside wine glasses and bottles and a dessert was laid out on the sideboard.

'I was prepared, madam, to overlook your scandalous behaviour with *that* man on board his yacht, but I find it hard to stomach you walking round Vauxhall Gardens at two in the morning like a common doxy!' His handsome face was distorted with disgust and Helena found her own anger rising at his hypocrisy.

She clung to the anger, gaining strength from it to fling back, 'Fine words indeed, sir, from a man with your history of dealing with women!'

Daniel laughed harshly. 'It is not at all the same thing! A man may stray where he will: for a woman of your social standing it is unthinkable. I cannot have my wife gaining the reputation of a slut.'

'Your wife! You still intend to marry me?' Helena demanded, seeing a thread of hope, the chance of release if he saw her as a threat to his future reputation and prospects.

Daniel's lips curled in a harsh smile and he gripped her wrist, pulling her towards him. 'Oh, yes, Helena, I intend to marry you. And once you are my wife, if you so much as look at another man, I will beat you black and blue—and run your lover through.'

To underline the threat his hand clenched on the hilt of his dress sword. As if on cue, Adam appeared from a side path and halted at the punch stall, casting around, obviously searching for someone.

'I see,' Daniel snarled. 'So that's the way the land lies.

Well, this will give me great pleasure.' As he spoke, he pushed Helena towards the back of the box and flung open the door.

Adam's head turned at the sound and the two men confronted each other across the trampled grass.

Chapter Eleven

Helena started forward, intent on staying Daniel's arm, but before she could reach his side there was a flurry of cerise silk and extravagant feathers and Portia Rowlett swept up to the door of the box.

Daniel stepped back sharply and Portia bestowed upon him a smile as brilliant as the diamonds clasping her throat. 'Lieutenant Brookes! Why, fancy encountering you here.' She turned to the party behind her and cried, 'Look, my dears, it is Lieutenant Brookes!'

The Lieutenant had no choice but to give way in the face of the incoming party and back into the box. Behind Portia, Helena could see Mr Rowlett and two other couples, one of whom she recognised as a Cabinet Minister and his wife.

Suddenly Portia saw her friend behind the Lieutenant and in a glance took in the stricken expression on Helena's face. Helena thought rapidly and, gathering her last shreds of composure, cried, 'Portia, dear! You see, I made it after all. You did say two o'clock, did you not? I am afraid I am a little late, but Aunt had the migraine and I would have been forced to return with her if I had not persuaded her to let me wait in your box.'

Mrs Rowlett might choose to present herself as a featherbrain, but her frivolous manner concealed a razor-sharp brain. Finding Mr Brookes uninvited in her box was puzzling, but Helena's presence was inexplicable. None the less, she recognised an emergency when she saw one. She rustled forward, picking up her fan from the table as she did so.

'Why, you bold thing, Helena,' she cried, tapping Daniel playfully on the sleeve as she passed. 'Gadding about unchaperoned and then inviting a gay blade like Mr Brookes into the box! Tut tut, my dear.' Portia turned to Daniel and added, in a tone of quite clear, if charming, dismissal, 'How nice to see you again, Mr Brookes, but I am sure we need keep you from your own party no longer. Good night.'

The Lieutenant was left with no option but to bow his way out with what grace he could muster. Helena cast a frantic glance around outside the kiosk, but Adam had melted into the darkness with Portia's arrival.

As the door closed behind Daniel, Portia cried, 'Sit down, everyone, sit down! You see our dessert is here. I did mention to you, did I not, Mr Rowlett, that Miss Wyatt was hoping to join us this evening? I am sure I did.'

James Rowlett was no fool; if Portia wanted to play games, then he would let her. 'So you did, dearest,' he responded placidly. 'Miss Wyatt, may I make known to you our other guests?'

Helena's brain whirled, but somehow she made the correct responses and joined in the chitchat as the party picked up their spoons and sampled the fruit mousse that had been laid out.

Under the table, Portia's hand sought hers and squeezed it reassuringly. Helena began to relax, but could not restrain a start of alarm when there was a knock at the door.

'Now, who can that be?' Portia asked gaily. 'We are having an exciting evening, are we not? Come in!'

The door opened to reveal Adam's coachman, his tricorn clutched in both hands. 'Good evening, ma'am. Lady Wyatt's compliments, Miss Helena, and I'm to drive you home directly. Your maid awaits you in the coach.'

'Oh, dear.' Portia sighed theatrically. 'That sounds very like a summons you cannot refuse, my dear. Doubtless your aunt has returned home to Brook Street to discover your mama did not approve of you remaining here with us. You had better go at once, or we will both be in your mama's disfavour!'

Helena, who had taken care not to let her cloak fall open to reveal the plain walking dress beneath, stood up with equal caution and made her curtsies and farewells. The coachman was silent as he walked a respectful two paces behind her towards the gate.

A ragged urchin was standing at the head of the horses and the man tossed him a copper coin before opening the door for Helena. Adam reached out and pulled her none too gently inside.

'Drive on!' he snapped, slamming the door and pulling up the blind.

The coach started with a jerk, sending Helena back into the squabs in an undignified heap. 'Adam—' she began to say.

'Be quiet,' he said evenly. 'I am thinking.'

Snubbed, she subsided into her corner, trying to descry his expression in the gloom, but failing. After a few minutes, she ventured, 'Where are we going?'

'I am taking you home, of course.'

'Of course,' she agreed dully. Of course he was taking her home. What else did she expect? What else did she want? Well, the answer to that was simple: she wanted him to take her in his arms, tell her he loved her and trusted her. More than anything else, she needed to see his face, for he was so still and so silent that he gave no clues as to what was going through his mind.

'May I pull down the blind? It is so stuffy in here.' She sensed rather than saw his nod of agreement and edged the canvas down until the gas lights gave some intermittent illumination to the interior of the coach.

She stole a sideways glance, but still found it impossible to read his face as the light flickered against his cheekbones. That he was tense she had no doubt; it was almost palpable in the confined space.

Helena fought back the urgent desire to get up and sit next to him, to feel his arms around her, his strength and warmth encircling her. Why did she love Adam Darvell so much? she wondered, as the carriage rattled over the cobbles. His reputation as a rake and a hellhound was not all unjustified; she remembered the contents of the chest in his cabin aboard the *Moonspinner*, full of gorgeous silks and satins, the discreet knowingness of the crew who were obviously used to his lordship's lady friends.

She remembered the ambivalent expression on the faces of the matrons at Almack's as their eyes followed him around the rooms. In some there had been a hint of soft recollection, in others, the caution of mamas with eligible daughters to protect.

Helena may have been brought up in the country, but she was not naïve; there were different rules for gentlemen and she did not grudge Adam his past. It was just that she wished to be his future…

She fell to dreaming, to remembering. She felt again his strength as he plucked her from the sea, the courage with which he had dived unhesitatingly to her rescue in the cold waves. She recalled the way he was with his crew and the respect in their faces when they looked at him. Her father would have said that he was a good leader, hard but fair.

Helena's mind drifted on to the meal they had shared in the inn in St Mary's. He had been kind and humorous and had listened to her talk of her family with warmth and interest. And the sharp edge of intelligence in his dark eyes fascinated her.

And when she and her mother had refused his offer of marriage he had taken it with dignity, although it must have come as a shocking blow to his pride.

Then there was the effect his touch had upon her; at first she had been scandalised at her response to him. She had feared she had all the makings of a loose woman. She had never been kissed by anyone, yet at the touch of his lips she tingled with desire and lost all vestige of discretion. But when Daniel had tried to kiss her—and he was a good-looking and personable man—she had felt nothing but revulsion and shame. She had felt shameless with Adam, but it had never felt wrong!

Loving him as she did only made the idea of marrying him for propriety's sake even more abhorrent to her. The thought that he would feel he had to be kind to her, perhaps would pity her, was more than her spirit could tolerate. And she could not hope that it would be a platonic marriage, for he would have every right to expect an heir. To share his bed, knowing he was only doing his duty...

Glancing up, she caught his eye and saw, for the first

time, uncertainty there. 'What is wrong?' she asked, startled into sharpness.

Adam hesitated, then said slowly, 'I think I can see a way out of your predicament.'

'What is it?' Helena asked eagerly. It seemed impossible that he could find a way for her to escape from Daniel's blackmail without either telling her uncle all, or risking the utter ruination of her reputation.

'I am not certain yet...you will be the first to know if I think it will work.'

The carriage pulled up and the coachman leaned down from the box, calling softly, 'Brook Street, my lord.'

Adam glanced out into the empty street, then up at the darkened house. 'Good, they are all abed.' The clock of Audley Street chapel chimed three as he spoke. 'Let me have the key.'

'Key?' Helena said stupidly as he began to open the carriage door. 'I have no key.'

'Then how do you intend getting back in? Has your maid left the garden door open for you?'

'No...oh, Adam, I was so eager to get out I never considered how I was going to get back in again!'

He did not bother to hide his exasperation. 'You tell me that you dressed up in a mask and a cloak and you escaped from the house without giving a thought as to how you could return to it?'

Helena looked at him, stricken. 'Yes.'

'Well, Helena, how do you intend to proceed now?' The exasperation had turned, inexplicably, to anger and his eyes on her face were harsh.

'I...I could hide down the steps in the area, near the coal cellar, until dawn when the servants open the doors. Then I could creep in through the kitchens...' Her voice died away; she was not convincing herself, let alone Adam.

'So you think I would abandon you to whatever drunks or vagabonds might be lurking about?'

Helena spoke rapidly as her mind at last began to work. 'Portia! You can take me to Portia's house!'

'I see.' Adam's voice was sarcastic. 'So we arrive unexpectedly at a house at three in the morning, not knowing whether the mistress or master are returned home or whether or not they have guests. The servants will, of course, not think this is in any way strange, despite the fact that you are entirely unchaperoned except by one of the most notorious rakes in London. What a splendid plan! Let us have a wager on how long the news would take to travel from the drinking houses the footmen use to their masters' ears. You would be the talk of the clubs within twenty-four hours.'

Helena was shocked by his cruelty. 'Adam! Why are you so *angry* with me?' For he was, indeed, very angry.

'Because you, madam, have been an infernal nuisance from the moment I picked you out of the sea.' He put his head out of the door and snapped, 'Home, Roberts!' then sat back, rigid, his arms folded across his chest.

For an incredulous moment she stared at him in the gloom, then a little sob escaped from her throat.

'Stop snivelling, Helena, it will solve nothing.'

'I am not snivelling!' she snapped back. 'But I cannot go home with you!'

Adam turned hard eyes on her. 'You are coming back with me because my home is the one place in London where the servants will not turn a hair at the sight of a cloaked woman entering in the small hours.'

The carriage drew up at his front door as he spoke. With a sharp glance around to make sure the Square was empty, Adam took Helena's arm and unceremoniously bundled her out of the carriage and up to the front door. 'Pull up your hood.'

The door was unbolted and opened silently with Adam's key, but even so the butler materialised from the baize door below the stairs. 'Thank you, Ogley, there is no need for you to wait up.'

If Ogley made the connection between the young lady he had admitted earlier that evening and the cloaked figure at the bottom of the stairs, he gave no sign of it, nor, in fact, did he acknowledge in any way that his lordship was accompanied. 'Goodnight, my lord.'

Blushing under her hood, Helena let Adam take her hand and hurry her up the stairs. His hand was warm, enveloping her chilly fingers, and she could feel his pulse beating strongly where their wrists touched.

At the head of the stairs on the second floor he opened a door and Helena found herself inside before she realised where she was.

The great four-poster dominated the room, its damask hangings lit to a dull sheen by the flickering firelight and the light from the many-branched candelabra on the dressing stand. The bed was turned down invitingly and a decanter stood with one wine glass on the table.

In a panic Helena turned to face him. 'I cannot stay here, this is your bedchamber!'

Adam looked down into her face, at the wide eyes and trembling mouth and said softly, 'Are you really so afraid of me, Helena?'

She stared back, wondering if she dared read tenderness in that voice, in the lines of his mouth. He unlaced the ties of her cloak with fingers that were not quite steady and it fell unheeded to the floor.

Her heart was beating like a drum, the pulse filling her

ears. Fatigue, anxiety and a dreadful yearning for him made her dizzy; when Adam reached out to cup her cheek in one hand, she flinched away from him as if stung.

Helena stumbled away from him and stood gazing into the fire, fighting down the wave of love and longing that threatened to send her running across the room and into his embrace. She was so tired, so vulnerable, she would never be able to conceal her feelings for him.

'There is no need to run from me, madam. A simple "no" would suffice—I am not Daniel Brookes.' His voice was cold, but she knew it had hurt him very much that she seemed not to trust him. 'I shall sleep in the dressing room.'

The door clicked emphatically behind him and only then did Helena dare turn from the fire. Slowly she dragged her leaden feet across the floor, blew out the candles and unbuttoned her outer clothing, letting the walking dress drop to the boards. Dressed only in her shift, she crept between the crisp sheets of the big bed and pulled the covers up to her chin.

The room was redolent with the scent of burning applewood from the fire, the familiar tang of Russian leather cologne and the indefinable sense of the man whose room it was.

She did not believe that sleep would claim her, but her eyes closed as soon as her head touched the pillow and she was plunged into feverish dreams, longings...

Images of Adam filled her mind: the recollection of his body hard against hers when he had first kissed her on the deck of the *Moonspinner*, the feel of his back under her spread palms as she yielded up her innocent lips to his experienced, tender mouth.

Helena tossed restlessly in the big bed, half-awake, half-asleep in that strange early morning state of waking and dreaming. The taste of the salt on his skin came back to her intensely, as did the thrilling feeling of powerlessness as his strong arms bore her down onto the bunk in that stuffy cabin.

Once more she felt the weight of him trapping her, his heart thudding over hers, the shock of finding how soft and hot his skin was. Part of her knew she was dreaming, for the pictures in her mind were silent; his lips moved in her hair but she heard no words.

Feverish desire was making the blood sing in her ears. The cabin faded and now she was in the Vauxhall Gardens and Adam was claiming her lips in a hard kiss of mastery and control, weakening her resistance, her ability to say no to him.

Now the shrubs faded too and her dreaming mind replaced the scene with the image of red damask bedhangings with flickering firelight playing across them. It was Adam's bedchamber, but she must still be dreaming for all was silent in the big room save for the beating of her pulse.

It seemed to Helena that the bed dipped, as though under another weight. Dreamily she turned and was taken, enfolded, in a burning embrace, held against a naked chest by bare arms. She moaned, but no sound escaped her lips.

A mouth trailed kisses down her throat, the touch as light as a butterfly's wing. Sensation coursed through her being out of all proportion to the sensitivity of the caress. Lips brushed across the fine muslin of her shift, over the curve of her breast and settled with shocking intimacy on the fabric covering her nipple.

Her flesh leapt to meet his questing mouth and the tongue that was now lapping agonisingly at the swollen peak through the dampened sheerness of the flimsy chemise, which was all that covered her aching body and separated it from the aroused male body which was molding against hers.

Instinctively Helena bent her head, brushing her eager mouth against Adam's hair. Her fingers tangled in the disarrayed locks, tugging and compelling his head up so that she could seek out his lips with hers. In her dream her eyes were tightly shut but still she had no difficulty finding Adam's mouth, her own softening, opening beneath his questing tongue.

One of his hands cradled the nape of her neck, the other moved with agonising slowness over the plane of her stomach until he reached the hem of her chemise and his palm began to stroke the satin skin of her thighs which quivered, responsive to his touch.

His hand gently, inexorably, moved upwards, nudging her thighs apart. The safety of the dream swept away all shame, all inhibition and seemed to give her the knowledge to respond to him as his body was demanding.

Adam's body shifted and as it did so a voice from the street shattered the early morning silence. 'Six of the clock and all's well!' In the hearth a smouldering log broke and fell in a shower of sparks and Helena's eyes flew open.

In the dawn light filtering into the room she found herself gazing into Adam's eyes, inches from her own. Her body, quivering with desire, clung to his bare limbs.

With a cry Helena twisted away, almost falling from the bed in shock. This was no dream, no feverish imagining concocted from the past. From the moment the bed had dipped it had all been real.

She scrambled back across the wide bed, dragging a sheet with her to cover her near-nakedness. The action revealed no dream but Adam, naked and aroused. For a long moment they stared at each other, both beyond speech, then Adam sat up against the pillows, pulling a cover across his lower body.

Hot colour suffused Helena's face, but she could not tear her eyes away from his. 'I thought...I believed I was dreaming,' she stammered.

A mocking smile curved his lips. 'Of course you did, Helena, and a very colourful imagination you have too.'

'How could you?' She accused him, furious with herself and with him. 'You said you were going to sleep in the dressing room and I *trusted* you!'

Adam put his hands behind his head and closed his eyes briefly. A rueful grimace crossed his features, but when he opened his eyes again Helena could read nothing in their dark depths. 'You can trust me to do the right thing, Helena,' he said evenly. 'And the right thing, as I have told you from the beginning of this sorry history, is for you to marry me.'

Her breath was forced from her lungs by the calculating way he could speak to her only moments after he had given her such pleasure. Her betraying body was still aching for him even though the scalding anger had replaced desire in her blood.

'And I have told you again and again I will not marry you.'

'I was fool enough to agree, against all my instincts and my honour. And now look at the mess you have got yourself into.' His voice was flat and hard. 'It was obvious that I could not persuade you to do the sensible thing, so I decided—reluctantly—to take extreme measures.'

Goaded beyond sense and endurance, Helena launched herself across the bed, her clenched fists raised to beat at his chest. He caught both wrists in one hand, holding her at arm's length as easily as if she were a child. In her impotence she blurted out, 'So you were forcing yourself to make love to me, were you?' Tears stung the back of her throat and she could not keep the hurt from her voice.

'I hate to hurt your pride, Helena, but a basic fact you will learn about men is that, with any halfway attractive woman, making love is really a matter of instinct.'

As a look of bleakness came across her face, he released her wrists and spoke more gently. 'Believe me, Helena, I only want to do the right thing and you have made it impossible for me. What choice did I have but to compromise you so totally that you had no option but to be my wife? But I would never force you—you must know that. I may be a rake, but I have never taken an unwilling woman.'

'And you have had so many, haven't you?' Helena was off the bed, her rigid back to him as she dragged on her creased dress and thrust her feet into her shoes without bothering to put on her stockings. Without looking back, she scooped up her cloak and ran to the door, wrenching it open.

Behind her she heard Adam cry, 'Helena! Wait!' but she was already halfway down the staircase.

Below in the hall Ogley glanced up, startled out his well-trained imperturbability. As she reached the door he stepped forward and hesitated, then, seeing the expression on her face, opened it for her to pass through.

Out on the street she forced herself to slow to a walk and threw the cloak around her shoulders, pulling up the hood. Adam could hardly chase her naked into the street and it would take him several minutes to dress. Walking briskly, she passed servants sweeping the paving slabs before their masters' great houses as they rubbed the sleep out of their eyes.

Reaching the corner of the Square, she turned left and walked on, attracting a curious stare from a milkmaid, her yoke across her shoulders, who was about to descend the area steps for her first delivery. Helena ducked her head and pulled the voluminous cloak more closely round her body.

No gentlefolk would be about at such an early hour, and if she had not been in such distress Helena would have been intrigued by the other world of the morning streets. Footmen in their shirtsleeves and baize aprons exchanged gossip over area railings; a porter with a basket of vegetables on his head sauntered along, whistling at any comely maidservant he encountered. Soapy water ran in rivulets down the broad front steps which led to the great panelled doors with their polished knockers as charwomen on their knees scrubbed them clean.

Helena had to watch her step as she dodged the water, very conscious of her bare, stockingless, ankles. The weak sunlight was slowly warming through the back of the cloak, but she was still chilled to the heart with the shock and Adam's betrayal.

The irony of it all was not lost on her as she made the short journey back to Brook Street. She loved Adam, heart and soul, and he would have had only to have spoken one word of love to her for her to have yielded to him joyfully against every tenet of her upbringing.

As she rounded the corner and turned into Brook Street, Helena paused and tried to compose herself. One of the footmen was polishing the dolphin knocker which Sir Robert had brought back from Portugal after one voyage, considering it suitable for a naval household.

Taking a deep breath Helena swept up the front steps with a calm, 'Good morning, Lovage.' The man's jaw dropped open and the knocker slipped from his fingers and crashed on to the striker plate with an unholy clang in the silent street.

'Oh...morning, Miss Wyatt. Begging your pardon, ma'am, you startled me.'

Summoned by the knocker Fishe appeared, a look of deep displeasure on his normally urbane features. 'Now, look here, my lad, this—Miss Helena!' If it had not been for her deep embarrassment, Helena would have laughed out loud, for the butler, in his amazement, was opening and closing his mouth like a fish. 'Forgive me, Miss Wyatt, I am not properly attired...' And, indeed, it was the first time Helena had ever seen him in his shirtsleeves, his horizontally striped waistcoat covered by his baize apron. 'I was not aware you were, er...abroad, Miss Helena.'

It was more a question than a statement. Acutely conscious of Lovage agog behind her, Helena managed a composed smile. 'Such a lovely morning, Fishe, do you not think? I could not resist slipping out to taste the early morning air. Will you have some chocolate sent up to my chamber?'

Orders for chocolate were at least a return to a semblance of normality and Fishe seized on the request with relief. He bowed. 'At once, Miss Helena. I will send your maid to you.'

Helena had begun to climb the stairs before she remembered her stockingless legs. Shrugging off the cloak, she let it drape from her shoulders, brushing the treads behind her, masking her feet and ankles. Even the loyal and discreet servants employed by Lady Breakey would be agog if the young mistress was seen coming home stockingless.

In the safety of her bedchamber Helena tore off her walking dress and pulled on her wrapper before sinking

down before the dressing table. Her hair, reflected to her
horrified eyes in the glass before her, was a veritable
bird's nest. One side was completely down—all the pins
lost somewhere in Adam's bed, she supposed. Hastily she
pulled out the few that remained at the back and was
fluffing out the tangles when Lucy tapped at the door and
slipped in.

'Oh, miss, where *have* you been?' The girl was agog,
her eyes shining with excitement.

'Just out for a walk, Lucy,' Helena replied calmly.
'Take the brush and brush my hair. I had to put the hood
of my cloak up, of course, and it seems to have made a
dreadful tangle.'

Glancing up Helena saw her maid's reflection. The girl
was gazing in half-horrified excitement at Helena's bed,
so obviously undisturbed, its covers and pillows as
smooth as they had been left last night.

'I do hope, Lucy, that you will not trouble my mother
or Lady Breakey with the intelligence that I took an early
morning stroll.' Her voice was even, but the tenor was
implicit.

Lucy dropped an agitated curtsy. 'Miss Wyatt...of
course I would not mention it, miss, I would have no call
to...'

Helena held her maid's gaze in the mirror. 'Good. By
the way...the walking dress I have put over the edge of
the screen—you may have it. I believe the colour does
little to flatter my complexion.'

The young girl bobbed again, before brushing gently
at the disordered curls beneath her touch. 'Thank you,
Miss Helena, I shall keep it for my Sunday best.' She
hesitated. 'It's very good of you, Miss Helena, but there's
no need, you know—I would never do anything to harm
you...'

Helena reached back over her shoulder with one hand and touched the girl's fingers. 'I know that, Lucy, my dear, but I would like you to have the dress anyway.'

As she dressed, Helena toyed with the idea of taking breakfast in her room, but decided to go down as usual. Despite the loyalty of her maid, she knew that below stairs would be buzzing with gossip about the young mistress's early morning excursion and skulking in her room would only increase the speculation.

The Commodore, after years on board ship, brought his habits of early rising to his own home and Helena found her uncle, aunt and her mama already in the breakfast room when she came downstairs. She circled the table, kissing each on the cheek as she did so before assuming her place.

'My word, my dear, you do look well this morning,' her uncle said with delight. 'I had feared this London air would not suit you after the sea breezes of Selsea, yet here you are with roses in your cheeks.'

Helena—who knew her cheeks were flaming after running the gauntlet of the curious glances of two footmen, the tweeny, and her uncle's valet who had somehow contrived to be in the hall when she passed through—had to force a smile in response.

Lady Breakey looked with mock severity at her husband. 'Oh, come, Sir Robert, you have been at sea too long! It is not the town air which has made our niece bloom, it is rather a handsome naval lieutenant of our acquaintance.' She leaned over and patted Helena's hand. 'Is that not so, my dear?'

Helena cast down her eyes to her plate as if in maidenly modesty, but was still conscious of her mother's steady gaze: Lady Wyatt was not entirely convinced of her daughter's happiness.

The party had hardly risen from the breakfast table when the knocker sounded and Fishe's voice saying, 'Good morning, Mrs Rowlett. I am not sure, ma'am, that her ladyship is at home.'

'Oh, never mind that, Fishe.' Portia had evidently fluttered past him into the hall. 'I do not want to disturb either of their ladyships, I just want to talk to Miss Helena.'

'Very well, ma'am, I will just ascertain...'

Helena hurried out of the door and took her friend's arm with little ceremony. 'That is all, thank you, Fishe. Portia, shall we go into the conservatory?'

Lady Breakey emerged from the breakfast room, a carefully modulated look of surprise on her face at the sight of a woman who rarely rose before eleven. 'Good morning, Mrs Rowlett, you are uncommonly early this morning. I trust I find you in good health?'

'Oh, it is such a lovely morning, you know, Lady Breakey,' Portia babbled cheerfully and unconvincingly. 'I just had to get out into the spring air, you know.'

Helena caught a glimpse of Fishe's face and detected a glimmer of relief: he obviously thought they had been on some jaunt together, but that at least meant that Helena had been chaperoned by a married lady.

Linking her arm through Portia's, Helena steered her friend into the conservatory, safe in the knowledge that no one else used the room until late morning when the sun had warmed it through.

The moment the door had safely shut behind them, Portia whirled round. 'My dear! What on earth was going on last night? I have not slept a wink all night—I do not trust that man.'

'Man?' Helena stammered stupidly. Adam was so at

the front of her mind that she assumed that somehow Portia knew what had happened.

'That man! That Lieutenant Brookes, of course! I am not usually wrong about men, and I liked him at first, but now I do not like him at all! The way he looked at you last night... Please tell me, my dear, that you have not committed some indiscretion with him.'

'Only become engaged to him,' Helena said hollowly, sinking onto a Gothick bench.

'Oh, Helena! But you told me you loved Adam Darvell!'

'I do, but Brookes is blackmailing me, and he has convinced my family that he is a good match for me. They all approve wholeheartedly, and if I refuse him he will ruin my reputation and destroy Adam.'

'But Lord Darvell has survived many scandals and the only damage it has done him is to give him the reputation of a rake. What harm can Brookes inflict upon him?'

For a moment Helena was tempted to pour out the whole story of the Frenchman, the papers and Adam's mysterious dealings. But then she remembered Mr Rowlett's position in the Government and realised that she could not put Portia in such an invidious position.

She took her friend's hands and looked into her eyes with an expression of deep seriousness. 'I cannot tell you what it is, but Adam has a secret that he cannot afford to have known. Please believe me—I cannot tell you.'

Portia looked into her friend's beautiful but troubled face. 'Very well, I will not plague you with questions you cannot answer. But tell me what was happening last night and how you came to be in my box. And where did you go when you left? I know that was not your aunt's coachman.'

Helena took a deep breath. 'No, it was Adam's man and I spent the night in Adam's bed.'

The expression of shocked amazement on Portia's face finally brought home to Helena the enormity of what she had just said.

Chapter Twelve

'Y ou did what?' Portia finally gasped out. Mrs Rowlett might be a flirt, a well-known social butterfly tolerant of dashing behaviour, but there were rules for the conduct of unmarried girls and Helena had just driven a coach and horses through most of them. After taking a deep breath, she finally managed to say with some semblance of calm, 'I think you had better tell me what happened from the beginning, Helena. How did you come to be in Vauxhall Gardens in the first place?'

Helena gave her friend a truthful, but carefully edited, account of her scandalous evening, leaving out Adam's rendezvous with the Frenchman. Portia would never betray her, but to tell that sort of secret to the wife of a Minister of the Crown would be trying her friend's loyalty too much. Fortunately, Portia was so swept up with the drama of the tale that she appeared not to notice that it was very odd of Adam to insist on keeping an appointment in Vauxhall Gardens, or that Helena should decide to leave the coach and follow him into the pleasure grounds.

'Well, I think I understand all that,' Portia said at length, 'and I must say, Lord Darvell seems to have acted with great presence of mind, sending his coachman to extricate you like that. But why, if he was taking you home, did you end up in Grosvenor Square, not Brook Street?'

'I had no key, no means to get in, without waking the household,' Helena confessed.

'Oh, Helena!' Portia threw up her hands in exasperation. 'Have you never crept out to go to a masquerade before?'

'Certainly not!' Helena retorted. 'I am not in the habit of sneaking out of the house.'

'No, but when you do, my dear,' said Portia archly, 'you certainly go the whole hog. Now, it is no good looking shocked—after all, you have spent the night with the man. Tell me, is he as wonderful a lover as rumour would have it?'

Helena's face flamed. Her friend had obviously assumed that Adam had taken her virginity and that they could now have a conversation almost as married women. 'I do not know…' she stammered.

'Well, of course, you have nothing to compare with. Lady M—'

'No!' Helena clapped her hands to her ears. 'Do not tell me about his other women, I could not bear to know their names.'

'Well, they all speak very highly of him.'

'*All?*' Helena asked, her tone desolate.

'Never more than one at a time, of course,' Portia said, believing she was reassuring her friend. 'And he is always very generous while an *affaire* lasts, by all accounts. Of course, there was that time with Lady—oh, all right, I shall not name her. When she got news that he had been seen dining with an opera dancer at Covent

Garden, she threw an entire shelf of Meissen figurines at him when he next called upon her.'

Despite her anguish, Helena's interest was piqued. 'My goodness! Did she hit him?'

'No, apparently he ducked them all.'

'Did he leave her?'

'Of course! Not because she threw the porcelain, but because she then demanded that he replace the figurines and he said that was too high a price to pay, especially if he had to give up the opera dancer as well. Anyway, never mind all that— Helena, just think what the consequences of last night might be!'

'Consequences? But no one but you knows I was there.'

'For heaven's sake, Helena! You could be with child!'

'No one else seems to worry about ''consequences'', from what you have just told me,' Helena retorted bitterly.

'Oh, do not be so naïve!' Portia said sharply. 'None of those Society ladies would dream of taking a lover until they have given their husbands an ''heir and a spare'', as they say. What happens thereafter is no one's business.'

'You mean...'

'Look around you and use your eyes! Think about that tall, red-headed daughter of Lady Langford's. The one that is the spitting image of Lord Ashwell.'

Helena's eyebrows shot up in astonishment. She knew she had been sheltered, living with her mother and John in Sussex, but for the first time she truly understood that a different set of mores prevailed in town. Loving Adam as she did, she knew she could never bear to share him in a way that appeared commonplace—nay, expected—in Society.

'And do you and Mr Rowlett play to these rules, Portia?'

'My dear Helena, James adores me. He would not look twice at another woman and I am happy with him and too content with my children and home to ever look elsewhere.'

Helena stood up, moving across to touch the velvety lip of an orchid. With her back safely turned to Portia, she asked in a voice that broke, despite her best intentions, 'Are there any children in town who bear an astonishing resemblance to Adam?'

'Helena, my dear, I think not.' Portia's voice hardened. 'But just because his other lovers have either been very careful or very lucky does not mean that you will be so fortunate.'

The face Helena turned to her friend was flaming, but she said steadily, 'There is absolutely no danger of that happening.'

A look of puzzlement crossed Portia's face. 'But you have told me you spent the night in his bed. Do you mean he was not in it after all?'

'Well, not at the beginning...'

'Then he did not make love to you?' It was obvious that Portia could not believe her ears.

'Yes, he did, but I thought I was dreaming and when I realised I wasn't he...stopped.'

Portia leaned back on the bench and shook her head in puzzlement. 'If he stopped, then why did he start?'

'So that I would have to marry him after all.'

Portia sprang to her feet and almost shouted at her friend, 'I thought that was what you wanted!'

'But he does not love me!' Helena cried out.

The two of them were standing confronting each other when the door to the salon opened and Lady Breakey swept in, the morning's *Times* brandished in her hand. She was too agog with her news to notice the crackling atmosphere between the two friends.

'Helena, darling! Look, the announcement of your engagement to Mr Brookes is in the Society pages: I had thought it submitted too late yesterday to make today's edition, but I was wrong. The whole of town will know about it this morning. People will be calling! Oh, I am so excited—now, what are you going to wear to receive them?' She looked critically at the modest sprig muslin her niece had donned that morning. 'Oh, dear, that gown will never do: I will speak to your maid.' She turned and almost ran from the room, calling, 'Sister! Sister! We have so much to do!'

The two young women gazed at each other thunderstruck. Somehow Helena had never believed it would really come to this, especially after last night's fiasco, but she had completely forgotten her uncle saying he was drafting the announcement yesterday afternoon.

Fishe appeared at the door and coughed tactfully. 'Lord Darvell, Miss Wyatt.'

His lordship strode into the room, his eyes fixed on Helena's white face; Portia realised that he had not even noticed her own presence. Devoted wife that Mrs Rowlett was, she could not repress a *frisson* of excitement at the sight of Adam Darvell. He was dressed for riding, breeches moulding the muscular length of his legs, his jacket sitting easily across broad shoulders. His hair, unfashionably long at the collar, was ruffled from the haste with which he had doffed his hat and he was quite obviously toweringly angry.

His riding gloves were in his left hand, and crushed in the same grip was a mangled copy of that morning's *Times*. Ah! Portia breathed under her breath. So, Lord

Darvell had finally been goaded enough to force Helena's hand, even if he had been too squeamish last night. Well, she had no intention of standing in his way.

'Helena!' he said in a voice of thunder. 'Have you taken complete leave of your senses?'

Helena simply stood there like a rabbit fascinated by the gaze of a stoat, too overwhelmed to make any response.

Portia cleared her throat and Adam swung round, seeing her for the first time. He sketched her the briefest of bows. 'Mrs Rowlett, good morning.' His expression contained not the slightest inducement for her to stay.

She began to draw on her gloves. 'Good morning, your lordship. A pleasant morning, is it not? However, I must get on. Goodbye, Helena dear.' Completely ignoring her friend's anguished expression, Portia nodded pleasantly to Adam, who sprang to open the door for her, and with a gay wave to Helena she swiftly departed.

Adam shut the door with great deliberation, tossed his gloves onto the bench and advanced on Helena, smoothing out the newspaper as he moved. 'Now, just what is the meaning of this?'

Helena finally found her voice. 'I told you he had proposed to me, and that I had had to pretend to accept him.'

'Yes, madam, and, if I recollect correctly, you told me last night that you had no intention of going through with it. However, what am I to construe when I read it in *The Times*? The whole of London knows by now: how are you going to get out of *that*?'

'Perhaps I have changed my mind,' she flared, not caring what she said so long as she hurt him as much as he had hurt her. 'Perhaps after last night I have decided that I prefer Daniel's overweening ambition to your cynical plotting. After all, you said yourself that I have to marry someone, and he is quite a good match. With my uncle's patronage he could go far, perhaps even up to flag rank.'

'You stupid little fool, have you not listened to a word I have told you about that man? He will use you, and when he has what he wants you will be as badly treated as all his other women.'

The fury swept from her toes to her scalp and she stalked forward to confront him, quivering with the force of her indignation. 'You hypocrite! You stand there and prate to me about Daniel's morals—well, sir, look to your own conduct! I know all about your other women—high-born and opera dancers both. You, sir, by all accounts, have the morals of a tom cat and it ill becomes you to tattle to me about Lieutenant Brooke's past when yours is the scandal of the town.'

Adam flinched as though she had hit him. 'I have never taken an unwilling woman...'

'And that makes it all right?' Helena's chin came up, her eyes sparked defiance. 'How many cuckolded husbands are there in town? How many by-blows have taken Darvell blood into other men's families? Well, sir, I will tell you plainly, I am the daughter of an admiral, of a man who laid down his life for his country and I have more pride than to accept *anything* you have to offer. At least with Daniel I know where I stand.'

In the aching silence that followed her outburst she had time to observe the tight, white lines of his mouth, the hardness of his eyes. As soon as the bitter words had left her mouth she regretted them, wished them unsaid: nothing on earth would induce her to marry Daniel Brookes. She knew the accusations she had thrown at Adam were cheap and shabby of her but, like a small child thwarted by its nurse, she had said what she knew would hurt and wound and now could find no way back.

Before she knew it, his hands came up to imprison her face between implacable fingers. 'By God, Helena, if any man had spoken to me like that I would kill him.' His voice was very soft, very dangerous. Helena quivered, opened her lips as if to say something, but no words came.

'Be quiet, madam,' he commanded, still with a voice like velvet. 'I doubt if there is anything left for you to insult me with. But I have not yet begun to insult you: you are no better than a whore, selling your body in marriage to a man you know is a bastard for ambition, for an easy life and—ultimately—to spite me.' She made a little whimper of horrified protest, but he merely tightened his fingers, compelling her face nearer to his own so she could feel his breath hot on her lips.

'Last night in my bed you responded to my caresses. You were wild, Helena, you were wild in my arms. You moaned for *me*, Helena—do you moan when *he* touches you? How do you respond when he does this?' And he bent his head and kissed her, claimed her, took her mouth, his tongue invading deeply in a crude demonstration of male mastery that shocked her to her very core.

Reaction gave Helena the strength to break free, to recoil from his hands; as she did so she hit out, slapping the taut cheek with a force that jarred her arm to the elbow. She stood there trembling, staring at him, her breath coming in deep gulps, and realised with a shudder of horror that by her actions and her words she had almost goaded him beyond endurance. But the man who stood rubbing his cheek, his eyes burning into hers, was Adam, and despite it all she loved him, was not afraid of him.

The entry of Fishe, preceded by one of the butler's habitual discreet coughs, was a shattering anti-climax.

Adam took a couple of jerky strides towards the garden door and Helena was left confronting Fishe, whose arms were encompassing the largest bouquet of flowers Helena had ever seen.

Tuberoses, hothouse lilies and myrtle filled the cool atmosphere of the conservatory with their exotic, cloying scent. 'These have been delivered for you, Miss Wyatt. There is a card. Shall I place them in this container here? No doubt you will wish to supervise their arrangement later today.'

'Thank you, Fishe, that will be all,' Helena managed to utter. The man bowed and left as quietly as he had entered and she went automatically to take the little card from its gilt-edged envelope amongst the profusion of blooms.

'Very touching,' Adam commented, his voice laconic from behind her. She jumped, not realising that he had moved from his position by the garden door. 'Quite the young lover, our gallant naval officer, is he not?'

Helena conned the message, but it was Adam who gave voice to the sentiments contained therein. '"*These fragrant blooms are but a pale imitation of your beauty and purity, my love. Before these fragile petals fall, let us name the day when we two shall be one, beloved. Yours, for ever, Daniel.*" I believe I am about to be sick. How any grown man can bring himself to write such drivel is beyond me.'

Yes, reflected Helena bitterly, the words 'my love' would never cross Adam's lips: they might commit him to something that spoke of permanency and obligation.

Adam reached over, plucked the card from her fingers and, with almost theatrical slowness, tore it into tiny pieces. He held them clenched in his fist, before releasing them to shower to the floor of the conservatory. 'I doubt

I shall be there to throw rose petals at your wedding, Helena. I wish you well of your choice.'

She was still staring blankly at the flowers when the door closed behind him. Slowly Helena sank to the bench and put her hot hands to her throbbing head. She felt sick to the stomach as the cloying perfume of the lilies met the roiling emotion inside her.

How long she sat she did not know, but her solitude was interrupted by the bustling arrival of her aunt. 'Thank goodness that dreadful man has gone! I came down immediately when I realised that Fishe had admitted him; I do not know what came over him not to tell me you were unchaperoned, especially given Lord Darvell's reputation.' She stopped, her eyes fixed on her niece's flushed face and heavy eyes. 'And now look at you! What did he do to upset you so?'

'Nothing,' Helena lied desperately. 'He came because he had seen the announcement. I am sorry if I seem discommoded, it is just that I am finding all this attention overwhelming. Look,' she said, rallying slightly in an effort to distract the sharp eyes of Lady Breakey, 'Mr Brookes has sent me these lovely flowers.'

'My word, what a beautiful bouquet, what tasteful colours. This bodes well, my dear!' She poked carefully amongst the blooms. 'Was there no card with them?' As she spoke her eyes fell on the drift of torn pieces at her feet, then rose to look assessingly at Helena's hot face. For a moment it seemed as if she was going to pass a comment, then she said gently, 'Yes, it is a very upsetting time, is it not? I remember it well. Sometimes it is difficult to know just what one does want. Come, my dear, luncheon is ready and then you must change, for I expect callers.'

* * *

The following week passed in a flurry of activity, with callers arriving as her aunt had predicted, and her mother methodically working through the preparations for the wedding. Once or twice she saw her mother pause, pen poised over yet another list of lingerie or wedding guests, and regard her with a sharp, questioning gaze. She wondered if she should confide in her mama, both about her feelings for Adam and Daniel's threats, but Helena shrank from the confessions which she knew could only lower her in her mother's estimation. Her only hope was to tell everything to her uncle.

The Commodore seemed rarely to be at home, and when he was he spent much time in his study. Helena guessed he would soon receive his orders and be at sea again and realised that much of the urgency her aunt felt about the wedding was to ensure that Helena would be given away by Sir Robert.

Helena racked her brains for a way of extricating herself from her engagement without either causing a scandal or putting Adam at risk. Without Adam at her side she did not feel capable of explaining in detail exactly what had happened on the *Moonspinner* and, therefore, why she would not marry Daniel Brookes. Her uncle was more than likely to either demand that Adam do his duty by her or instigate an Admiralty enquiry into his activities.

Pressure of business at the Admiralty and his new duties also kept Daniel from visiting for more than a few minutes at a time; to Helena's surprise and relief, her mother chaperoned her closely on every occasion. There was an odd edge of formality to Lady Wyatt's conversation with her future son-in-law, which the Lieutenant, not knowing her well, did not recognise.

* * *

Four days after that shattering scene with Adam in the conservatory, Helena had written him a note. It had taken her hours, and many false starts, to pen even the brief lines she finally dispatched, begging his forgiveness for her intemperate words. The temptation to pour out her feelings, tell him she loved him, confess her despair at losing him, had almost overwhelmed her once or twice, but she had curbed it ruthlessly, knowing that it was hopeless.

The footman returned with her note undelivered, reporting that the knocker was off his lordship's door and the remaining skeleton staff had told him that Lord Darvell had returned to his Sussex seat.

Helena had been in the depths of despair. She could not bear to think that Adam thought she meant those things she had said to him, yet she dare not entrust the missive to the mails. Her black mood was not helped by Lucy, who had been listening to the footman's account of the comfortable gossip he had had with Adam's footman in the Red Lion.

'Lovage says that his lordship has gone down to Sussex to hold an orgy at his big house,' she reported as she dressed Helena's hair. 'What's an orgy, Miss Helena? It sounds very wicked. Are there…you know, loose women and things?'

'Stop prattling about things you do not—and should not—understand,' Helena retorted sharply. 'And dress my hair more carefully today, several curls fell out yesterday.' Lucy had sulked for the rest of the day, which mirrored Helena's mood exactly. She could not believe the story of orgies, but she could well believe that he had a comfortable houseparty and was doubtless not short of compliant female company.

* * *

Lady Wyatt interrupted these black thoughts and hesitated, as though on the brink of speech. 'Helena, are you sure... Oh, never mind. The Dowager Lady Grantchester is below, do come and receive her congratulations.'

Helena moved through the social niceties of the visit like an automaton at Merlin's Magical Museum, where she had taken John one wet afternoon. She smiled and blushed and said everything that was proper in response to the old lady's questions and was finally able to retreat from the centre of attention and pour tea. Listening to her aunt and the Dowager chatting happily about the wedding plans, she realised with a sudden rush of resolution that no one was going to rescue her from this predicament but herself and that she had to seize the bull by the horns and take her uncle into her confidence.

The Dowager's visit seemed interminable, especially as Helena heard the door of her uncle's study open and shut as she was refilling cups. Once Lady Grantchester was safely seen to her carriage Helena marched up to the study door before she could lose her resolution.

Her hand was raised to knock when she heard voices within and the door opened to reveal not only her uncle but another man of similar age, also wearing the uniform of a Commodore of the Royal navy. He was a stranger to Helena, a short man with mouse-brown hair, heavy eyebrows and a decided twinkle in his eyes when he saw who was standing on the threshold.

'Good afternoon, Miss Wyatt.'

'Good afternoon, sir.' Helena bobbed a slight curtsy wondering how the stranger had recognised her.

'Helena, my dear, allow me to present Commodore Sir William Thorn. Commodore, my niece Miss Wyatt.'

They shook hands and Sir William tucked Helena's hand under his arm as he walked towards the door. 'I knew your father, young lady, a brave man and a fine sailor.' He looked at her piercingly. 'You look just as you have been described to me.'

It seemed unlikely that he would truly recall her father's description of his young daughter, or that she had changed so little, but Helena was grateful for his attempt to recall her father to her.

'Lady Thorn would like to meet you, my dear,' he continued. 'Perhaps you would care to join us on my yacht in the Solent some time.'

Helena cast him a startled glance, but he was regarding her with smiling, intelligent eyes and without a hint of guile on his face. It had to be a coincidence, that was all. She must learn not to react guiltily to that sort of chance remark. 'Thank you, sir, that would be delightful. I do not think I would be a very good sailor, however.'

'No, no, you would be quite at home.' He freed her hand at the door, turning to take his cocked hat and gloves from Lovage. 'Would you not like to stand on deck with the wind in your hair, or hear the howling of the Wolf Rock or watch the Isles of Scilly come up on the starboard bow?'

Helena was so taken aback that her uncle was descending the steps beside Sir William before she had the opportunity to ask him to stay and speak with her a minute. Shaken, she turned back inside. Who was Sir William? Did he know about her adventure on the *Moonspinner* and was he now taunting her with that knowledge?

It was that same evening that Helena found herself entirely alone with Daniel Brookes. She had hoped to find her uncle alone when he returned, but the opportunity did not arise. After an early dinner the rest of her family had gone off to see a new play at Drury Lane, but she had pleaded tiredness and remained alone in the small salon. Her embroidery lay disregarded in her lap after the first few stitches and Helena sat gazing into the fire, no thoughts of any consequence in her weary mind.

She was vaguely aware of the front-door knocker, but did not heed it for callers at that hour were likely to be from the Admiralty for Sir Robert. When Lovage opened the door and announced, 'Mr Brookes, Miss Wyatt,' she jumped up, sending her embroidery hoop curving across the floor.

Lovage bowed himself out without waiting to ascertain whether Helena wished to call for her maid, and it occurred to Miss Wyatt that the man had probably received half a sovereign for his pains.

'Mr Brookes! I did not look to see you this evening,' Helena stammered. 'My family are all at the theatre.'

He stooped to retrieve her embroidery hoop and handed it to her, dropping into the wing chair opposite hers without invitation and crossing his long legs at the ankle.

'Yes, I know they are. I thought it was about time we had a little talk, Helena.'

'About the wedding?' she hazarded, a little too brightly, wishing he would not make himself quite so much at home. And yet this was the opportunity she had been steeling herself for. If she could not tell her uncle, she would just have to face Daniel down, convince him that she would no longer yield to his blackmail. Her uncle's decanters stood ready by the side of the chair he had taken and Daniel reached out a casual hand and poured himself a generous measure of port.

'No, not about the wedding. About that little incident at Vauxhall Gardens.' He took a thoughtful sip of the red liquor.

Helena's heart leapt with hope, but she managed to keep her face serious. 'Yes, that was rather an ill-judged romp, I am afraid. Mr Brookes, are you come to tell me that on reflection you feel my behaviour unfits me to be your wife?' Despite her best efforts to sound chastened, a tiny hint of hope must have shown in her voice for his face hardened.

'On the contrary, my dear Helena, I have come to ensure that arrangements are proceeding as planned. Indeed, it was a "romp" and I should be interested to know exactly what that was about, and what part Lord Darvell played in it.' He leaned forward, suddenly large and threatening in the subdued light of the room. 'I will not be deterred by such behaviour—after all, I have long reconciled myself to the fact that in you I am getting used goods—but I warn you, you will not have the opportunity for the slightest indiscretion once we are married. I will keep you under lock and key if need be.'

'How dare you threaten me?' Helena retorted. 'It is about time I ended this farce once and for all: I am not going to marry you and nothing you can say or do will change my mind. Now leave, please.' She stood, hoping to lessen the power of his presence, but he stood too, looming above her. 'Go,' she almost shouted, 'or I will ring for the servants! Adam warned me...'

'Ah, yes, Darvell. You will marry me, Helena, because I have an account to settle with that man.' The hatred dripped from every word.

'No.' She stood up straight and defied him. 'I will not be blackmailed. Adam has done nothing wrong and you will never prove that he has!'

'But, my dear, gullible young woman, I have evidence of exactly what he has done. Even as we speak he is meeting with his French spy and his fellow traitors in

Sussex under the guise of a wild houseparty. I set out tonight to apprehend them and even now a squad of dragoons from Chichester has the house surrounded. I can do one of two things, my dear, and the choice is yours.'

Helena stammered, 'I do not believe you, I do not believe he is a traitor!'

Daniel's teeth were very white in the gloom as he smiled at her wolfishly and continued as though she had not spoken. 'If you are very, very nice to me, my dear, I can send ahead and warn him, give him the chance to escape to France on his yacht. But if you are not—' he reached out and let his hand trail shockingly down over the curve of her breast '—I will arrest him and you can see him hang.'

Before she could move, before she could protest, he was kissing her, his mouth wet and open on hers, his hands straying intimately over her body. Helena threw herself away from him, dragging the back of her hand across her mouth to expunge the taste of him and almost threw herself on the bellpull.

Daniel tugged down his uniform jacket and hissed, 'Oh that's not nice, Helena, not nice at all. I am afraid Lord Darvell will bear the consequences of that.'

To Helena's immense relief Fishe appeared, his brows drawn together in disapproval at seeing the young mistress alone and obviously distressed.

'Fishe, see Mr Brookes out. And, Fishe, I will not be at home to Mr Brookes at *any* time in the future.'

'Very good, Miss Wyatt. Your hat, sir.'

Fishe reappeared minutes later to find Helena seated at the escritoire, feverishly penning a note.

'Miss Helena, are you all right?'

'Yes, thank you, Fishe. Please send this note with all speed to Mrs Rowlett's house. If she is not at home, the man must find where she has gone and take the note to her. And Fishe—do not send Lovage.'

'Indeed not, Miss Helena. Lovage will find himself without a position this very evening,' the butler replied stiffly.

Helena almost ran up to her chamber, surprising Lucy, who was turning down the bed.

'Lawks, miss, you did give me a shock,' the girl cried, clutching her throat. 'Whatever is the matter?'

'I have to travel down to Sussex this night and I have sent to Mrs Rowlett to lend me her second carriage and coachman. Pack me an overnight valise and a bag for yourself.'

Lucy had just finished her task and Helena was shaking the sand over a hasty note to her uncle when they heard the sound of carriage wheels in the street below.

She hastened downstairs, followed by Lucy, and found Portia, in full evening dress, standing in the hall in agitated conversation with the butler. On seeing her friend, Portia rushed over and hugged her. 'My dear, what is happening? Your note was so strange!'

'It is imperative I go to Sussex; Adam is in grave danger and I must warn him.'

'Then I am coming with you,' said Portia with determination. 'It is inconceivable that you should travel that distance alone and at night.'

'Thank you, my friend, I am so grateful. Come, Lucy, hurry with the bags. Fishe, please give this note to my uncle the minute he returns—it is of vital importance that he sees it this evening.'

As the coach bounced over the cobbled streets Helena recounted the full story of her voyage with Adam without leaving out any details about the mysterious Frenchman or Daniel's accusations and threats.

Portia sat silently agog, only the sound of Lucy's exclamations and gasps of horror interrupting Helena's narrative. At the end Portia leaned across and took Helena's cold hand in hers. 'I believe, like you, that a man like Adam Darvell would never be a traitor. Something else must be going on; there is a rational explanation for his behaviour, I am certain, and I will do everything I can to help you both.'

Mr Rowlett kept not only a fine stable, but went to the added expense of maintaining his own change of horses on the routes he most often travelled, including to his mother's estate in Hampshire. Portia, therefore, had no trouble in securing fresh horses and a rapid change at each posting inn and the progress they made was remarkable.

The moon was full, illuminating the road ahead of them and allowing the coachman to obey his mistress's demands to 'Spring them, Jevons!'

They finally entered West Itchenor as the church clock was striking three, and made a more sedate progress down the country lane that lead to Adam's house.

Lucy, worn out by the hour and the unaccustomed excitement, slept heavily in one corner, but both Helena and Portia were wide awake, their eyes fixed on the darkness ahead. As they wended their way through the narrow country roads the silence was riven by a vixen barking in the wood behind them and moths fluttered up from the vergeside, their wings white in the moonlight.

The carriage turned in off the lane past a pair of lodges. The gates were open and, peering out, Helena could just glimpse the dull gleam of metal and a flash of pipe-clayed bandoleer in the shadows of the buildings. Her heart leapt in her chest and she clutched Portia's arm. 'The dragoons! They are in place already, we are too late!'

'If they are still out here, it means that Brookes has not yet arrived,' Portia reassured her. 'And that means we are in time to alert Adam. He can still make good his escape.'

'He has done nothing wrong!' Helena cried, and Portia shushed her.

'Better to live and fight another day,' she said grimly.

Ahead of them the house blazed with light despite the hour. It seemed every room on the ground floor was occupied, and many bedchamber windows were also lit. Despite her fears for Adam, Helena's heart sank at the sight: she had no wish to walk in and find him in the arms of some doxy.

It was love that sent her hurrying down the steps as soon as the coachman opened the door, love that compelled her to push wide the huge front door and walk unannounced across the hall and into the room from where most noise came.

Helena threw off Portia's restraining arm and stood on a threshold of a large salon lit by multiple branches of candles on every available surface. Her horrified eyes took in a scene which could have been straight from one of her mother's translations of Ovid. Perhaps half a dozen young men, their shirts open at the neck, their jackets and cravats discarded, lounged around the long central table. Each had a girl with them, young but painted, their flimsy gowns jarringly bright to Helena's eyes. Some sat on the laps of their companions, others hung over the backs of their chairs, but all eyes were riveted on the one girl who was dancing on the table top, discarding garments as she did so in an impromptu dance of the seven veils.

The cries and catcalls echoed off the walls as the dancer swirled surefooted amongst the debris of dinner: wine glasses and empty bottles, a great Stilton cheese and the wreck of half a dozen capons.

Of Adam there was no sign. The dancer removed her penultimate veil and the men began to shout at her to wait. 'Where's Darvell? Damme, he can't miss this!' one young buck yelled. No one had yet spotted Helena, rooted to the spot on the threshold.

'In the library with you know who—I don't think he'll want to be disturbed,' one of his companions responded. Her heart sinking, Helena backed into the hall.

'What are you going to do?' Portia whispered.

'Find him, of course. I wonder which is the library?'

'No, Helena, do not go in there! What if he is—?'

'Oh, never mind, that does not matter,' Helena retorted impatiently, throwing open one door after another. She was greeted with cries of 'Get out!' from one room, and found another empty except for a number of discarded garments.

Pausing before the last door in the hallway, she took a deep, tumultuous breath. How could she prepare herself for what she was going to find behind its concealing panels? With a trembling hand she turned the knob and pushed open the door. The room was lit with one branch of candles and the light of the fire. At the sound of the door opening, the two figures on the hearthrug turned from their mutual absorption. Across the room Helena's wide eyes met and locked with Adam's shocked gaze.

Chapter Thirteen

'Helena!' Adam straightened up, looking at her with a thunderstruck expression that held none of the embarrassment she had expected to see written there. 'What the devil are you doing here?'

Someone cleared his throat, and Helena, dragging her eyes away from Adam's, saw clearly for the first time that his companion was not female. Both men, who had been standing in conversation at the fireside, had turned at her entrance.

'*Mademoiselle,*' the Frenchman said gravely, placing his glass of brandy on the mantelshelf before bowing formally. It was the man from St Mary's and from Vauxhall Gardens. 'We meet at last: Adam has told me so much about you that I feel that I already know you. But then…' his thin lips twitched with suppressed amusement '…you have been at my heels for some while, *n'est-ce pas?*'

Adam, too, put down his glass. Any amazement he had felt at seeing Miss Wyatt in his country house at three in the morning was no longer evident on his expressionless face. 'I feel the time has come to make my friend known to you, Miss Wyatt. May I present Henri, le comte de Provins.'

Utterly bewildered, Helena permitted her hand to be taken and her fingertips kissed with utmost Gallic gallantry. It was almost as if she were outside her own body, observing herself go through these ludicrous social formalities. 'Monsieur le comte,' she murmured in response.

Then through a haze of tiredness her brain began to work again. 'You are a Royalist?'

'Mais oui, mademoiselle. What did you think I was? Surely not a supporter of that usurping Corsican dog?' He turned and spat into the fire, the sizzle demonstrating his contempt for Napoleon Bonaparte as words could not. '*Pardon, mademoiselle,*' he apologised swiftly.

Suddenly Helena's legs could support her no longer and she sat down hastily in the nearest wing chair. 'Thank heavens,' she whispered, 'thank heavens I was right.'

Adam was by her side in two swift strides, his hand on her arm. With his other hand he gently smoothed back her disordered hair and looked deep into her eyes. 'Helena, tell me, why are you here? How did you get here?'

'I have come to warn you that Daniel Brookes believes you are a traitor and has set a trap for you. Portia and I drove down together as soon as I discovered what he intended.'

'But you do not believe I would betray my country?' He was looking down at her steadily; behind him, the Count melted tactfully into the shadows. 'You were spying on me at the inn, were you not?'

'I did not set out to, but what I glimpsed, did, I admit, make me suspicious. Adam, I could hardly credit what I feared, but I had to be sure. I am, after all, an admiral's daughter—one who gave his life for his country.'

'So at what point did you decide to trust me?'

'When we were boarded by the excisemen—I knew you were hiding something before you gave me the packet of papers.' Helena shook her head, as if to clarify her thoughts. 'It was strange, I could not have put into words why I trusted you, but I did. I sensed, I think, that you were a man of honour, one who, if he truly believed in the revolutionary cause, would have gone openly to fight for the Emperor, not traded in secrets for his own gain.'

She bit her lip and could not meet his eyes. 'There is something else, is there not?' he asked gently.

'Yes…I knew you would do nothing to hurt me. If those papers had been treacherous, you would never have entrusted them to my care, knowing that if they had been found on me, it would have been my neck in the noose as a result.'

Adam half turned away, pushing his hair back with one hand. 'You trusted me, yet I did not behave like a gentleman to you on the *Moonspinner*, did I, Helena?'

'And I did not behave like a lady, as you told me on the beach that Sunday morning,' she said calmly, meeting his gaze again. 'You did not force me, Adam, and I know you would not have taken…advantage of me.'

'But Brookes—why the devil did you play with fire with him? Why did you let the engagement go so far?'

'Because he was blackmailing me.'

'I know that…'

'No, Adam, he was threatening not just to ruin me, but to expose you and whatever your activities were.'

'But you have just said you believed me, that I could not be a traitor.'

'It is not that simple. How was I to know what the real truth was? You could be innocent of treachery, but still be smuggling! I did not want to see you hauled off to prison and that man triumphant.'

Adam fell to his knees beside her chair and took her cold hand between his own warm ones. 'Why did you not tell me this the other evening when you came to me?'

'I was determined never to do anything to put you in a position where you again felt obliged to marry me.' Despite the fact that I love you, she wanted to shout out, but she could not.

'And yet tonight you put yourself in peril for me.' There was an unspoken question in his voice.

'Adam, I had to…' But she was unable to finish. In the hall outside the heavy front door swung open with a crash, there was the sound of boots on the marble and the shout of orders.

Helena sprung to her feet, her hands pushing Adam back towards the curtained window. 'The dragoons! You must both run or he will have you shot out of hand!'

'Dragoons? Who the devil—'

'It is Daniel Brookes's doing. Adam, I told you, he thinks you are a traitor and by exposing you he will do his own career much good—you must flee, both of you.'

'I will be damned if I will be chased like a dog from my own home by that bastard. Wait here,' he snapped at Helena as he strode to the door, his face like thunder.

Neither Helena nor the Count obeyed him, but the Frenchman held Helena back in the doorway, drawing her back into the shadows of the room. 'Wait,' he said, low-voiced. 'He would not want you to be seen by the soldiers.'

The hall was a scene of chaos. An elderly, portly butler confronted a sergeant of dragoons and his six men, their rifles glinting menacingly in the candlelight. The four young men had spilled out of the dining room: two were

hastily pulling on their jackets while the others pushed
the girls back into the room and firmly shut the door on
their excited chattering.

'What is the meaning of this outrage?' the butler was
demanding. 'How dare you enter his lordship's house
without his leave?' His grey hair was disordered and his
face an alarming shade of puce.

The sergeant sneered at the elderly man, pushing him
hard in the chest. 'You just get out of the way, granddad.'

He had hardly a chance to turn before a crashing right
hook caught him on the chin and sent him sprawling
across the chequered marble. Adam stood over him, rubbing and flexing his fingers. 'That will teach you to have
a little more respect for your elders and betters.' He shot
a hard glance at the soldiers who had stepped forward,
weapons at the ready. 'Stand back! If your sergeant has
no more sense than to make a scene in a private house
without authority, then you should have.'

'But, my dear Darvell,' a voice said silkily, 'they have
every authority— the King's authority. And you,' Daniel
Brookes said with a look of pure venom as he stepped
into the light, 'have now added assault to a long list of
treasonable activities.'

Henri stepped forward to his friend's side, his hands
clenching. 'You insult my friend *monsieur*, you will answer to me.' It was a clear challenge to a duel and
Daniel's face darkened with anger.

'I do not duel with spies and foreigners, only with
gentlemen,' he snarled back.

One of the young blades by the door straightened up,
a look of purpose on his face. 'Sir,' he said, looking
directly at Adam, 'this has gone far enough. Shall we
throw them out?'

The look on Daniel's face would have been comic if

there had been any room for humour in the situation. For the first time he looked round, taking in the four men who now stood, sobered and grim, by the dining-room door. 'Frensham! Cooper? My God, are you all in this?' The sergeant groaned, rubbing his jaw and Brookes shoved him in the ribs with his foot. 'Get up, man, and arrest the lot of them!'

Adam stepped forward, facing his enemy across the sprawled soldier. 'I warn you, Brookes, you are making a very grave mistake.'

Helena, unable to bear the crackling tension any longer, took an involuntary step forward to Adam's side.

'So—' Daniel grinned without humour '—your *whore* is here too. How very indiscreet of you.'

'You will withdraw that remark immediately, sir, and apologise to the lady, or meet me and answer for it,' a voice cut across Adam's furious response.

'Uncle Robert!' Helena ran across the hall and threw herself into her uncle's arms. He hugged her close, pressing her face against the buttons of his full dress uniform.

'There, there, dear. Sir William and I came with all dispatch as soon as I received your note. Now, you go with Mrs Rowlett and find the housekeeper, we will attend to this.'

Dazedly Helena realised that Portia was standing with Sir William Thorn, concern and dismay on her pretty face. Helena gazed in disbelief at the Commodore whom she had met only hours before in her uncle's house.

'You men,' Sir William ordered, 'get out and take your sergeant with you. I am Sir William Thorn of His Majesty's navy and I am taking command here.' As the door closed behind the baffled troop, Sir William turned to his colleague. 'Commodore, you know perfectly well that naval officers may not duel.'

'He has offered a very great insult to my niece,' Sir Robert Breakey ground out between clenched teeth, 'and he will answer for it.'

'He has indeed insulted Miss Wyatt,' Adam said pleasantly. 'He has insulted her repeatedly, and for that he will meet me. And I believe you would agree, sir, that as he has publicly accused me and my guests of treason, my right to satisfaction takes precedence over yours.'

'So be it,' Sir Robert replied grimly. 'So long as someone sees to the dog, I care not.'

'He is not a bad naval officer, you know, Sir Robert,' Sir William remarked judiciously, regarding with some amusement the flushed, scowling face of Daniel Brookes. 'Unfortunately, he appears to have the morals and character of a total scoundrel.'

'Your choice of weapons, Brookes?' Adam demanded.

'I say, sir,' Frensham broke in, 'isn't that damned irregular? I mean, we need seconds and what have you...'

'Be quiet, lieutenant,' Adam commanded. 'I intend to kill the swine now, not wait until he has the chance to bruit this lady's name abroad any further.'

'Lieutenant?' Helena whispered, totally confused.

'They all are,' Sir William replied, low-voiced. 'Part of my secret service—which does not exist, of course,' he added with a twinkle.

'And Adam?'

'Oh, he is a civilian, I never could get him to obey orders, although he works with my group,' the Commodore whispered back. So that was how Sir William had known so much about her! It was not her father, but Adam, who had spoken to him of her.

'His friendship with the Count and others like him bring us constant intelligence. Darvell uses his parties as a cover to exchange information and to brief my young officers. No one questions the presence of numerous young men at one of his lordship's notorious weekends.'

He broke off to eye the preparations for the duel. 'Darvell warned me that Brookes was getting too close—his hatred for Darvell and his overwhelming ambition have pushed him to act beyond his remit or orders. His lordship and I became so concerned that I decided to speak to your uncle yesterday. Darvell was determined that the engagement should be broken.' Sir William looked at her wryly. 'His lordship was extraordinarily insistent on that point.'

Helena shook her head dazedly; it was all too much to take in. A few hours ago she would have been in heaven to know that Adam's name was cleared of all suspicion, that she was free from Daniel Brookes. But now there was the impending duel to face.

'Swords,' she heard Daniel say, and she gasped at the memory of Adam's joking words in Vauxhall Gardens about Daniel's inability with a pistol to hit the nearest barn door, but his expertise with a rapier.

'Adam, no, please do not fight him,' she implored, running to his side and grasping his arm. 'I am free of him, it does not matter what he says, he is too discredited for anyone to pay any heed.'

Firmly but gently Adam pushed her back into her uncle's arms and turned to his butler, who was proffering an open case of duelling swords to Brookes.

Daniel took one and flexed it with an evil grin on his face. 'A grave mistake to challenge me, Darvell. Have you forgotten how at Eton I would best you every time we fenced?' He shrugged out of his coat and threw it onto the hall chest, then turned back his cuffs and stood waiting.

Adam too discarded his jacket and flexed the remaining weapon. The others pressed back against the walls to leave the centre of the long room clear and Portia tried, vainly, to pull Helena back into the library.

'*En garde!*' the Count called and the rapiers engaged with a sickening clash and scrape. Helena clenched her fingers on Portia's arm and fought down a wave of nausea and dizziness. How could it have come to this? But she knew she was powerless to prevent Adam defending both her honour and his own, even though it might end in his death.

The two men prowled and circled, sizing each other up, each seeking for a sign of weakness and advantage. Suddenly there was a swish of steel through air and Adam lunged forward. Daniel parried skillfully, his own blade sliding off Adam's own, then with lightning speed he lunged himself.

Adam jumped back, his sword up to meet the challenge and guard his heart and with consummate skill Daniel turned his wrist at the last moment and brought the point of the rapier scoring down his opponent's arm.

A sharp line of red stained the white linen and Helena bit back a cry of horror. The candlelight flickered, the duellists seemed to ebb and flow in her unfocused sight, the gorge rose in her throat and she clenched her fists until the nails bit painfully into her palms. Portia put a supporting arm around her friend, but made no further attempt to remove her from the scene of the duel.

Adam stepped back with a sharp hiss of pain, then thrust forward again. His rapier began to flicker and dance and he began to beat back Daniel's challenge, sending the other man backing down the length of the hall. 'It is a long time since we were boys at Eton, Brookes,' Adam said, his breath coming short with exertion. 'I have learned a few lessons since then.'

He appeared to drop his guard fleetingly. With a grunt of triumph Daniel lunged, then reeled back as the point of Adam's weapon buried itself in his right shoulder. His sword fell, clattering to the marble, and he staggered, holding the wound as the blood welled between his clenching fingers.

Frensham jumped forward, a linen napkin bunched in his hand. 'Sit down, man, let me see the wound.' He looked up and addressed the room at large. 'He'll live, but we better get him to bed and send for the surgeon.'

Sir William regarded the fallen officer with a frown. 'You will not want him on the premises any longer than is necessary, my lord. When the surgeon has patched him up I will take him back to London with me.'

'What are you going to do with him?' Sir Robert asked grimly.

'He is too good an officer to lose in time of war. I think a spell in the West Indies would suit his talents and keep him out of mischief, provided, that is, he does not succumb to the fever. Come on, get him up to a bed-chamber.'

The hall seemed suddenly empty, with only Adam, her uncle and Portia left. The butler was wrapping a clean white cloth tightly around his master's forearm.

'It's just a graze, man, do not fuss.'

'Adam...' It was all Helena could manage to stammer out. She was weak with relief, too unsteady to walk towards him.

He met her gaze, and for the first time she saw in his eyes a longing that in its very intensity caught her breath in her throat.

When he spoke it was as though there was not another soul in the room. 'You are free now, Helena. You do not have to marry Brookes, you do not have to marry me.

But one thing you do need to know: I love you, Helena. Do you understand me, my darling? I only want what is best for you, and if that is your freedom, well, I will accept it.'

Portia caught her breath on a sob, but Helena did not hear her. The room tilted and swayed and she fell, a long way, down into darkness.

Before she succumbed to the depths of it she was vaguely conscious of strong arms encircling her, lifting her; of lips in her hair and warm breath as someone murmured words she could not discern, before oblivion swept over her.

When Helena awoke she had no idea where she was. Very early sunlight was just touching the undraped windows and outside the birds were singing. She was in bed, warm under the covers, but she was not alone.

Someone else was breathing beside her, their breath rising and falling on the faintest of snores. Helena turned her head and saw Portia's tumbled curls on the pillow beside her. 'More damson preserve,' Portia remarked in her sleep, 'more...' her voice trailed off and she sighed and turned over.

Cautiously Helena levered herself up against the pillows. She felt light-headed and, seeing the covered glass of lemonade beside the bed, took a grateful drink. It was sharp and refreshing in her mouth and she found she could think clearly.

She was obviously still in Adam's house. Somewhere, presumably, her uncle had been given a room for what had remained of the night. And what a night! A tinge of remembered fear stole over her as she recalled the events, the duel, the blood.... Then she remembered Adam's words.

He loved her. He had said so in front of witnesses when he had no need to. She remembered the scorching look of longing and recognised now that it truly was love she had seen there.

But he had set her free, and the last thing she wanted to be was free of Adam. Yet if she told him that, in his pride and honour he would assume she was only trying to repay him for his defence of her. How could he believe otherwise after the cruel, wounding words she had thrown at him, after her defiant declaration that she would rather marry her blackmailer than him?

Suddenly she knew what she had to do. She swung her legs carefully out of the bed, and tiptoed to the door. Helena was out in the corridor before she realised just how flimsy the nightgown she was wearing really was. It was another of the diaphanous muslin slips that she had found on the *Moonspinner*, fastened loosely at the neck with silk ribbons. The house was silent, but surely the servants would soon be about their duties.

Casting swiftly round her, Helena guessed that the master bedroom would be at the front of the house, commanding a fine view of the park. She ran lightly down the corridor to the heavy panelled door and pushed it cautiously open. Yes, it was Adam's room.

Despite the gloom his dark blond hair showed clearly on the pillow. He was lying on his stomach, deep in sleep, one bare leg thrust out from under the covers which extended to his waist. His torso was bare, its only covering a light bandage on his left forearm.

Helena tiptoed forward, and stood gazing down at him, a wave of love and longing coursing through her. She put out one hand and smoothed back the hair from his brow, thankful to feel the cool skin under her fingertips. Thank God, his wound had not given him a fever.

Adam stirred and murmured, 'Helena...' but he was still asleep. Without letting herself think what she was doing, Helena pulled back the covers and slipped into the big bed next to the man she loved. Her slight weight hardly disturbed the mattress as she snuggled up against his long flank, placing one arm over his broad back.

Greatly daring, she curled her ankle round his bent leg, only realising when she met the warmth of his skin how cold her feet were. Adam turned his head on the pillow, and with his face towards her she could see him frown as the surprise of her cold feet penetrated his consciousness.

His eyes opened slowly until he was regarding her, his eyes almost black under their heavy fringe of lashes. To Helena's amazement he did not speak, only half turned to take her in his arms.

With a soft groan he kissed her like a parched man at a spring, his mouth wide and tender on her softness, drinking her in with an intensity he had never shown before. The kiss went on and on, Helena in her turn investing in it all the love she had never been able to show him.

Her hands moved as if of their own volition, trailing down the strong planes of his back to the tautness of his buttocks. He froze and his eyes opened blue and intense on her face.

'Bloody hell! You are not a dream!'

'No, of course I am not,' Helena murmured, her hands still exploring his hard flanks. Against the filmy muslin of her nightgown she was overwhelmingly aware of the heat of him, of the burning desire of him.

'What are you doing here?' With a superhuman effort Adam forced himself away from her, rolled onto his back and sat up against the pillows. 'No, do not touch me!'

he warned as Helena twisted round to wrap her arms around him again. 'You are making this very difficult for me, you have no idea how much I want you.'

'And I want you, Adam,' Helena confessed softly, staring deep into his eyes. 'I love you, I want you. Please—do not start being noble again.'

There was a quivering silence then Adam said slowly, 'Are you sure you are not being the noble one, Helena? Are you doing this because you think you owe me a debt of honour? Well, I do not want a willing sacrifice.'

Furious, Helena jumped off the bed, hands on hips. 'Will you listen to what I am saying to you, you... provoking man?'

Little did she realise that her hands stretched the fine fabric taut over her slender hips, rendering it virtually transparent. Adam clenched his fingers on the sheet and tried to ignore the thrust of rosy nipples, the dark shadow between her thighs. 'Helena, it is you who are provoking—I warn you, I cannot contain myself much longer.'

Helena sighed. She had thought Adam would sweep her up in his arms, make passionate love to her and all would be right. But the man had a will of iron! Very well, then, this called for desperate measures. Her fingers went to the silken ribbons at her neck.

Adam watched her in fascination, unable to do all the things he knew he ought: get out of bed now, wrap her in his dressing gown, march her back to Portia's chaperonage. But he loved her so much and he had waited so long... The diaphanous robe whispered as it met the floorboards and she was naked, blushing under the heat of his eyes in the classic pose of every naked nymph, one arm across her creamy breasts, one hand creeping to hide the tangle of dark curls.

His resolve shattered into a thousand pieces and he

held out his arms to her. Helena came to him trustingly, her eyes full of love for him. How had he ever been so blind, missed the message that innocent gaze was sending him so clearly?

Adam laid her against the pillows and looked at her. Helena blushed a rosy pink but held his gaze. Her fingers reached up to him, fastening in his hair, pulling his head down to her breast.

At the first touch of his warm mouth on her agonisingly taut nipple Helena arched against him, her whole body filled with an aching, longing to be part of him.

'Helena,' he ground out, his mouth buried in the soft swell of her breast, 'are you quite sure about this? Because if you are not, you had better say so now.'

'I am sure, my love, but that does not mean I am not...'

'Do not be afraid.' Adam rolled her over, shifting his weight to cover her. 'I am going to make love to you.'

And so he did, at first with infinite tenderness and then, as she answered his passion with her own, with a surging intensity that took her beyond all barriers to a plane of pleasure she had never imagined existed.

Afterwards they lay sated and at rest in each others' arms. The sun began to fall across the bed in a golden bar and Adam reached out and pulled the tangled sheets up and over their still-entwined bodies.

At length Helena murmured, 'What time is it?'

As if in answer there was a tap at the door which began to open. 'Not now!' Adam called, and the door swiftly shut to. 'Seven o'clock—that would have been my valet.'

Helena stirred and sat up against the pillows, stretching like a satisfied cat. She was so happy that she felt almost overwhelmed by it. Adam had twisted round and was regarding her very seriously.

'Helena, I must know. Will you marry me?'

'I have little choice, my lord,' she responded primly. 'After all, I am now completely ruined. You are honour bound to marry me, I'm afraid.'

She saw the doubt in his eyes, and realised with a surge of amazement that this strong, hard man was vulnerable, was in her power. Instantly she regretted her levity. 'Of course I will marry you, Adam. I love you, more than life itself. I cannot believe you truly love me—why did not tell me before?'

'When I made that first declaration I could not imagine that any lady in your circumstances would have rejected me: I could only assume your dislike for me outweighed the overwhelming necessity to protect your reputation. And my pride was hurt—badly.' He looked rueful. 'As you yourself observed, I have never had to try very hard to secure feminine companionship.'

'Hmm.' Helen regarded him between narrowed lids. 'Portia told me about your lady-friends. She seemed to think that the fact that you only had one at a time made it all right.'

'There were hardly dozens of them,' Adam defended himself with a smile. 'And I never dallied with any innocents. They all knew exactly what they were doing—and all of them were very well able to look after themselves.'

'Yes, I heard about the Meissen.'

Adam looked startled. 'Good God, is that widely known? Georgiana was always crashingly indiscreet, and extremely expensive.'

Looking at the shuttered expression on her face, he cursed himself for a fool. It was so easy to talk to her—

she had led him into talking about other women minutes after she had given him everything and with a passion and love he had never found before.

'Helena, I am sorry, I should never have spoken so. They were diversions, doing harm to no one, and are over forever since I met you. I love you and I want nobody else. I may be a rake, Helena, but I vow, from this moment on, I am a reformed one.'

Helena glanced up at him from under her lashes, warmed and secure in his love. 'Does that mean, Lord Darvell, that you will not expect me to be taking a lover after I have done my duty by you and presented you with an heir?'

'Helena, you are teasing me. But I promise you this— any man who touches you will answer for it with his life. I love you, I have made you mine. If you are not convinced, Miss Wyatt, I had better show you all over again.'

And he did.

* * * * *

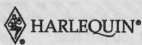

HARLEQUIN®

makes any time special—online...

eHARLEQUIN.com

your romantic magazine

—Romance 101—
♥ Guides to romance, dating and flirting.

—Dr. Romance—
♥ Get romance advice and tips from
our expert, Dr. Romance.

—Recipes for Romance—
♥ How to plan romantic meals for you
and your sweetie.

—Daily Love Dose—
♥ Tips on how to keep the romance
alive every day.

—Tales from the Heart—
♥ Discuss romantic dilemmas with other
members in our Tales from the Heart
message board.

All this and more available at
www.eHarlequin.com

HINTL1R2

If you enjoyed what you just read,
then we've got an offer you can't resist!

Take 2
bestselling novels FREE!
Plus get a FREE surprise gift!

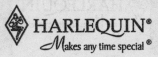